DEMON PRINCE NO. 4

"Lens Larque is said to be enamored of the whip; he considers it a trusty friend and a convenient instrument for the punishment of his enemies. He uses it often to this end, judging it preferable to other methods. At Sadabra he owns a great house with a semi-circular room where he sits to take his victual. For savor he keeps by his side a fine short-handled whip, with a lash twelve and a half feet long.

"Around the wall stand Lens Larque's enemies, manacled to rings as naked as eggs. To the buttocks of each is pasted a heart-shaped target three inches in diameter. To enliven his meal Lens Larque attempts to snap off the targets with the flutter of his whip, and his skill is said to be fine."

—quoted from an article by
Erasmus Heptor in *The Galactic Review*

JACK VANCE
in DAW Editions:

The "Demon Princess" novels

1. STAR KING
2. THE KILLING MACHINE
3. THE PALACE OF LOVE
4. THE FACE
5. THE BOOK OF DREAMS*

The Tschai novels

1. CITY OF THE CHASCH
2. SERVANTS OF THE WANKH
3. THE DIRDIR
4. THE PNUME

Others

WYST: ALASTOR 1716

SPACE OPERA

EMPHYRIO

* Forthcoming (Title tentative)

THE
FACE

Jack Vance

DAW BOOKS, INC.

DONALD A. WOLLHEIM, PUBLISHER

1633 Broadway
New York, N.Y. 10019

PUBLISHED BY
THE NEW AMERICAN LIBRARY
OF CANADA LIMITED

FIRST PRINTING, NOVEMBER 1979

1 2 3 4 5 6 7 8 9

DAW TRADEMARK REGISTERED
U.S. PAT. OFF. MARCA REGISTRADA.
HECHO EN U.S.A.

PRINTED IN CANADA
COVER PRINTED IN U.S.A.

Part I: ALOYSIUS

Chapter 1

From *Popular Handbook to the Planets*, 330th edition, 1525:

Aloysius, Vega VI

Planetary constants:
Diameter .... 7340 miles
Sidereal day .... 19.836218 hours
Mass .... 0.86331 standard
Etcetera ....

Aloysius, with its sister planets Boniface and Cuthbert, is accounted among the first worlds to be colonized from Earth, and the traveler who enjoys the ambience of antiquity will here find much to please him.

Contrary to popular assumption, the first settlers were not religious zealots but members of the Natural Universe Society, who dealt gingerly with the new environment, and built nothing at discord with the landscape.

The NUS is long gone, but its influence still permeates the system, and almost everywhere will be noted a sedate reverence for native customs and textures.

The axis of Aloysius inclines to an angle of 31.7 degrees from its plane of orbit; there are seasonal fluctuations of notable severity, mollified somewhat by a dense and moist atmosphere. Of the seven continents Marcy's Land is the largest,

with New Wexford its chief city. The least of the
continents is Gavin's Land, on which is situated
the city Pontefract.

It may here be noted that each land, during
the Sacerdotal Epochs, represented the diocese of
a cardinal and bore his name, thus: Cardinal
Marcy's Land, Cardinal Bodant's Land, Cardinal
Dimpey's Land, and so forth. The appellative has
fallen into disuse and is rarely heard.

Through a policy of low taxes and favorable
regulations, both Pontefract and New Wexford
have long functioned as important financial cen-
ters, with influence reaching everywhere across
the Oikumene. Many important publishing
houses also make their headquarters at these
places, including the prestigious *Cosmopolis* magazine.

Religions, sects, creeds, movements, counter-
movements, orthodoxies, heresies, inquisitions:
this is the stuff of early Vegan history; emphati-
cally so on Aloysius which derives its name from
the patron saint of the Aloysian Order. The Ambrosians, who preceded the Aloysians, founded
the city Rath Eileann beside Lake Feamish, at
the center of Llinliffet's Land. The conflicts between these nominally devotional brotherhoods
make a fascinating chronicle.

Indigenous flora and fauna are not particularly
noteworthy. Through intensive effort by the original settlers, terrestrial trees and shrubs are wide-
spread, the conifers especially finding a hospitable
environment, and the seas are stocked with
selected terrestrial fish.

Jehan Addels, after his meticulous habit, arrived ten
minutes early to the place of rendezvous. Before alighting
from his car he took pains to scrutinize the surroundings. The
scenery was dramatic but apparently devoid of menace; Addels found nothing to excite his misgivings. To the right stood
Phruster's Inn, with timbers blackened by centuries of wind
and rain, and the Dunveary Crags beyond, rising crag upon
buttress, finally to disappear behind high mist. To the left

Phruster's Prospect confronted three-quarters of a full circle and several thousand square miles of territory, varying with whims of the weather.

Addels alighted from his car, cast a single skeptical glance up the awesome Dunveary slopes, and walked out upon the observation platform. Leaning against the parapet he hunched his shoulders against the wind and waited: a thin man with parchment-colored skin and a high balding forehead.

The time was close upon mid-morning; halfway up the sky Vega glowed pale through the mist. A dozen other folk stood along the parapet. Addels subjected each to a careful inspection. Their flounced and tasseled garments in muted reds, browns and dark green, marked them for country folk; residents of the town dressed only in shades of brown, with an occasional black ornament. This group seemed innocent. Addels turned his attention to the panorama: Lake Feamish to the left, Rath Eileann below, vaporous Moy Valley to the right. . . . He frowned down at his watch. The man whom he awaited had given precise instructions. A lack of punctuality might well indicate crisis. Addels gave a sniff, to express both envy and disdain for a way of life so much more eventful than his own.

The time of the appointment was at hand. Addels noticed a path which, originating at the edge of Rath Eileann far below, slanted back and forth up the hillside, to terminate at a flight of steps cut into the rock nearby. Up this path came a man of average stature, unobtrusively muscular, with rather harsh cheekbones, flat cheeks, thick dark hair cropped short. This was Kirth Gersen, of whom Addels knew little except that by some mysterious means, no doubt illegitimate, Gersen had come into the possession of vast wealth.* Addels earned a large salary as Gersen's legal adviser, to date with his scruples, such as they were, intact. Gersen seemed well acquainted with IPCC** procedures, which in times of stress afforded Addels a degree of nervous comfort.

Gersen ran up the steps, paused, saw Addels and crossed the observation deck. Addels took dispassionate note that after a climb which would have reduced Addels to a state of gasping exhaustion, Gersen was not even breathing deeply.

* Cf. *The Killing Machine*
** Interworld Police Coordinating Company

Addels performed a stately gesture of greeting. "I am pleased to find you in good health."

"Exactly so," said Gersen. "Your journey was pleasant?"

"I was distrait; I hardly noticed," said Addels in a measured and meaningful voice. "But certainly you are enjoying your stay at the Domus?"

Gersen assented. "I sit in the lobby for hours absorbing the atmosphere."

"For this reason you remain here at Rath Eileann?"

"Not altogether. This is what I want to discuss with you, where we won't be overheard."

Addels looked right and left. "You suspect eavesdroppers at the Domus?"

"Up here the risk is at least minimized. I have taken the usual precautions; no doubt you have done the same."

"I have taken all the precautions I thought necessary," said Addels.

"In that case, we are almost certainly secure."

Addels' only response was a frosty chuckle. For a moment the two men stood leaning on the parapet, overlooking the gray city, the lake, and the misty valley beyond.

Gersen spoke. "The local spaceport is at Slayhack, north of the lake. A week from today the *Ettilia Gargantyr* will arrive. The registered owner is the Celerus Transport Company based at Vire on Sadal Suud Four. This ship was at one time the *Fanutis,** registered to Service Spaceways, also at Vire. The registrations are both nominal. The ship then was the property of Lens Larque, and so presumably is now."

Addels pursed his lips in distaste. "In our conversation you mentioned his name. Somewhat to my distress, I must admit. He is a notorious criminal."

"Quite so."

"And you intend to conduct business with him? Inadvisable. He is not to be trusted."

"Our business runs along different lines. As soon as the *Ettilia Gargantyr* arrives, I want a lien, or some other such instrument, placed against ship and cargo, so that the ship is impounded without any possibility of departure. I want title to the ship attacked, so that the actual owner—not his

---

* At the Mount Pleasant raid, where Gerson lost home and family, the *Fanutis* had been employed as a slave transport.

agent or his legal representative—must come here to protect his interests."

Addels frowned. "You want to bring Lens Larque here to Rath Eileann? An extravagant hope."

"It is worth a trial. He will naturally use another identity."

"Lens Larque standing before a court of law? Absurd."

"Quite so. Lens Larque enjoys absurdities. He is also avaricious. If the action appears legitimate, he won't want to lose his ship by default."

Addels gave a grunt of grudging acquiescence. "I can tell you this, at least. The most convincing disguise for legitimacy is legitimacy itself. There should be no trouble discovering a basis for action. Spaceships trail a rash of small complaints in their wake. The difficulty is one of jurisdiction. Has this ship touched Rath Eileann before?"

"Not to my knowledge. Ordinarily it works the Argo Fringe."

Addels said in a formal voice, "I will give the matter my best attention."

"An important point to remember: Lens Larque is not an amiable man, for all his tricks and fancies. My name—I hardly need emphasize this—must not be used. You yourself would be wise to act discreetly."

Addels ran nervous fingers through his sparse blond hair. "I don't care to confront him at all, discreetly or otherwise."

"Nevertheless," said Gersen, "the ship must be immobilized here at Rath Eileann. Use a writ of attachment, or replevin or some such document. The real owner must definitely appear, or else lose title by default."

Addels said peevishly, "If the ownership is corporate, or vested in a limited society, no such result is possible. The action is not all that easy."

Gersen gave a grim laugh. "If it were easy, I'd do it myself."

"I quite understand," said Addels in a morose voice. "Let me think the matter over for a day or two."

Three days later, in Gersen's chambers at Domus St. Revelras, a musical tone signaled an incoming call. Gersen touched the "Monitor" button; a cascade of exploding asterisks certified that the line was free of interference. A few seconds later Addels' fine-boned face appeared on the screen.

"I have made guarded inquiries," spoke Addels in his most didactic voice. "I have obtained definite judicial opinion to the effect that an action of the sort you envisage is valid only if a local citizen has suffered substantial damage, that debt or damage having optimally occurred locally and at a recent time. As of now we satisfy none of the requirements. Therefore we could not obtain a valid writ."

Gersen nodded. "I expected as much." He waited patiently while Addels pulled at his bony chin and selected words.

"In connection with the *Ettilia Gargantyr* itself, I have searched records for liens, debts and other actions under litigation. As ships of space pass from port to port, they often incur small debts or inflict minor damages, which usually no one troubles to pursue. The *Ettilia Gargantyr* is no exception. Two years ago an incident occurred at Thrump on David Alexander's Planet. The captain provided a banquet for a group of local freight agents, employing ship's stewards and other personnel to prepare and serve the meal. Instead of the *Gargantyr's* mess hall, he chose to use a chamber at the spaceport. The Thrump Victuallers Guild asserted that such a process contravened local ordinance. They registered a claim for lost wages and punitive damages. The ship departed before a summons could be served, so the action remains in abeyance, pending the ship's return, which is unlikely."

Addels paused to reflect. Gersen waited patiently. Addels made delicate adjustment of his thoughts and spoke on: "The Victualler's Guild meanwhile negotiated a loan with a certain Cooney's Bank, chartered at Thrump on the same David Alexander's Planet. Along with other assets they pledged the cause of action against the *Ettilia Gargantyr*. A month or so ago the Guild defaulted on the debt, and the suit has now been transferred to the interest of Cooney's Bank." Addels' voice took on a speculative tone. "It has often occurred to me that your affairs might most flexibly be handled through a bank. Cooney's Bank, while essentially sound, suffers from a tired old management. The stock sells at a reasonable price and you could easily buy control. Branches might then be established wherever it became expedient to do so: for instance at Rath Eileann."

"The lawsuit could then be transferred, so I assume."

"Quite correct."

"And a lien could be laid so as to hold the ship here at Rath Eileann?"

"I have made inquiries, in terms of hypothetical cases. I find that the suit may not be filed either at the City Podium nor the Land Court, but only at the Court of Interworld Equity, which sits three times a year at the Estremont under a Circuit Propounder. I have taken counsel with a specialist in interworld equity. He feels that Cooney's Bank's case might well be prosecuted if the *Ettilia Gargantyr* arrives at Rath Eileann; it's physical presence would provide *in rem* jurisdiction. He is certain however that no magistrate would issue a mandamus requiring the presence of the ship's owner on grounds so trivial."

"That, however, is the essence of the matter! Lens Larque must come to Aloysius."

"I am advised that this can not be enforced upon him," said Addels complacently. "I suggest that we now turn our attention to other matters."

"Who is the Propounder sitting at the court?"

"We can't be sure. There are five such magistrates, and they travel a circuit around the Vegan system."

"The court is not now in session?"

"It has just completed its calendar."

"And presumably won't sit again for months."

"Exactly. In any case, the Propounder would almost certainly throw out any motion requiring the presence of the *Gargantyr's* owner."

Gersen nodded pensively. "That is inconvenient."

After a moment Addels inquired. "Well then—what of Cooney's Bank? Shall I make acquisition?"

"Let me think things over. I'll call you tonight."

"Very well."

Chapter 2

From *City of the Mists,* in *Cosmopolis,* May 1520:

On a map Rath Eileann shows like a twisted T. Along the top horizontal, from right to left, are the Ffolliot Gardens, Bethamy, Old Town, the Orangery with the Domus behind, then Estremont on a Lake Feamish islet. The T's vertical straggles to the north for miles, through the Moynal district, then Drury, Wigaltown, Dundivy, Gara with its Dulcidrome, and finally Slayhack with the spaceport.

Of all these districts Old Town exerts the most beguiling charm. Despite streaming mists, oddsmelling vapors, crooked streets, crotchety buildings, this district is far from dull. The local folk wear garments only in shades of brown: sand and taupe, through the middle tans, through oak and other wood into the deepest umbers. When they go abroad in the fitful Vega-light, their costumes against the stone, black iron and sooty timbers create an effect of peculiar richness, the more so for an occasional dark red, yellow, or dark blue turban. At night Old Town flickers to the light of innumerable lanterns hung by ancient ordinance before the doorway of every ale house. Since the crabbed streets and innumerable little alleys have never been named, much less have known the presence of a name-sign, the stranger quickly learns to steer a course by means of the ale houses' lanterns.

The Ambrosian monks, first to settle beside Lake Feamish, built in contemptuous disregard for order, in accordance with the hectic fervor of

12

their creed. The Order of Aloysians who came
forty years later (and who gave the world its
name) half-heartedly tried to modify Old Town,
then lost interest and after establishing the new
Bethamy Quarter gave all their energies to the
construction of Temple St. Revelras.

Gersen left the Domus and sauntered north along the central parade of the Orangery: a formal garden of twenty
acres, inappropriately named since, among the carefully
clipped trees, were to be found no oranges, but only yews,
limes and the indigenous green-glass tree.

At the Grand Esplanade Gersen turned east around the
bend of the lake and presently crossed over a causeway to the
Estremont, a massive structure of silver-gray porphyry, built
on four staggered levels, surmounted by four tall towers and
a central dome. At the Justiciary Gersen made a number of
inquiries, then, even more thoughtful than before, returned to
the Domus.

In his chamber he took paper and stylus and worked out a
careful schedule of times and events, which he pondered with
care. Then, turning to the communicator, he brought the
image of Jehan Addels to the screen. "Today," said Gersen,
"you outlined a procedure in regard to the *Ettilia Gargantyr*."

"It was no more than a tentative idea," said Addels. "The
scheme breaks down as soon as we reach the Estremont. The
Circuit Propounder would never make us a favorable ruling."

"You are altogether too pessimistic," said Gersen. "Strange
things happen; the courts are unpredictable. Please act along
the lines we discussed. Acquire Cooney's Bank and immediately charter a local branch. Then, as soon as the *Gargantyr*
opens its hatch, hit it with every kind of paper you can think
of."

"Just as you say."

"Remember, we are dealing with people who are careless
of legal responsibility, to say the least. Make sure that the
ship is secure. Serve the papers with at least a platoon of constables, and immediately put the crew ashore. Pull the
power-bar, seal the junctions with a destruction-lock; chain
open the cargo hatch. Then post a strong guard, with at least

six armed men on duty at all times. I want to make sure that the ship stays down in Rath Eileann."

Addels essayed a morose pleasantry. "I'll move into the captain's cabin and guard the ship from within."

"I've got other plans for you," said Gersen. "You won't escape so easily."

"Remember, the court of Interworld Equity has jurisdiction. There won't be another session for months, depending on the calendar."

"We want to give the owner time to appear," said Gersen. "Make sure that our action alleges malice, conspiracy, and a deliberate policy of interstellar fraud—charges that only the owner can properly deny."

"He'll go into the dock, deny everything. The Benchmaster will throw out the case, and you'll be left to sweep out the courtroom."

"My dear Addels," said Gersen. "You clearly don't understand my intentions—which is just as well."

"Just so," said Addels bleakly. "I don't even care to speculate."

A month later Gersen once more met Addels on Phruster's Prospect.

The time was middle afternoon; mists over the Dunvearys had dwindled to a few wisps; the landscape showed a stark grandeur to the cold glare of Vega-light.

As before Gersen had climbed the trail which led up from the Ffolliot Gardens at the western edge of Rath Eileann. He stood leaning on the parapet as Addels sedately arrived in his car.

Addels crossed the road and joined Gersen at the parapet. In a heavy voice he said: "The *Gargantyr* has landed. The documents have been served. The captain made an outcry and attempted to return into space. He was removed from the ship and charged with attempted flight to evade the court's jurisdiction. He is now in custody. All precautions have been taken. The captain has sent off an information to his home office." By this time Addels had learned the details of Gersen's program and had not altogether recovered his composure. "He has also retained an attorney, who presumably is competent and who well may wreak enormous grief upon us all."

Gersen said: "Let us hope that the Lord High Benchmaster shares our view of the case."

"An amusing concept," growled Addels. "Let us hope that we will find our terms in the Carcery no less amusing."

Chapter 3

From *Life*. Volume I, by Unspiek, Baron Bodissey:

If religions are diseases of the human psyche, as the philosopher Grintholde asserts, then religious wars must be reckoned the resultant sores and cankers infecting the aggregate corpus of the human race. Of all wars, these are the most detestable, since they are waged for no tangible gain, but only to impose a set of arbitrary credos upon another's mind.

Few such conflicts can match the First Vegan Wars for grotesque excess. The issue concerns, in its proximate phase, a block of sacred white alabaster the Aloysians intended for Temple St. Revelras, while the Ambrosians claimed the same block for their Temple St. Bellaw. The culminating battle on Rudyer Moor is an episode to tax the imagination. The locale: a misty upland of the Mournan Mountains; the time: late afternoon, with Vega darting shafts of pallid light here and there, as roiling clouds allow. On the upper slopes stand a band of haggard Ambrosians in flapping brown robes, carrying crooked staves carved from Corrib yew. Below is gathered a more numerous group of the Aloysian Brotherhood; small shortlegged men, plump and portly, each with ritual goatee and scalp-tuft, carrying kitchen cutlery and garden tools.

Brother Whinias utters a cry in an unknown language. Down the slope bound the Ambrosians, venting hysterical screams, to fall upon the Aloysians like wild men. The battle goes indecisively for an hour, neither side gaining advantage. At sundown the Ambrosian Cornuter, by the creed's rigorous rule, sounds the twelve-tone call to vespers. The Ambrosians, in accordance with their invariable habit, place themselves in devotional attitudes. The Aloysians quickly set to work and destroy the entire Ambrosian band well before the hour of their own devotions, and so ends the Battle of Rudyer Moor.

Back into Old Town creep the few surviving Ambrosians, in secular garments, where eventually they become a canny group of merchants, brewers, ale-house keepers, antiquarians, moneylenders and perhaps pursuivants of other more furtive trades. As for the Aloysians, the order disintegrates within the century; their fervor becomes no more than a quaint tradition. Temple St. Revelras becomes the Domus, grandest of all the Vegan hostelries. Temple St. Bellaw is only a sad tumble of mossy stone.

Gersen sat in the public lobby of Domus St. Revelras, the ancient nave where cenobites had sweated under the gaze of the Gnostic Eye. Patrons of the contemporary Domus knew little of Gnosis, even less of the Eye, but few could look about the great chamber without awe.

The wavering sound of a thousand year old gong marked the hour of late afternoon. Into the chamber stepped a tall thin young man with a thin keen nose, gray eyes of great clarity, and an air of jaunty intelligence. This was Maxel Rackrose, local correspondent to *Cosmopolis*, now assigned to the assistance of "Henry Lucas"—the identity Gersen used in his role as special writer for *Cosmopolis*.

Maxel Rackrose dropped into a chair beside Gersen. "Your subject is both elusive and sinister."

"All of which makes for interesting copy."

"No doubt." Rackrose brought forth a packet of papers. "After a week of scouring I've turned up little more than common knowledge. The fellow has a genius for anonymity."

"For all we know," said Gersen, "he is sitting here in the Domus lobby. That's not as improbable as you might suppose."

Rackrose gave his head a confident shake. "I've just spent

a week with Lens Larque; I'd smell him out if he were within a mile."

Such convictions were not necessarily to be dismissed out of hand, thought Gersen. "That large man yonder, with the nose-piece; might he be Lens Larque?"

"Definitely not."

"You're sure?"

"Certainly. He exudes patchouli and ispanola, but none of the reek Lens Larque is said to exhale. Secondly, he corresponds to descriptions of Lens Larque only in that he is big, bald and dressed in ugly clothes. Thirdly—" Rackrose uttered a careless laugh "—it so happens that I know the man to be one Dett Mullian, who manufactures antique tavern lamps for the tourists."

Gersen smiled wryly, ordered tea from a nearby attendant, then gave his attention to Rackrose's documents.

Some of the material he had already seen, such as an excerpt from *The Mount Pleasant Raid*, by Dauday Wams, published in *Cosmopolis*:

> When the Demon Princes met to affirm their compact, the massive personalities often collided. Howard Alan Treesong mediated the disputes in a casual manner. Attel Malagate proved as obdurate as stone. Viole Falushe took positions based upon malicious caprice. Kokor Hekkus, while unpredictable and innovative, charmed no one. Lens Larque's arrogance aroused much antagonism. Only Howard Alan Treesong maintained equability. What a wonder that the venture succeeded in any degree whatever! It is a tribute to the professionalism of the group.

The next paper, headed *Lens Larque the Flagellator*, was the work of Erasmus Heupter. Immediately below title and byline appeared the drawing of a near-naked man of immense size, with a supple and sleek muscularity. The head was small and shaven, narrow at the cranium, wider at the jaws. Heavy eyebrows joined over a long drooping nose; the face looking out of the picture expressed an inane and lewd euphoria. The man wore only sandals and short tight trousers over heavy and unpleasantly meaty buttocks, and in his right hand he flourished a short-handled whip of three long thongs.

Rackrose chuckled. "If that's our man, I think we'd recognize him, even here at the Domus."

Gersen shrugged and read the text:

> Lens Larque is said to be enamored of the whip; he considers it a trusty friend and a convenient instrument for the punishment of his enemies. He uses it often to this end, judging it preferable to other methods. At Sadabra he owns a great house with a semi-circular room where he sits to take his victual: great heaps of hork and pummigum* consumed with tankards of must. For savor he keeps by his side a fine short-handled whip, with a lash twelve and a half feet long. The pommel is ivory and engraved with the whip's name: PANAK. The reference has never been elucidated, to this writer's knowledge. The lash terminates in a bifurcated flap of leather four inches long: the "scorpion." Around the wall stand Lens Larque's enemies, manacled to rings and naked as eggs. To the buttocks of each is pasted a heart-shaped target three inches in diameter. To enliven his meal Lens Larque attempts to snap off the targets with the flutter of his whip, and his skill is said to be fine.

Underneath, in a different type face appeared the note:

> The piece duplicated above appeared originally in the *Galactic Review,* and probably is no more than the exercise of a perfervid imagination, especially in regard to the illustration. Report makes Lens Larque out to be a large man, but the giggling giant depicted above is hardly a credible representation.

> It is instructive to note that the author, Erasmus Heupter, dropped out of sight soon after

---

* Pummigum: a pudding of yellow meal, meat, tamarinds, ogave, scivit and like fruits, served in a thousand variants at restaurants catering to spacemen across the human universe.

publication of the article and was never seen
again. One of his associates received a short letter:

> Dear Cloebe:
> I am hard at work elucidating the
> meaning of the name PANAK. Already I
> have discovered several clues, but the
> work is not without its little surprises.
> The weather is fine, still I would as lief
> be home.
> In all sincerity, Erasmus.

Gersen gave a soft grunt. Rackrose said: "The skin tingles
a bit, does it not?"

"Yes, quite so. Are you still willing to cooperate in this
project?"

Rackrose winced. "Please don't use my name."

"As you like." Gersen examined the next item: a sheet of
typescript, apparently the work of Rackrose himself:

> The name Lens Larque is probably a pseudo-
> nym. Criminals tend to use false names and ali-
> ases. A true name can be traced to a home locale
> where photographs and intimate connections are
> discovered; secrecy and security are thereby frac-
> tured. Again, when the criminal succeeds at his
> illicit business, he ordinarily feels the impulse to
> return to his home community and there play the
> magnate among those who despised him in the
> past. The pretty girl who rejected him for a con-
> ventional husband: he now can patronize her, es-
> pecially if she has lost her good looks and lives in
> hard circumstances. All this is possible only if he
> is not identifiably a criminal; hence, he feels
> compelled to use a name of operation other than
> his own.

> These concepts, once they are pointed out,
> seem quite obvious; still, they take us to the ques-
> tion: what is the derivation of an assumed name?
> They come in two varieties: first, those names

selected at random and intended to be non-descript, and second, those with symbolic significance. The latter predominate among criminals of personal force and flamboyance, of whom Lens Larque is an excellent example. Therefore, I assume the name "Lens Larque" to be an alias which carries symbolic import.

I visited the local UTCS* and ordered a search of all the languages and dialects of the Oikumene and Beyond, past and present, for homonyms to the name "Lens Larque."

I attach the result.

Gersen examined an orange-bordered sheet displaying a UTCS print-out:

LENS LARQUE—homonyms, with definitions.

1. Lencilorqua: a village of 657 inhabitants on Vasselona Continent, Reis, sixth planet to Gamma Eridani.
2. Lanslarke: a predacious winged creature of Dar Sai, third planet of Cora, Argo Navis 961.
3. Laenzle arc: the locus of a point generated by the seventh theorem of triskoid dynamics, as defined by the mathematician Palo Laenzle (907-1070).
4. Linslurk: a moss-like growth native to the swamps of Sharmant, Hyaspis, fifth planet of Fritz's Star, Ceti 1620.
5. Linsil Orq: a lake of the Blissful Plains, Verlaren, second planet to Komred, Epsilon Sagittae.
6. Lensle Erg: a desert. . . .

The list continued through twenty-two entries, ever more distant from the standard.

Gersen returned to Rackrose's analysis:

I decided that, granted the hypothesis, the second entry appeared the most likely possibility.

* Universal Technical Consultative Service

From UTCS I extracted full particulars regarding the *lanslarke*. It is a four-winged creature with an arrow-shaped head and a stinging tail, reaching a length of ten feet exclusive of the tail. It flies over the Darsh deserts at dawn and twilight, preying upon ruminants and occasionally a lone man. The creature is cunning, swift, and ferocious, but is now rarely seen, though as a fetish of the Bugold Clan it is privileged to fly freely above their domains.

So much for the lanslarke, and on to Item No. 8 of the attached papers. This is the single and only account on record of a meeting with Lens Larque, at a relatively early stage of his career. The narrator never identifies himself but would seem to be the official of an industrial concern. The locale of the meeting is also indefinite; discretion held full sway.

Gersen turned to Item No. 8.

Excerpt from "Reminiscences of a Peripatetic Purchase Agent," by Sudo Nonimus, as published in *Thrust*, a trade journal of the metallurgical industry. (The author's name, as presented, is quite evidently a pseudonym.)

We met (Lens Larque and I) at a public eating house a hundred yards down the road from the village. The structure was an exercise in massive crudity, as if some monstrous entity had carelessly piled great concrete blocks one on the other, almost haphazard, to create a set of rambling irreglar enclosures. These blocks, whitewashed and in the sun's full glare, fairly dazzled the eyes. The spaces within however were cool and dim and once I had overcome my fear of blocks toppling about my ears, I judged the effect quaint and memorable.

Making inquiry of a languid serving-boy, I was directed to a corner table. Here Lens Larque sat to a great platter of meat and legumes. The food gave off a great waft of sour spice, harsh and offensive to the nostrils; nevertheless a purchase agent knows no qualms, so I took a seat opposite and watched him as he ate.

For a period he ignored me as if I were no more than one of the puff-bugs drifting lazily about the room; I therefore took occasion to measure him on my own terms. I saw a large man, heavy almost to the point of corpulence, cloaked in a voluminous white garment, the hood draped close about his face. I could see his complexion, a rich russet-bronze, like the haunch of a bay horse; I could likewise discern something of his features which were large but oddly pinched together, or even compressed. His eyes, when at last he troubled to glance at me, burnt with a yellow intensity which might have daunted me, had I not met many another such gaze in the course of my ordinary work, and which most often resulted from avaricious hope. No so in this case!

Finishing his meal, the man began to speak, in phrases selected as if by random and conveying no plausible import. Was this a novel bargaining trick? Did he hope to addle my thinking under a coil of perplexities? He did not know his man; as ever, I intended neither to be jockeyed nor hoodwinked, much less swindled. I heeded each word he spoke, taking care to make no assents nor dissents, lest these signs should be considered to form the basis of a bargain. My patience seemed to work an opposite effect upon this strange man. His voice became strident and harsh, and his gestures cut the air like flails.

At last I managed to interpose a quiet suggestion into the harangue. "In connection with our business, may I inquire your name?"

The question caught him up short. In a baleful voice he asked: "Do you question my fidelity?"

"By no means!" I made haste to reply, since the man was obviously truculent. I have dealt with many such in the course of my business, but none like this surly fellow. I continued in an affable tone. "I am a businessman; I merely wish to verify the identity of the person with whom I am dealing. It is a matter of ordinary commercial practice."

"Yes, yes," he muttered. "Quite so."

I pressed home my advantage. "Gentlemen settling to a bargain use conventional manners, and it is only polite that we address each other by name."

The fellow nodded thoughtfully and produced a most remarkable belch, redolent of the spice he had consumed. Since he took no heed of the matter, I gave no sign that I had noticed.

Again he said, "Yes, yes; quite so." And then: "Well, it is really no great affair. You may know me as Lens Larque." Leaning forward, he leered at me through the folds of his cloak. "This name suits me well, do you not agree?"

"On such short acquaintance I could not pretend to hold an opinion. Now, our business. What are your offerings?"

"Four tons of duodecimate* Black, SG 22, prime quality."

We had no difficulty in arriving at a bargain. He named a price. I could take it or leave it. I resolved to demonstrate that others than himself could act with dignity and decision, without wheedling, haggling or feigned outrage. I immediately accepted his tender, subject to proving out the quality. My stipulation stung his vanity, but I managed to allay his annoyance. In the end he saw reason, and became alarmingly jovial. The serving boy brought two great tankards of a vile mouse-flavored beer. Lens Larque quaffed his portion in three gulps and by the exigencies of the situation I was forced to do likewise, all the while giving fervent if silent thanks to the iron

---

* Duodecimates: those stable transuranic elements of atomic number in the 120's and beyond. Duodecimate Black is an unrefined sand consisting of various duodecimate sulfides, oxides and similar compounds, with a specific gravity here stipulated as ('SG-22.')

belly and matchless capacity developed by my
many long years as a purchasing agent.

Gersen replaced the papers in their folio. "Very good
work. Lens Larque takes on substance. He is a large fleshy
man with a large nose and chin, which might now be surgi-
cally altered. His skin on at least one occasion was reddish-
bronze. Naturally he can use skin-toner as easily as anyone
else. Lastly, his place of origin might well be the world Dar
Sai, from the evidence of his name and also the mention of
duodecimates, which are mined on Dar Sai."

Rackrose sat up in his chair. "Are you acquainted with
Wigaltown?"

"Not at all."

"It's a coarse and dismal neighborhood with a dozen or
more off-world enclaves. Altogether unfashionable, of course;
still, if you like odd smells and peculiar music Wigaltown is
the place to wander. There's a small Darsh colony and they
patronize a public house on Pilkamp Road. Tintle's Shade,
the place is called. I've often noticed the sign which reads
'Fine Darsh provender.'"

"That is interesting news," said Gersen. "If Lens Larque is
Darsh, and if he happened to pass through the neighborhood,
we might expect him to visit Tintle's Shade."

Maxel Rackrose glanced over his shoulder. "Even Dett
Mullian begins to look sinister. Why do you suppose that
Lens Larque is nearby?"

"I don't hold any firm opinion. Still, he might arrive at any
time."

"Mathematical probabilities guarantee at least this much."

"Exactly. We should acquaint ourselves with Tintle's Shade
for just this contingency."

Rackrose winced. "The place reeks with strange odors; I
wonder if I'm up to it."

Gersen rose to his feet. "We'll try 'fine Darsh provender'
for our supper. Perhaps we'll become devotees."

Rackrose reluctantly hoisted himself erect. "We had best
alter our gear," he grumbled. "Dressed for the Domus, we'd
be remarkable at Tintle's Shade. I'll disguise myself as a roof
mender and meet you there in an hour."

Gersen glanced down at his own garments: an elegant
loose blue suit, a loose-collared white shirt, a crimson sash. "I

feel as if I'm already in disguise. I'll change clothes and go as myself."

"In one hour. Pilkamp Road, in the dead middle of Wigaltown. We'll meet in the street. If you go by omnibus, get off at Noonan's Alley."

Gersen left the Domus and walked north through the dusk along the Orangery Parade. He wore a dark blouse, gray trousers caught in at the ankles and soft low boots: typical garments of the working spaceman.

At the Esplanade he mounted a transport platform and waited. The lake reflected the final glimmers of sunset color: rust-red, apple-green, somber orange. As Gersen watched they disappeared and the lake became a gunmetal shimmer, illuminated by a few faint lights along the far shore. . . . An open-sided omnibus approached. Gersen stepped aboard, seated himself, dropped a coin in the slot, that he might not be ejected at the next halt.

At the bend of the lake the Esplanade became Pilkamp Road. The omnibus slid north through Moynal and Drury under an endless chain of blue-white street lamps.

The bus entered Wigaltown. At that ramp nearest Noonan's Alley Gersen alighted.

Dark night had come to Wigaltown. At Gersen's back buttresses of black rock hunched into the lake. Across Pilkamp Road narrow buildings pushed their roofs high, to put unlikely shapes and odd angles against the sky. Some of the tall narrow windows showed light; others were dark.

Diagonally across the street hung an illuminated sign:

TINTLE'S SHADE

Fine Darsh provender:
Chatowsies
Pourrian
Ahagaree

Gersen crossed the street. From the shadows of Noonan's Alley came Maxel Rackrose, wearing brown corduroy trousers, a checkered brown and black shirt, a black vest decorated with tinsel blazons, a loose black cap with a metal bill.

Gersen read from the sign. " 'Chatowsies. Pourrian. Ahagaree.' Do you have your appetite with you?"

"Not really. I am a fastidious eater. I may taste a bit of this and that."

Gersen, who often had gulped down food he dared not think about, only laughed. "A keen journalist doesn't know the word 'fastidious.' "

"Somewhere we must draw the line," said Rackrose. "It may be here, at Tintle's Shade."

They pushed through the door into a hall. Ahead stairs led up to the upper floors; to the side an arch opened upon a white-tiled chamber heavy with a musty stench. A dozen men drank beer at a counter tended by an old woman in a black gown, with straight black hair, dark orange skin and a black mustache. Posters announced exhibitions and novelty dances, at Rath Eileann and elsewhere. One of these read:

The Great Rincus Troupe
Witness a hundred marvelous feats!
See the bungles dance and play while
the thongs whistle and keen!

Swister Day,
at Fuglass Hall.

Another:

Whippery Ned Ticket
and
his lively bungles!
How they leap! How they caper!

Whippery Ned sings songs of sliding leather
and chides his troupe for errors or
insufficient zeal, perhaps with a
smart tingle of the flick!

The woman behind the bar called out: "Why do you stand like hypnotized fish? Did you come to drink beer or to eat food?"

"Be patient," said Gersen. "We are making our decision."

The remark annoyed the woman. Her voice took on a

coarse edge. " 'Be patient,' you say? All night I pour beer for crapulous men; isn't that patience enough? Come over here, backwards; I'll put this spigot somewhere amazing, at full gush, and then we'll discover who calls for patience!"

"We have decided to take a meal," said Gersen. "How are the chatowsies tonight?"

"The same as always, no worse than any other. Be off with you; don't waste my time unless you're taking beer. . . . What's this? Smirk at me, will you?" She seized a mug of beer to hurl at Maxel Rackrose, who alertly jumped back into the anteroom, with Gersen close behind.

The woman gave her black mane a scornful toss, twisted her mustache between thumb and forefinger, then turned away.

"She lacks charm," grumbled Rackrose. "She will never know me as a habitué."

"The dining room may surprise us," said Gersen.

"Pleasantly, so I hope."

They started up the steps, which, like the beer-chamber, exhaled an unpleasant vapor: a compound of strange cooking oils, off-world condiments and a stale ammoniacal waft.

At the first landing Rackrose halted. "Candidly, I find this all a bit unsettling. Are you sure that we actually intend to dine here?"

"If you have qualms, go no farther. I myself have known places both better and worse."

Rackrose muttered under his breath, and trudged on up the steps.

A pair of heavy wooden doors opened into the restaurant. At widely separated tables small groups of men huddled like conspirators, drinking beer or eating from platters immediately below their faces.

A massive woman stepped forward. Gersen judged her no less formidable than the woman who tended the beer spigot, though perhaps a few years younger. Like the woman below, she wore a shapeless black gown and her hair hung in a rank tangle; her mustache was not quite so full. With glittering eyes she looked from one to the other. "Well then, do you wish to eat?"

"Yes; that is why we are here," said Gersen.

"Sit yonder."

The woman followed them across the room. When they

were seated she leaned forward portentously with hands on the table. "What is to your taste?"

"We know Darsh food by reputation only," said Gersen. "What are your special dishes?"

"Ah ha! Those we reserve for our own eating. Out here we serve *chichala**, and you must make the best of it."

"What of the fine Darsh provender you advertise? The chatowsies, the pourrian, the ahagaree?"

"Look about you. Men are eating."

"True."

"Then that is what you must eat."

"Bring us portions of all these dishes; we will give them a try."

"As you like." The woman departed.

Rackrose sat in glum silence while Gersen looked around the room. "Our man is not among those present," said Gersen at last.

Rackrose glanced skeptically from table to table. "Did you seriously expect to find him here?"

"Not with any confidence. Still, coincidences occur. If he were passing through Rath Eileann, this is where we would hope to find him."

Maxel Rackrose surveyed Gersen dubiously. "You are not telling me all you know."

"Should that surprise you?"

"Not at all. But I'd like a hint as to what I'm getting into."

"Tonight you need fear only the chatowsies and perhaps the pourrian. If our research continues, it might entail danger. Lens Larque is a sinister man."

Rackrose glanced nervously around the room. "I would prefer to give the fellow no offense. He has a rancorous disposition. Remember Erasmus Heupter? Whatever the word 'Panak' means, I don't care to know."

The woman approached with a tray. "Here is the beer which men customarily take with their food. It is also usual for newcomers to provide a bit of entertainment. The shadow-box is yonder; a coin will produce a troupe of amusing figments."

---

* *Chichala*: an indelicate term. In the present context the word metaphorically connotes food prepared for and served to men.

Gersen turned to Rackrose. "You are expert in such affairs; you shall make the choice."

"With pleasure," said Rackrose rather heavily. He went to the shadow-box, read the list of offerings, pulled a toggle and dropped a coin into the hopper. A shrill voice called out: "It's Javil Natkin and the Sly Rogues!" To a clattering music of blocks and chinklepins, the entertainers appeared in projected image: a tall thin man in white and black diaper, carrying a whip, and a band of six small boys wearing only long red stockings.

Natkin sang a set of doggerel verses lamenting the faults of his charges, then performed an eccentric prancing jig, snapping his whip this way and that, while the boys hopped, whirled and scampered with extraordinary agility. Natkin, expressing dissatisfaction with their antics, flicked his whip at the plump buttocks. The boys so stimulated turned frantic somersaults, until Natkin stood surrounded by tumbling boys, whereupon he threw up his arms in triumph and the images disappeared. Patrons, who had given earnest attention to the display, muttered and grumbled and returned to their food.

From the kitchen came the black-gowned woman, with bowls and platters. She thumped them down upon the table. "Here is the food. Chatowsies. Pourrian. Ahagaree. Eat your fill. What you leave returns to the pot."

"Thank you," said Gersen. "By the way, who is 'Tintle?' "

The woman gave a derisive snort. "Tintle's name is on the sign. We do the work; we chink the coin. Tintle keeps his distance."

"If possible, I'd like a few words with Tintle."

The woman gave a derisive snort. "You'd like nothing whatever from Tintle; he's stupid and dull. Still, for what it's worth, you'll find him in the back yard counting his fingers or scratching himself with a stick."

The woman moved away. Gersen and Rackrose gingerly addressed themselves to the food. After a few moments Rackrose said: "I can't decide what tastes worst. The chatowsies are fetid, but the ahagaree is ferocious. The pourrian is merely vile. And the lady seems to have washed her dog in the beer. . . . What? Are you eating more?"

"You must do the same. We want to establish a pretext for returning. Here; try some of these remarkable condiments."

Rackrose held up his hand. "I have taken quite enough, at least on the basis of my present salary."

"As you wish." Gersen gulped down a few more mouthfuls, then thoughtfully put down his spoon. "We have seen enough for this evening." He signaled to the woman. "Madame, our account, if you please."

The woman looked over the platters. "You have eaten ravenously. I will need two or, better, three svu from each of you."

Rackrose cried out in protest. "Three svu for a few mouthfuls of food? That would be exorbitant at the Domus!"

"The Domus serves insipid gutch. Pay your account or I will sit on your head."

"Come now," said Gersen. "That is no way to attract a steady clientele. I might add that we are waiting to meet a certain member of the Bugold Clan."

"Bah!" sneered the woman. "What is that to me? A Bugold outcast robbed the Kotzash warehouse, and so now I live here in this place of dank winds and curdled rheum."

"I've heard a somewhat different story," said Gersen with an air of careless omniscience.

"Then you heard nonsense! The Bugold rachepol and that scorpion Panshaw connived together. They should have been broken and not poor Tintle. Now pay me my coin and go your way. This talk of Kotzash has put me out of sorts."

Gersen resignedly put down six svu. The woman, with a triumphant leer toward Maxel Rackrose, swept up the coins. "As for the gratuity, another two svu will be considered adequate."

Gersen handed over the coins and Madame Tintle departed.

Rackrose gave a snort of disgust. "You are far too obliging. The woman's avarice is matched only by the vileness of her cuisine."

Madame Tintle spoke over his shoulder. "By chance I overheard that remark. On your next visit I will boil up my crotch-strap for your chatowsies." Once again she swept away. Gersen and Rackrose also took their leave.

Out on the street they stood a moment. Mist hung over the lake; street-lamps north and south along Pilkamp Road showed as receding aureoles of pale blue light.

"What now?" asked Rackrose. "Is it to be Tintle?"

"Yes," said Gersen. "He is conveniently close to hand."

"That vulgar female mentioned a back yard," grumbled Rackrose. "We will find it around yonder, there, up Noonan's Alley."

The two men walked around the corner of Tintle's Shade, up the hill beside a wall which presently showed a gate of metal bars, giving on Tintle's back yard. To the rear stood a line of ramshackle sheds, one of which showed a light.

At an upper window someone created a clangor by striking a pan against the wall, then lowered a pot on a length of string.

"It appears," said Gersen, "that Tintle is about to dine."

The door to the shed opened, to reveal the silhouette of a squat heavy-shouldered man. He ambled across the yard, detached the pot from the line and carried it back to the shed.

Rackrose called through the gate: "Tintle! Hoy, Tintle! Over here by the gate!"

Tintle halted in surprise, then turned and ran spraddle-legged to his shed. The door closed behind him; the lights were immediately extinguished.

"That's all from Tintle tonight," said Gersen.

The two returned to Pilkamp Road, boarded the next omnibus and rode south to Rath Eileann Old Town.

Chapter 4

From *The Demon Princes* by Carol Carphen:

The author of this monograph, as he ponders the Demon Princes and their marvelous deeds, often becomes confused by the multiplicity of events. To cure this condition he resorts to generalizations, only to see each such edifice collapse under the weight of qualification.

In basic fact the five individuals have but a single aspect in common: their total disregard for human pain.

Thus, as we hold Lens Larque up for comparison to his peers, we find no correspondence save in this single quality. Even that anonymity and secrecy which one might suppose to be a basic element of the craft is, in the case of Lens Larque, distorted into something rude and brash, so that it seems almost a craving for public attention. Lens Larque at times appears almost eager to exhibit himself.

Still, when we sum up what we know about Lens Larque, we discover few definite facts. He has been described as a tall man of considerable bulk who, through his burning gaze and abrupt movements, gives the impression of a passionate and volatile disposition. No clear descriptions of his face are extant. According to rumor, he is expert in the use of the whip and takes pleasure in so punishing his enemies.

The essay concludes with the summation:

Once again, as I succumb to the allure of generality, let me put forward the following propositions:

The evil magnificence of the Demon Princes cannot be quantitatively compared. On a qualitative basis they can be, perhaps intuitively, characterized.

1. Viole Falushe is as malignant as a wasp.
2. Malagate the Woe is inhumanly callous.
3. Kokor Hekkus enjoys horrifying pranks.
4. Howard Alan Treesong is inscrutable, devious, and very likely insane, if the concept is at all applicable to such folk as these.
5. Lens Larque is brutal, revengeful, and extravagantly sensitive to slights. Like Kokor Hekkus he is not unknown to sadism, in grotesque variation. Occasionally one finds references to a "reek" or "coarse effluvium" in connection with his person, but whether this is psychological aura or actual bad odor is never made clear. Still, Lens Larque would seem to be the most physically unappealing of all the Demon Princes, with the possible exception of Howard Alan Treesong, whose aspect is unknown.

Trails of rain from a pre-dawn storm swept the north end of Lake Feamish; over Rath Eileann clouds scudded and raced, and let blazing shafts of Vega-light down upon the gray city. So, in alternate shine and shadow, Gersen and Jehan Addels walked along the Esplanade toward the Estremont.

Addels went stiffly and without enthusiasm, his shoulders hunched, his face dour and bleak. As they neared the causeway he stopped short. "Do you know, this is sheer madness."

"But in a good cause," said Gersen. "Someday you'll congratulate yourself."

Addels grudgingly proceeded. "The day I'm discharged from Frogtown Pits."

Gersen offered no reply.

At the causeway Addels halted once again. "You should come no farther. We must not be seen together."

"Quite right. I'll wait here."

Addels continued across the causeway. The great doors of glass and iron opened before him; he entered a silent foyer paved in white marble and stelt*.

Addels ascended to the fourth floor and marched despondently to the offices of the Chief Clerk. Outside in the corridor he halted, drew a deep breath, threw back his shoulders, licked his lips, relaxed his face into a mask of serenity and confidence, then stepped through the door.

A marble counter crossed the room. At the back four underclerks in dark red gowns scrutinized documents. They looked up with empty expressions, then returned to their work.

Addels gave a peremptory rap on the marble. One of the clerks made a sad face, rose to his feet and approached the counter. "What may be your business?""

"I want to consult the Chief Clerk," said Addels.

"At what time was your appointment?"

"My appointment is now," snapped Addels. "Announce me and be smart about it!"

The clerk spoke a languid word or two into a mesh, then ushered Addels into a high-ceilinged chamber, illuminated by a crystal globe of a hundred facets. Rose velvet drapes hung across the high windows; a semi-circular desk in the Old Empire style, enameled ivory-white with gilt and vermilion accents, occupied the center of a pale blue carpet. Here, at his ease, sat a balding middle-aged man, well-fleshed and round-faced, with a benign expression. Like the under-clerks he wore a dark red gown, as well as a square white cap displaying the official emblem of Llinliffet's Land. As Addels stepped forward, he rose courteously to his feet. "Counsellor Addels, it is both my duty and my pleasure to serve you."

"Thank you." Addels seated himself in the chair indicated.

The Chief Clerk poured tea into a cup of frail Beleek and placed it within Addels' reach.

"Most gracious of you," said Addels. He sipped. "Superb. Lutic Gold, to hazard a guess? With a bit of something to sharpen the edge?"

---

* Stelt: a precious slag mined from the surfaces of burnt-out stars.

"You have a fine discrimination," said the Chief Clerk. "Lutic Gold it is, from the north slope, with an ounce of Black Dassaward to the pound. For brisk mornings such as this I consider it quite appropriate."

For a few minutes the two discussed tea, then Addels said: "Now, as to my business. I represent Cooney's Bank, now chartered at Rath Eileann. As you may know we have instituted action against Celerus Transport Company, of Vire, Sadal Suud Four; the ship *Ettilia Gargantyr*; and others. I have conferred with the Honorable Duay Pingo who will stand for the ship. He is anxious to expedite the case and I quite agree. In effect I speak for both parties to the action. We request the earliest possible place on the calendar."

The Chief Clerk, pursing his lips and blowing his cheeks, consulted a document which lay in front of him. "It so happens that we can schedule a relatively prompt hearing. A certain Lord High Benchmaster Dalt has been assigned to the circuit."

Addels raised his sandy eyebrows. "Would that be Benchmaster Waldemar Dalt who benched Interworld Court at Myrdal on Boniface?"

"The same. There's quite a piece about him in the *Legal Observer*."

"The *Legal Observer*, eh? I have not seen this journal before."

"It's the first issue, published at New Wexford. I received a complimentary copy, no doubt by virtue of my office."

"I must find an issue," said Addels, "if only to read up on Dalt."

"It makes interesting reading. They compliment Dalt for his precision, but they describe him as a bit of a martinet."

"That's my recollection." Taking up the magazine Addels studied the article. A photograph depicted a harsh-featured man wearing black and white judicial costume, the black frontal fringe of the traditional headdress hanging low across his forehead. Black eyebrows emphasized his extreme pallor. A clenched mouth and narrow glinting eyes suggested inflexibility and perhaps severity.

"Hmmf," said Addels. "That's Benchmaster Dalt. I've seen him in action. He's as hard as he looks." He put the magazine down. The Chief Clerk picked it up and read aloud.

"Sometimes regarded as over-abstract and over-rigorous,

Benchmaster Dalt is by no means a dreamy-eyed theorist; to the contrary, he insists upon full etiquette. Court officials consider him a stern disciplinarian."

With a faint smile Addels asked: "And what do you think of that?"

The Chief Clerk shook his head ruefully. "He seems a tyrannical old griffin, for a fact."

"He's not all that old; in fact some say he leans over backward on that account."

"Yes, yes," muttered the Chief Clerk. "I've heard much the same story, from one source or another."

"Smarten up your bailiffs," said Addels. "Provide your stentor the best throat lozenges—because Benchmaster Dalt is coming to enliven your court. He watches like an eagle. If someone scamps his duty, he's flayed to the bone. Personally, I'd prefer a more affable judge. Won't someone else be working the session?"

The Chief Clerk gave his head a troubled shake. "You'll have to deal with Dalt, and so will I. Many thanks for your advice; I'll warn my bailiffs, and Benchmaster Dalt will have no complaint."

The two men sipped tea in thoughtful silence. Then Addels said: "Perhaps I'm lucky to draw Dalt after all. He's draconic against swindlers and he'll cut through technicalities to deal out justice; still it's a mixed blessing. So when will we have our hearing?"

"Maasday next, at half morning."

Maasday morning a storm drove down Lake Feamish, piling up whitecaps to pound against the Estremont foundations. The tall windows of the courtroom admitted only a wet gray light, and the three chandeliers, symbolizing the three Vegan planets, glowed at full power. The Chief Clerk sat at his desk wearing immaculate scarlet and black robes with a black cushion hat. By the door a pair of bailiffs stood, erect, alert and mindful of Benchmaster Dalt's reputation for irascibility. To the right sat Counsellor Duay ˉPingo with his clients, to the left Counsellor Jehan Addels with officials of Conney's Bank. A half-dozen casual spectators were on hand for reasons best known to themselves. Silence held the room. Only the far whisper of waves against stone could be heard.

A chime sounded the hour of half-morning. From the rear

chamber came Lord High Benchmaster Dalt, a personage of middle size, spare of physique, wearing full High Court regalia. The headpiece fringed his forehead and hung black swafts over his ears. Looking neither right nor left he mounted to the bench, then glanced swiftly around the room, his chalk-white pallor and taut uncompromising features creating an effect of austere elegance.

Across the centuries the rituals of the Vegan judicial system had been simplified, but were still notorious for symbolic homologies. The Lord High Benchmaster no longer rode to the bench in a chair carried by four blind virgins, but the bench itself—the "Balance"—still rested upon a wedge-shaped fulcrum, even though most progressive Benchmasters stipulated stabilizing struts to dampen the quivering Needle of Justice.*

Benchmaster Dalt had ordained rigid stabilizers for the Balance, to hold the needle fixed at equilibrium.

The stentor appeared on a balcony behind the bench. "Be it now heard; oyez! This sacred court, ruled by Lord High Benchmaster Waldemar Dalt is now in session!" He threw three white feathers into the air to symbolize the liberation of three white doves. Holding his arms on high, he called: "Let the wings of truth fare far across this land! The Court of Interworld Equity now sits in session."

Lowering his arms, he backed into his alcove and disappeared from view.

Benchmaster Dalt rapped with his gavel, and glanced at a memorandum. "I will hear preliminary statements in the case of Cooney's Bank vs. the Celerus Transport Company, the ship *Ettilia Gargantyr*, its officers and all its lawful owners. Are the parties at contest present?"

"Ready for the plaintiffs, your Lordship," said Addels.

"Ready for the defendants, your Lordship," said Duay Pingo.

Benchmaster Dalt addressed Addels. "Be so good as to construct your complaint."

"Thank you, your Lordship. Our plea for damages is based

---

* The Benchmaster who rode the Balance so rigidly that the needle showed no motion, in the sly vernacular of the courtroom, was said to be "stiff of arse," while a more restless official, under whose shifts and shrugs the needle swung back and forth, might become known as "old flitter-britches."

upon the following sequence of events. On a date, which when translated into Gaean Standard time, becomes Day 212 of the year 1524, at the city Thrump on David Alexander's Planet, the owner of the ship *Ettilia Gargantyr* maliciously and spitefully conspired with the ship's commanding office, a certain Wislea Toom, so to defraud the local Victualler's Guild of moneys legally and rightfully due them and thereupon put their nefarious plan into effect, by the simple and shameless process—"

Benchmaster Dalt rapped with his gavel. "If Counsellor will control his indignation and favor the court with a simple explanation of the facts, and allow me to decide the applicability of such terms as 'nefarious' and 'shameless,' we shall proceed much more crisply with this case."

"Thank you, your Lordship. No doubt I anticipate my full presentation, but we are pleading for punitive as well as actual damages, on the basis of malice and fraud with premeditated intent."

"Very well, proceed. But remember, I am not partial to subjective presentations."

"Thank you, your Lordship. The defalcation occurred, as I have stated. The injured parties filed local action; however, the *Ettilia Gargantyr* had vanished, as had the Celerus Transport Company.

"In due course the cause of action was transferred to Cooney's Bank.

"The arrival of the *Ettilia Gargantyr* at Rath Eileann laid *in rem* jurisdiction in this court and, pursuant to our writ of attachment, we prepared a new action. The *Ettilia Gargantyr* is now immobilized at Slayhack Spaceport. We pray for actual damages to the amount of twelve thousand eight hundred and twenty-five svu. We declare that the owner of the ship, through the apparently fictitious 'Celerus Transport Company,' maliciously and in arrogant contempt of lawful process conspired with Captain Wislea Toom to the detriment of the plaintiff's assignors. We feel that conduct of such description is all too common and merits a vigorous rebuke, and this is the basis of our plea for punitive damages."

"You use the term 'owner' of the *Ettilia Gargantyr*. I abhor circumlocution. Please identify this person by name."

"I am sorry, your Lordship! I do not know his name."

"Very well, then." *Rap* went the gavel. "Counsellor Pingo, do you have a statement?"

"Simply this, your Lordship. The action is monstrous and extravagant. It is a mischievous exploitation of what at worst was a rather trivial oversight. We do not challenge that a claim against the ship at one time existed. We adamantly deny the competence of Cooney's Bank to act in this regard and we consider the charges of malice and conspiracy inapplicable."

"You will be given opportunity to demonstrate as much, through the testimony of your principals." Benchmaster Dalt surveyed Duay Pingo's clients. "The lawful and registered owner of the ship is now present?"

"No, your Lordship, he is not.'

"'Then how do you expect to defend against the charges?"

"By demonstrating their total absurdity, your Lordship."

"Aha, Counsellor! There you insult my intelligence. In my experience dozens of apparent absurdities have turned out to be unassailable facts. I will point out that the action is specific. It alleges malice, fraud and conspiracy, and these charges may not be countered by either rhetoric or obfuscation. You are wasting the time of this court. How long will you need to produce the proper respondents?"

Pingo could only shrug his shoulders. "One moment, your Lordship, if you please." He went to consult his clients, who muttered uncertainly among themselves. Pingo returned to face Benchmaster Dalt. "Your Lordship, I point out that my clients are undergoing unnecessary hardship, due to the costs of operating the ship, including salaries, insurance, berth rental and the like. May we post bond as guarantee to the payment of some fair settlement, should in fact your judgment go against us, and so let the ship be on its way? This is only simple justice."

Dalt glared at Duay Pingo. "You are appointing yourself, in my court, as the arbiter and explicator of justice?"

"By no means, your Lordship! It was merely a way of speaking. An unhappy phrase, for which I apologize!"

Benchmaster Dalt appeared to reflect. Jehan Addels, lifting his arm as if to scratch his head, muttered into his sleeve: "Specify full value of ship and cargo. No bondsman in town or anywhere else will risk so much."

Benchmaster Dalt spoke. "I rule in favor of the defendant's

request, provided that he posts bond to the full value of ship and cargo, which would represent the maximum indemnity."

Duay Pingo winced. "That may well be impossible, your Lordship."

"Then produce your proper witnesses and let us try the case properly! You can't have the situation both ways! What good is a defense action without facts or pertinent testimony from responsive witnesses? Get your case together or you must lose by default."

"Thank you, your Lordship, I will hold immediate consultation with my clients. May I request a short postponement?"

"Certainly. For how long?"

"I am not at this point certain. I will presently notify the Court Clerk, if such suits my esteemed colleague and your Lordship."

"I am content," said Jehan Addels, "so long as the continuance does not exceed a reasonable time."

"Very well, so ruled. Let us be quite definite, Counsellor Pingo. I require direct testimony from the principal of the case. He will be the person who owned the ship at the time of the alleged infraction, together with proof as to his ownership. I will not accept depositions, proxies or agents. So long as this is understood, I grant a continuance of two weeks. If you require more time, please apply to the Court Clerk."

"Thank you, your Lordship."

"Court is adjourned."

The Lord High Benchmaster stalked to his chambers. The Chief Clerk mopped his face with a blue kerchief and muttered to a bailiff, "Have you ever seen such a griffin?"

"He's a bad one, for sure, touchy as a blastiff with boils. Glad I am that I'll never need to face him in court."

"Bah!" muttered the Chief Clerk. "Belch once in his court and he'll order your gizzard toasted. I'm all in a sweat from holding my breath."

During the evening Gersen received a call from Jehan Addels.

"Miraculously," Addels noted, "we are still out of jail."

"It's a pleasant sensation," said Gersen. "Enjoy it while you can."

"Everything is so fragile! Suppose a diligent journalist looks in the Legal Record? Suppose the Chief Clerk gossips with someone from Boniface? Suppose he places other cases into the docket?"

Gersen grinned. "Benchmaster Dalt no doubt will dispense equity."

"More properly, Benchmaster Dalt should plead indisposition," declared Addels. "Remember, not all lawyers are fools!"

"No need to borrow trouble. Pingo is sending messages across the galaxy. There will be a great disturbance somewhere."

"How true! Well then—what next?"

"We wait to see who appears when the hearings resume."

Chapter 5

From *Dar Sai and the Darsh*, by Joinville Akers:

The Darsh whip-dances constitute a highly structured art form. I say this flatly and without qualification, after having devoted considerable time to the subject. A savage and repellent art form, granted; an art form grounded in a whole cluster of sexual aberrations, i.e: pederasty, flagellation, sado-masochism, voyeurism, exhibitionism: so much is conceded. It is an art form to which I personally am not attracted, though at times it exerts a certain horrid fascination.

The intricacies of whip-dancing totally elude the uninitiated. During the ordinary routine the whip-wielder, contrary to appearances, seldom injures or even inflicts serious pain upon the dancers. Like other apparently horrendous exhibitions, a great part is show. The thematic material to the outsider seems repetitive and limited and more often than not depends upon a simple tried and true premise: the whipmaster and his troupe of prankish, unruly or insubordinate "bungle" boys. The variations upon this theme, however, are intricate, subtle, often ingenious, often amusing, and inexhaustibly popular with Darsh males. Darsh females, on the other hand, observe these spectacles with contemptuous indifference, and consider them merely another aspect of masculine fatuity.

Gersen and Maxel Rackrose alighted from the omnibus, then stood for a moment looking across Pilkamp Road at Tintle's Shade. "It presents no braver face by daylight," said

43

Rackrose. "In fact, I can now discern peeling paint and windows hung all askew."

"No matter," said Gersen. "The dilapidation is picturesque and will enhance our lunch."

"Today," said Rackrose, "I lack all appetite. Still, don't let me deter you from your own meal."

"Perhaps something on the menu will tempt you."

They crossed the street, pushed through the door, passed the beer counter by and mounted the dank steps to the restaurant.

Only a few tables were in use. Madame Tintle stood idly by the kitchen pass-through, twirling the tip of her mustache. Languidly she signaled them to a table and ambled over to inquire their needs. "So the two of you are back. I never thought to see you again."

Gersen essayed a gallantry. "We were drawn as much by your colorful personality as by the food."

"What would you mean by that?" demanded the woman. "You are aspersing either me or the food. Either way you'll get a pot of slops over your head."

"No offense intended," said Gersen. "In fact I can put you in the way of some money, if the prospect suits you."

"Of all races Darsh are most avaricious. What is the proposal?"

"A friend of mine will shortly be arriving from Dar Sai, or so I expect."

"He is Darsh?"

"Yes."

"The situation is hardly possible. Darsh men make no friends, only enemies."

"This gentleman is, if you prefer, an acquaintance. When he arrives, he will surely visit Tintle's Shade, to eat familiar food. I want you to notify me of his arrival, so that we may renew our acquaintance."

"Easily done, but how will I recognize him?"

"Just inform me or my friend whenever a new Darsh comes to Tintle's Shade.'

"Well—it's not particularly convenient, I can't sort over every odd goumbah* who creeps in from the street. My curiosity would arouse frivolous comment."

___
* A pejorative term used by Darsh women in reference to men: a person of vulgar futile stupidity.

"Perhaps Tintle himself might be pressed into service," suggested Rackrose.

"Tintle?" The woman made a rasping sound in her throat. "Tintle's been smirched and broken. He's not allowed up here; everyone would hold their noses and leave. I can barely tolerate his presence in the yard."

Gersen asked: "How did this come about?"

Madame Tintle looked around the room, then finding no better use for her time, condescended to reply. "It was on the whole a sad misfortune, which Tintle never earned. At the Kotzash warehouse Tintle was the proud guard. But when they came to loot and steal, Tintle slept rather than guarded and failed to throw the switch. All the duodecimates were taken. Then it was learned that Ottile Panshaw the bursar had neglected insurance, so all was lost. Panshaw could not be found, so the whole countryside came down on Tintle. He was fixed under the public latrine for three days, and everyone expressed themselves as the mood took them. Tintle and Dar Sai no longer could stomach each other, so we came to this dreary bog. That is the story."

"Hmmf," said Gersen. "If Tintle had been a friend of Lens Larque, affairs might have gone differently."

The woman eyed him with dour suspicion. "Why do you speak of Lens Larque?"

"He is a famous man."

"Infamous, rather. It was Lens Larque who robbed the Kotzash warehouse; why should he be a friend of Tintle? Though that was the accusation."

"Then you know Lens Larque by sight?"

"He is a Bugold and none of my affair."

"He might be sitting across the room at this moment."

"So long as he finds no fault and pays his account, what do I care?" She looked contemptuously around the room. "He is not here today, that is certain."

"Well and good," said Gersen, "but back to our arrangement. When a strange Darsh appears—Lens Larque or any other—notify me or my friend Maxel Rackrose, who will take his lunch here every day. Each time you point out a strange Darsh, you will be paid two svu. Point out Lens Larque and earn ten svu. And should you lead me to my friend, you shall earn twenty svu."

Madame Tintle compressed her black brows in perplexity.

"A most unusual arrangement. Why do you want Lens Larque? Most folk would pay ten svu or more to avoid him."

"We are journalists. I consider him a prime subject for an interview, should he appear. Certainly we can not expect such good luck."

Madam Tintle shrugged. "I have nothing to lose. Now, what will you eat?"

"I'll take a few bites of ahagaree," said Gersen.

"The same for me," said Rackrose, "but less sulfur and iodine than usual."

"What about chatowsies?"

"None today."

Leaving the restaurant Gersen and Rackrose walked around to the back of the building and approached the iron gate. Through the bars they saw Tintle hunched in the pale sunlight before one of the sheds. Each of his three-inch earlobes terminated in a dangling metal ornament; Tintle amused himself by flicking these with his finger and letting them swing. Gersen called out: "Tintle! Hey, Tintle!"

Tintle rose slowly to his feet: a squat man with copper-colored skin and lumpy features. He came a few steps forward, then halted, to peer in suspicion toward the gate. "What do you want with me?"

"You are that Tintle who guarded the Kotzash warehouse?'

"I know nothing about it!" bawled Tintle. "I was asleep and innocent in every respect!"

"But you were broken."

"It was a gross error!"

"And you ultimately plan to vindicate yourself?"

Tintle blinked. "I had not thought so far ahead."

"We would definitely like to hear your version of the case."

Tintle came slowly toward the gate. "Who are you, asking such questions?"

"Investigators in the cause of justice."

"I have had enough justice. Investigate Ottile Panshaw and break him; I will lead the line to the latrine." Tintle turned and started back toward his shed.

"Just a moment!" called Gersen. "We have not discussed benefits."

Tintle came to a tentative halt. "What benefits?"

"First a fee in payment for the value of your time. Second, punishment of the robbers."

Tintle made a sound of incredulous amusement. "Who intends to punish Lens Larque?"

"Anything might happen. At the moment we only wish to hear details of the case."

Tintle looked from one to the other. "What is your official status?"

"Don't inquire too closely. High officials can't offer fees."

Tintle at last showed flexibility. "How much are you offering?"

"That depends upon what you tell us. Five svu, at the least."

"That is no vast sum," Tintle grumbled. "Still, I suppose that it will suffice." He looked up toward the windows at the back of the restaurant. "There she stands, a great rat glaring down from its hole. Let us transfer our business to Groary's Tavern, across the way."

"As you wish."

Tintle unharnessed the gate and passed through into the alley. "She'll be sorely vexed to see us going off to the tavern, and I'll eat slops for a week. Still, let's be away. A man must never heed the woman's roar."

Black piles emerging from the waters of Lake Feamish supported the rear deck of Groary's Tavern. The three men took seats at a wooden table. Tintle hunched forward, and Gersen thought to perceive the inkling of a sickly stench. Imagination? Tintle? A bubble up from the lake-bottom slime?

"I believe that five svu was mentioned," said Tintle.

Gersen put money on the table. "We are interested in the Kotzash robbery. Remember, if the loot was recovered, you might well be vindicated and indemnified."

Tintle gave a harsh laugh. "Do you take me for a fool? In this life events bend to no such kindly patterns. I'll tell you what I know and take your money and that will be the end of it."

Gersen shrugged. "You were guard at Kotzash warehouse. What exactly is 'Kotzash?' "

"Ottile Panshaw formed the corporation. The miners brought in duodecimates and placed them with Panshaw, who paid off in shares of Kotzash Mutual. The shares were ostensibly redeemable in svu at any time. So it went, and the warehouse at Serjeuz bulged with packets of fine duodecimate. How could Lens Larque not be tempted? Some say that Ottile Panshaw notified him when the warehouse could hold no more. So Lens Larque dropped his great black ship into the compound during the night. His villains came bounding into the warehouse and I was lucky to make my escape, for surely they would have killed me. This consideration failed to quell the general rage. They demanded why I, the designated guard, had failed to protect the warehouse, and why the great gate had been left ajar. I blamed Ottile Panshaw, but he was absent. Therefore I was dragged to the Central Sump and broken."

"A sorry tale," said Gersen. "Still, how do you know that Lens Larque was responsible?"

Tintle gave a fretful toss of the head which set his pendules to jerking. "Enough that I tell you as much. It is not a name to be discussed at length."

"Nevertheless, the guilty man must be brought to justice, and your contribution may be of assistance."

"'And when Lens Larque hears of my verbosity, what then? I dance ten fandangos to the music of Panak."

"Your name will not be spoken." Gersen brought forth another five svu certificate. "Tell us what you know."

"It is nothing very much. I am of the Dupp Clan; Lens Larque is a Bugold. I knew him well in the old days. At Naidnaw Shade we played hadaul* and everyone joined a cabal against him. But he had worked a counter-strategy, and it was I whose bones were broken."

"What sort of man is he?"

Tintle shook his head at a loss for words. "He is a big man. He has a long nose and fleering eyes. At the Kotzash warehouse he wore a thabbat**, but I knew him by his voice and his fust.***"

"If he stepped into Tintle's Shade, would you know him?"

Tintle gave a gloomy grunt. "I am not tolerated in the

* Hadaul: a Darsh game, combining elements of conspiracy, double-dealing, cunning, trickery and a general free-for-all melee.
** Thabbat: the Darsh hood, usually of white or blue cloth.
*** Fust: an odor exuded by Darsh men.

Shade. He could come and go a dozen times; I'd never be the wiser."

"When you played hadaul, what name did he use?"

"That was long ago. Then he was simple Husse Bugold, though already he was rachepol."

"You have photographs of Lens Larque?"

Tintle snorted. "Why should I cherish such mementos? He is high, I am low. He exudes a fust of meriander and fine koruna and red-oil ahagaree; I reek of the sump."

Gersen pushed the money across the table. "If you should see Lens Larque, be wary. Claim no acquaintance; don't let him recognize you. Communicate at once with Maxel Rackrose." He wrote on a card and pushed it across the table.

Tintle twitched his mouth in a quick uneasy wince. "It seems that you expect Lens Larque."

"We can only hope," said Gersen. "He is an elusive man."

Tintle began to have second thoughts. "I might not know him now. It is said that he has changed himself. Have you heard how the Methlen taunted him? He wanted to live in a fine house, but the neighbor wouldn't allow it. He said he wanted no ugly Darsh face hanging over the garden walls. Lens Larque was exasperated and changed his face at once. Who knows what he looks like now?"

"Use your intuition. What happened to Ottile Panshaw?"

"He crossed to Twanish on Methel. For all I know he's there yet."

"And what of Kotzash: does the corporation still function?"

Tintle spat upon the floor. "I paid in four hundred ounces of good black sand—a true fortune—and I received forty shares of stock. I gambled at hadaul and I now have ninety-two." From a greasy wallet he extracted a packet of folded papers. "There are the certificates. Their value: nil."

Gersen examined the papers. "They are bearer certificates. I'll buy them from you." He placed ten svu upon the table.

"What?" cried Tintle. "For almost a hundred shares of prime Kotzash stock? Do I seem such a dunderhead? Each share represents not only ten ounces of sand but other values: rights, options, leases. . . ." He looked askance as Gersen picked up the ten svu. "Not so fast! I accept your offer."

Gersen slid the money across the table. "I suspect that you

have made the better bargain, but no matter. If you chance to notice the man whom we have discussed, inform us and you will be rewarded. Is there anything else you can tell me?"

"No."

"If you supply us more information, we'll pay you well."

Tintle vouchsafed only a surly grunt. He finished his beer at a gulp and departed the tavern, with both Gersen and Maxel Rackrose leaning back from the waft of his passage.

Chapter 6

From *Life*. Volume I, by Unspiek, Baron Bodissey:

The evil man is a source of fascination; ordinary persons wonder what impels such extremes of conduct. A lust for wealth? A common motive, undoubtedly. A craving for power? Revenge against society? Let us grant these as well. But when wealth has been gained, power achieved and society brought down to a state of groveling submission, what then? Why does he continue?

The response must be: the love of evil for its own sake.

The motivation, while incomprehensible to the ordinary man, is nonetheless urgent and real. The malefactor becomes the creature of his own deeds. Once the transition has been overpassed a new set of standards comes into force. The perceptive malefactor recognizes his evil and knows full well the meaning of his acts. In order to quiet his qualms he retreats into a state of solipsism, and commits flagrant evil from sheer hysteria, and for his victims it appears as if the world has gone mad.

At noon on St. Dulver's Day, Maxel Rackrose presented himself at Gersen's chambers in the Domus. His manner was subdued; he spoke tersely. "During the last two weeks I have monitored travelers incoming at Slayhack, New Wexford and Pontefract spaceports. Twenty originated in the Cora system, but only three described themselves as Darsh. The others are Methlen. None of the Darsh fit specifications. Three of the Methlen might conceivably be our man. These are the photographs."

Gersen looked over the faces: none held meaning for him. Rackrose placed down another photograph with the air of a magician performing a feat. "This man is Ottile Panshaw, who forgot to pay the Kotzash insurance premiums. He arrived yesterday and is now here at the Domus."

Gersen studied the spaceport photograph, which depicted a middle-aged man, thin and frail with a small luxurious paunch, a large head with alert lucent eyes, a long thin flexible nose, a delicate mouth drooping at the corners. To either side of a bald forehead hung sparse russet curls; his skin had been toned a bitter yellow. Ottile Panshaw wore stylish and ornate garments: a square black velvet hat piped with scarlet and silver, dove gray trousers, a pale pink shirt with a rolled black collar, a fawn-colored jacket.

"Interesting!" said Gersen. "I hope to ask Panshaw a question or two."

"That should be easy enough; he's not a hundred yards away. Getting honest answers might be more of a problem, to judge from his face."

Gersen nodded thoughtfully. "This is not the face of a candid man. It's also not the face of a man who forgets insurance premiums."

"Yes; that's a puzzling situation. Perhaps the premiums were exorbitant. That's not unlikely so close to Beyond."

"And so close to Lens Larque. Perhaps the insurance officials refused coverage on this theory."

"Or—which is even more likely—Panshaw simply pretended payment and put the money in his own pocket."

Gersen once again examined the clever face of the photograph. "I certainly wouldn't want Ottile Panshaw in command of my money. . . . Perhaps he had reason to depreciate Kotzash stock."

Rackrose frowned. "What would induce him in that direction?"

"I can think of several possibilities. One might be voting control of the company."

"If it were bankrupt?"

"Tintle mentioned other assets: leases, options and the like."

"I suppose anything is possible."

Gersen reflected a moment, then, turning to the communicator, brought the pale foxy face of Jehan Addels to the screen. "There is a new aspect to our business," said Gersen. "The Kotzash Mutual Corporation, based at Serjeuz, on Dar Sai in the Cora system. Might there be information available at New Wexford?"

Addels showed one of his rare grins. "You'd be astonished as to what information we can command. If this Kotzash has done business to the value of one svu with any bank of the Oikumene, information is on hand."

"I am interested in assets, officers, control procedure, anything else which might seem interesting."

"I will discover what there is to know."

The screen went dark. Turning, Gersen discovered a thoughtful expression on Rackrose's face. "For a simple journalist, you exert surprising authority," said Rackrose.

Gersen had forgotten his role as Henry Lucas, special writer for *Cosmopolis.* "No great affair; Addels is an old friend."

"I see. . . . Well, what shall we do about Ottile Panshaw?"

"Watch him closely. Hire professional help, if necessary."*

Rackrose said dubiously: "A man like Panshaw will surely notice such attention."

"If so, his conduct will be interesting."

"As you like. How will I pay the detectives?'"

"Make out vouchers payable by *Cosmopolis.*"

With a sigh of languid despair, Rackrose stood to his feet and departed.

Presently Addels's face returned to the communicator. "Kotzash is a queer business. The Serjeuz warehouse was robbed of ore worth twenty million svu. The comptroller had neglected insurance and the company fell apart. No formal bankruptcy, mind you: the loss was only to the stockholders. The stock, needless to say, is worthless."

"And who owns the stock?"

"The Kotzash charter was filed at the Chanseth Bank, in Serjeuz; copies subsequently reached the association office here at New Wexford. It specifies that anyone holding twenty-five percent or more of the shares becomes a director,

---

* Vegan law prohibited the use of motile spy-cells and like devices. Rigorous penalties attached to the use of such equipment and detectives relied upon traditional methods of surveillance.

with a vote in proportion to his holdings. There are forty-eight hundred and twenty shares outstanding. Twelve hundred and fifty shares, something over twenty-five percent, are registered in the name of Ottile Panshaw. The rest are distributed in unregistered small holdings."

"Very strange."

"Strange and significant. Panshaw is the only director; he controls Kotzash."

"He must have bought up depreciated stock," said Gersen. "Certainly he never put up half a ton of duodecimates."

"Not so fast. Panshaw is a man of style. Why spend hard-earned money for worthless stock?"

"Why indeed? I am burning with curiosity."

"Kotzash evidently maintains an office on Methel; the prospectus lists both Serjeuz and Twanish addresses. Kotzash is, therefore, an interworld corporation and files a yearly report. Last year's report listed as assets: mining charters, leases and exploration rights, as far afield as the asteroid Granate and the moon Shanitra. Kotzash also owns fifty-one percent of Hector Transit and Trading Company, of Twanish. Who owns the remaining forty-nine percent? Ottile Panshaw. He would seem, as Kotzash comptroller, to have issued twelve hundred and fifty shares of Kotzash stock and paid them over to himself for fifty-one percent of Hector Transit and Trading."

"And what do the records say of Hector Transit and Trading?"

"Nothing. It has never filed a prospectus."

"I find this most confusing," said Gersen.

"It is not confusing," said Addels. "It is merely a case of juggling and paperwork, to ease unscrupulous persons past their responsibilities."

"Is Kotzash stock listed on the exchange board?"

"The index indicates a nominal value of one centim per share, with no tenders either to buy or sell. In essence the stock is dead."

"Put out feelers," said Gersen. "If any Kotzash comes on the market, buy."

Addels gave his head a sad shake. "It is money cast into the sea."

"Ottile Panshaw thinks otherwise. He is staying at the Domus, evidently."

"What? Amazing! There now is cause for conjecture!'"

"I am no less perplexed than you. But take comfort; court convenes tomorrow. Benchmaster Dalt allows no evasiveness; he'll set the matter straight."

"If we escape shame and incarceration. We walk a tight-wire! Panshaw is highly astute!"

"If all goes well, Panshaw can go his way in peace, so far as I am concerned."

"When you say 'if all goes well' do you mean the appearance of Lens Larque at Estremont?"

"Exactly."

Addels gave his head an emphatic shake. "I am sorry to say this, but you are chasing foxfire. Maniac, brute, tor-turer—all these Lens Larque may be, but he is not a fool."

"Well, we shall see. Now you must excuse me; it is time for Benchmaster Dalt to take his lunch."

Precisely on the hour Benchmaster Dalt made a stately en-trance into the Domus restaurant: a rigidly erect man, white of skin, with black curls massed around his cold and austere face. His garments reflected a formal elegance decades out of date; heads turned to watch the striking implacable jurist cross the room to his table.

He consumed a frugal meal of salad and cold fowl, then sat in portentous meditation over a cup of tea. A thin man of no great stature who had been sitting across the room ap-proached his table.

"Lord High Benchmaster Dalt? May I join you for a mo-ment?'"

Benchmaster Dalt turned a leaden stare upon the peti-tioner, then spoke in a dry and measured voice, "If you are a journalist, I have nothing to say."

The other man laughed politely as if in appreciation of Benchmaster Dalt's little joke. "My name is Ottile Panshaw, and I am definitely no journalist." He eased himself deftly into the chair opposite Benchmaster Dalt. "Tomorrow you are hearing Cooney's Bank versus the *Ettilia Gargantyr, et al.* Would you think it an impropriety if I were to discuss the case with you?"

Benchmaster Dalt, inspecting Ottile Panshaw, saw a ma-ture man of slight physique, with a large head, flexible features and a gracious expression, wearing a dapper suit of plum and umber.

Panshaw bore the Benchmaster's stare with polite aplomb. Benchmaster Dalt finally put a curt question: "What is your standing in the case?"

"In an accessory sense, I am associated with the defendant, but naturally I came to make no importunities. The case is extraordinary and certain elements may never be introduced formally; still they might well illuminate your overall picture."

Benchmaster Dalt's eyelids took on a languid droop; his expression became more remote than ever. "I am uninterested in special representations."

"This goes without saying. Be assured that I wish only to present a few items of background information; they will carry their own burden of conviction."

"Very well; speak on."

"Thank you, sir. To begin, I represent the ownership of the *Ettilia Gargantyr*. The vessel is under lease to the Hector Transit Company, a subsidiary of Kotzash Mutual, a company of which I am the managing director. All well and good, but the ultimate owner of the ship is a certain Lens Larque. Is that name familiar to you?"

"He is a notorious criminal."

"Exactly. He would be loath to stand before a Vegan court and identify himself. The idea is actually whimsical. I therefore suggest that the testimony of myself, the functioning owner, be accepted in lieu of that of Lens Larque."

Benchmaster Dalt's pallid face altered by not so much as a twitch. "At the preliminary hearing I ruled that only the owner in actuality at the time of the alleged tort can offer germane testimony. I see no reason to alter this ruling. The special quality of this witness is quite beside the point, and does not affect the ruling."

"Quite so," said Ottile Panshaw, with a rueful grin. "Your point of view is that if Lens Larque wished to testify in the Vegan courts, he should not have become a criminal."

Benchmaster Dalt allowed the merest ghost of a smile to bend his lips. "Exactly. Court convenes tomorrow. Is this Larque person at hand to testify?"

Ottile Panshaw lowered his voice. "Our conversation is presumably unofficial and confidential?"

"I can make no such commitment!"

"In that case, I can tell you nothing."

"Your caution implies a great deal. I must assume that this person is at hand."

"Let us pose a hypothesis. If Lens Larque were at hand, would you be willing to take his testimony *in camera*?"

Benchmaster Dalt frowned. "I expect that he will testify to advance his own case. Reputedly he has looted, tortured and murdered; why should he hesitate at perjury? Can he supply corroboration to his testimony?"

Ottile Panshaw gave a soft gentle laugh. "You and I, sir, for all our disparities, are ordinary human beings. Lens Larque is something quite different. I could not venture to predict his testimony. Corroboration may or may not exist. Indeed in your previous ruling, you indicated that you needed only the owner's testimony."

Benchmaster Dalt considered. "The case of Cooney's Bank versus the *Ettilia Gargantyr* is obviously out of the ordinary. I can only render the most accurate equity possible without reference to the antecedents of the principals. It is my earnest goal to try each case on its own terms. Therefore, despite my personal preference for formal proceedings, I will undertake to hear this man's testimony *in camera*. You may bring him to my suite here at the Domus in two hours time. I feel that I am leaning well over backwards in the interests of fairness and equity."

Ottile Panshaw smiled diffidently. "Would you come with me now to a place of my choice?"

"Certainly not."

"You must understand this person's trepidations."

"Had he lived a blameless life he could walk with careless step."

"Oh, his step is careless enough." Ottile Panshaw rose to his feet and hesitated several seconds. The corners of his mouth jerked down in a clownish grimace. "I will do what I can."

The Benchmaster's suite, the finest and most exquisitely appointed at the Domus, included a parlor furnished with antique pieces in that style known as "Dravan Commandeer." In a massive armchair sat the Benchmaster. He had elected to wear his robes of office in order to emphasize the solemnity of the occasion. His face, toned cadaverous white, with its lean cheeks, hard jaw and short straight nose, was in stark contrast with the luxuriant black curls of the ceremonial wig. The Benchmaster's hands, strong and spare, with straight strong fingers, seemed also a trifle incongruous; they seemed more the hands of an active man, accustomed to the feel of tools and weapons.

Jehan Addels sat across the room, in an attitude of anxiety; clearly he would have preferred to be elsewhere.

A chime sounded; Addels rose to his feet, went out into the foyer, touched a button. The door slid aside, to admit Ottile Panshaw and a tall heavy-fleshed man in a hooded white cloak. Under the hood showed a face flat and moonish with ruddy-bronze skin, a lumpy nose, heavy lips and round black eyes.

Benchmaster Dalt spoke to Ottile Panshaw. "You are acquainted with counsel for the plaintiff, the Honorable Jehan Addels. Inasmuch as all issues conceivably may be resolved here and now, I deemed it proper to notify him of our meeting."

Ottile Panshaw gave his head a quick bird-like nod. "I understand, Lord Benchmaster. Allow me to introduce a principal in the case. I will not utter his name; there is no need to embarrass anyone—"

"To the contrary," said Benchmaster Dalt. "We are here precisely so that identities may be authenticated and unequivocal responses be made to questions of fact. You, sir, what is your name?"

"I have used many names, Benchmaster. Under the name 'Lens Larque' I assumed ownership of the ship *Ettilia Gargantyr*. During my time of ownership, I have performed no acts under the influence of malice or vindictiveness. I am innocent of the conspiracy alleged by Cooney's Bank. Against these statements I lay my great oath."

"We require something more than oaths in cases of this sort," said Benchmaster Dalt. "Counsellor, be so good as to summon the clerk."

Jehan Addels opened a side door, beckoned; into the room came the Chief Clerk, wheeling an instrument before him.

Benchmaster Dalt said, "Clerk, allow this gentleman to authenticate his statements."

"At once, Holy Law." The clerk slid the machine toward

the man in the white cloak. "Sir, this is a harmless device which reads emanations from your conceptualizer. Notice this luminous indicant: truth excites a green light; falsity is shown by red. I will place the register against your temple; allow me to shift the hood."

Drawing back in annoyance, the man muttered to Ottile Panshaw, who returned only a half-smiling half-crestfallen shrug. The clerk, gingerly slipping back the hood, placed an adhesive patch upon the ruddy-bronze temple.

Benchmaster Dalt spoke. "Counsellor Addels, ask your questions, but only to the effect of establishing identity and ascertaining motivation at the time of the alleged tort."

Ottile Panshaw said in a silky tone: "May I suggest, Holy Law, that exact dispassion might better be approximated if you yourself put the questions?"

"I am intent only upon truth. So long as Counsellor Addels pursues truth, we must all approve. Counsellor, ask your questions."

"Sir, you state your name to be Lens Larque?"

"Yes; this name has been applied to me."

The indicant glowed green.

"What is your name in actuality?"

"It is Lens Larque."

"How long have you been known by this name?"

Ottile Panshaw cried out: "Holy Law, the fact has been made clear and verified by the indicant! Must we incessantly pursue a sterile inquisition?"

"Holy Law, I submit that the identification is not yet unequivocal."

"I agree. Continue."

"Very good. Where were you born?"

"On Dar Sai. I am Darsh." An almost foolish smirk widened the man's mouth.

"And what was your born, or given, name?"

"That is a matter of no consequence." The red light flickered, then the green light glowed.

"Odd," mused the Benchmaster. He himself put a question. "How long then have you been known as Lens Larque?"

"That is not important." The red light glowed bright.

"Has someone recently—within the last week or two—fixed the name 'Lens Larque' upon you?"

The Darsh's eyes bulged, and he made lurching motions with his shoulders. "That is an insulting question."

Benchmaster Dalt leaned sharply forward. "That is not the proper tone to take. Either you are Lens Larque, whereupon we come to grips with the case; or you are not, whereupon you and Mr. Panshaw have committed a most serious impropriety."

"The whole matter is a farce," grumbled the Darsh. "Accept the fact that I am Lens Larque and ask your questions."

Benchmaster Dalt's eyes glittered. "If you are Lens Larque, answer this. Who were your associates at the Mount Pleasant raid?"

"Bah, I forget such details."

"What does the name 'Husse' suggest to you?"

"I have no skill with names."

"That may well be. You are evidently not the real Lens Larque. For the last time, state the identity under which you have lived for the last twenty years."

"I am Lens Larque." The indicant glowed red.

"And I denounce you and Ottile Panshaw as conspirators, perjurers and frauds. Clerk, place these men under arrest! Take them into custody and lock them in separate dungeons."

The clerk blew out his cheeks and stepped cautiously forward. "The pair of you must now consider yourselves in the custody of the Estremont. Stand quietly; hold now! Not a move! I represent the full force of Vegan law!"

Ottile Panshaw's eyelids drooped in worry and despondency. "Lord High Benchmaster, I beg your understanding! Please be aware of the special circumstances!"

Benchmaster Dalt spoke in cold tones. "You have seriously prejudiced your case. I am disposed to find for the plaintiff, unless Lens Larque presents himself at once. You may use this telephone to call him. I am bored with tricks."

Ottile Panshaw showed his sad twisted smile. "Lens Larque is notorious for his tricks." He paused, then continued in an almost confidential tone: "Cooney's Bank will never enjoy a judgment against Lens Larque, I can state this much."

"What is your meaning?"

"Ships disappear. In not one, but by many modes. Remember the tricks! Now, accept my truly sincere apologies, and allow us to leave."

"Halt!" cried the clerk. "You are in my custody!"

The Darsh looked toward Ottile Panshaw. "All of them?"

Panshaw gave a delicate shrug, from which the Darsh seemed to derive exact information. He stepped back and produced a peculiar implement: a foot-long handle terminating in a small spiked knob. The Chief Clerk stood back aghast, then turned and ran for the door. The Darsh swung his haft; the spiked ball was propelled into the back of the clerk's head; he threw up his arms and fell forward. In the same rhythmic motion the Darsh turned, swung the haft and the ball darted toward Benchmaster Dalt. Jehan Addels uttered a croak of outrage and lurched forward, only to be tripped by the dapper foot of Ottile Panshaw. The Benchmaster had dodged low to the side; the projectile struck the wall at his back. He ran crouching forward, black robes fluttering, face white under the black curls. The Darsh drew back a step and flourished the haft. Benchmaster Dalt seized the upraised wrist, kicked at the Darsh's knee, thrust an elbow under the heavy red jaw. The Darsh stumbled to the floor. The Benchmaster wrenched away the haft; the Darsh groped and dragged him to the floor. They tumbled about the room, white robe and black, like monstrous black and white moths. Ottile Panshaw skipped here and there holding a small hand-weapon. He looked toward Jehan Addels who instantly threw himself flat behind a couch. Panshaw turned away, to stand rapt in astonishment while the languid and elegant jurist broke first the Darsh's wrist, then his jaw, then produced a glittering black sliver with which he stabbed the Darsh in the back of the neck.

Ottile Panshaw half-heartedly pointed his weapon. Jehan Addels, watching from behind the couch, uttered a sharp cry and threw a bronze vase. Benchmaster Dalt reached for the Darsh's ball-whip; Ottile Panshaw stepped quietly to the door, bowed and departed with the aplomb of a successful conjurer.

The Benchmaster pushed aside the Darsh corpse and jumped to his feet. Jehan Addels emerged from behind the couch. "What an appalling situation!" cried Addels. "If we are discovered with these dead things, we will be immured forever!"

"In that case we will depart. It is the only sensible course."

The Benchmaster removed his wig and doffed the black

robes. He looked down at the corpses in gloomy dissatisfaction. "Failure. The scheme is bankrupt." He indicated the huddle which once had been the Chief Clerk. "Provide well for his kin; we can at least do that."

"I fear for myself and my own kin," Addels fretted. "Is there to be no end to this violence? And these corpses: we are vulnerable! Panshaw from sheer spite may call in the alarm!"

"Quite so. Benchmaster Dalt must now dissolve into nowhere. A pity: he was truly an admirable fellow, with flair and style. Good-bye, Benchmaster Dalt!"

"Bah," muttered Addels. "You should have been a theatrist rather than an assassin, or whatever you consider yourself. Must we loiter here forever? The kindest dungeons are at Maudley; far worse are the Frogtown Holes."

"I hope to visit neither." Gersen flung wig and gown aside. "Let's be gone from here."

In his own chambers Gersen removed the white skin-tone; then, while Addels watched in lambent disapproval, he dressed in his ordinary gear. Addels finally could no longer contain his curiosity. "Where are you off to now? The sun is setting; don't you ever think of rest?"

Gersen, in the act of arming himself responded half apologetically: "Did you hear Panshaw's hints? How Cooney's Bank should never consider the *Ettilia Gargantyr* a reliable asset? How famous is Lens Larque for his tricks? Lens Larque is evidently close at hand. I want to watch his trickery."

"I lack all such curiosity! When I think of what I have undergone, I am horrified! I am a legalist and a financial expert, I admit as much; but my disregard for the law goes no further. I need time to rest. I must recover my sense of reality. I bid you good evening." Jehan Addels departed the chamber.

Five minutes later Gersen left the suite. The placidity of the Domus seemed untroubled; Ottile Panshaw evidently had not called in an alarm.

In front of the Domus Gersen signaled down one of the city's venerable hacks and climbed into the passenger dome. He called into the mesh: "To Slayhack Spaceport, as fast as possible."

"Aye, sir!"

The hack trundled along the Esplanade and around the bend into Pilkamp Road. As they drove, the afterglow faded

and dusk glimmered across Lake Feamish. Through Moynal
and Drury they went and into Wigaltown, and Gersen saw
ahead the yellow sign advertising Tintle's Shade. The upper
windows showed red and yellow lights and flickered with
moving shadows: merriment tonight at Tintle's Shade! From
Wigaltown into Dundivy, then Gara and finally into Slayhack, where the spaceport floodlights lit up the sky. Gersen
leaned forward in his seat, trying to induce speed upon the
lumbering old hack by sheer force of will. . . . An explosion
of light across the sky, a shuddering burst of yellow-white
glare, and seconds later a great belch of sound. Staring from
the cab, Gersen saw black fragments hurtling across the light,
upon which his imagination put the semblance of human
shapes.

The light subsided into a cloud of roiling smoke.

The cab driver cried out in fear: "Sir, what shall I do?"

"Keep going!" called Gersen, then a moment later: "Stop
here!"

He alighted from the cab and looked across the field. In
the place of the *Ettilia Gargantyr* lay a few smouldering
shards. Gersen stood rigid with rage and dismay. Predictable!
he told himself between clenched teeth. Lens Larque plays
quaint tricks! He destroys lawsuit and ship together, and col-
lects full insurance! These premiums Ottile Panshaw will not
have neglected!

"I have become complacent," he muttered. "I have lost my
hard edge!" He swung around in disgust and returned to the
cab. He asked the driver: "Can you drive out on the field?"

"No, sir, the field is forbidden to us."

"Then continue along the road a bit."

The cab skirted the field. In the illuminated area beside the
repair shops, Gersen noticed a swarming group of men, apparently in a state of shock, or hysteria. Gersen called to the
driver: "Take that access lane yonder, toward the warehouses."

"I may not leave the public road, sir."

"Very well; wait here." Gersen jumped to the ground.

From behind the shops darted a small warehouse truck,
driven erratically. At full speed it fled across the field, toward
the access lane. The men at the shop reacted instantly. Some
pursued on foot; others leapt aboard vehicles and so gave
chase. The truck, gaining the access lane, bounded at full

speed toward the road. As it passed under a floodlight Gersen saw the driver's face, which was wide, red-bronze and heavy, with staring eyes: the face of Tintle. He lacked skill in guiding the truck and drove off the lane into a rut. The truck jerked and bumped, and, slewing to the side, overturned. Tintle was thrown through the air, kicking and sprawling,; he fell half on his back, half on his side, and lay for a moment inert. Then, laboriously, he lurched to his feet, threw a wild glance over his shoulder and started at a hobbling run for the road. His pursuers caught him under one of the floodlights, and in the circle of blue-white radiance struck him great blows with fists and metal tools. Tintle staggered back and forth, and fell to the ground. The men kicked him and jumped upon his head and body until Tintle was bloody, ruptured and dead.

Gersen, arriving at the scene, spoke to a young man wearing mechanics' overalls. "What goes on here?"

The young mechanic turned him a stare half-apprehensive, half-defiant. "Don't you see the wreckage? That hulk yonder? This man exploded it, and half a dozen of our fellows as well! Bold as brass he drove his truck under the cargo hatch and set down a great crate. It was frack, that's what it was! Then he drove off and a minute later the blast all but knocked us down, over by the shops. There were four guards aboard and six day-shift men going off to their homes. All gone in the blast!" Overcome by indignation and the importance of the occasion the young mechanic began to bluster: "And who are you to come asking why we should capture the drot?"

Without troubling to reply, Gersen turned away. He marched back to the hack, where the driver waited nervously in the darkness. "Sir, where now?"

Gersen turned a last look across the field where, in the glaring floodlights, the group of workmen, waving, stamping, gesticulating, still surrounded Tintle's corpse. "Back into town," said Gersen.

Away from Slayhack, south along Pilkamp Road, into Gara and Dundivy rolled the cab. Gersen stared unseeingly ahead along the line of street-lights which curved in a luminous chain all the way back to Old Town. Gersen's brooding was interrupted by the sight of a sign: TINTLE'S SHADE. As before colored lights and moving shadows played along the upper windows. Tonight, while Tintle lay dead in Slayhack, Tintle's Shade pulsed with jovial activity.

An eery emanation tingled the edge of Gersen's mind. For an instant he sat indecisively, then called the hack to a halt. "Wait for me; I won't be long."

"Aye, sir."

Gersen crossed the street. From Tintle's Shade came muffled sounds of revelry: piping music, occasionally a howl and yelp of foolish glee. He pushed through the entrance. The old woman in black looked stonily across the beer hall but spoke no word.

Gersen mounted the stairs to the upper floor. Passing through the door, he found himself behind a row three deep of ranked bodies, heads and sloping shoulders silhouetted against the pink illumination beyond.

At the center of the room an entertainment was in progress. Two musicians on a platform played drums and tweedle-pipes. Below and visible only in glimpses past bald heads and dangling earlobes, a wizened youth cavorted with a pneumatic dummy dressed as an old Darsh woman. He sang in a nasal voice, urgent and breathless, the Darsh jargon* not altogether intelligible to Gersen:

> *I first saw light at Gaggar's Shade beneath the*
> *nephar tree;*
> *They gave me bottom beer to drink, then good*
> *ahagaree.*
> *My dangle coiled all curlicue to everyone's*
> *despair;*
> *A kitchet wandered past the door; it straightened*
> *then and there.*
> > *Tinkle tankle winkle wankle finkle fankle fime*
> > *All the aeons gone before are simply wasted*
> > *time.*

---

* Darsh men and women use distinctly different idioms, both rich in epithets. The song is phrased in male jargon.

A young girl is a "chelt." After adolescence and until she grows her facial mustache, usually after six to eight years, she is a "kitchet." Thereafter she may incur any number of epithets, usually derogatory.

The women use an equivalent set of terms in reference to the men.

I saw a chelt in native pelt and felt a queer condition.
The heartless creature jeered and mocked my meager proposition.
Every day I chased the chelts and prowled the shade by night,
Wondering where the kitchets went when Mirassou shone bright.
    Tinkle tankle winkle wankle finkle fankle fun
    The chelts though brash wear no mustache, the kitchets only one.

Oh where do all the kitchets go on midnight promenade?
Oh what compels the tender things so far from Gaggar's Shade?
They walk to Dobbin's Fountain; they climb Knobkelly Row;
Out upon Bagshilly Sand the tender kitchets go.
    Tinkle tankle winkle wankle finkle fankle fex
    A fearful thrill to pit your skill against the female sex!

When I became a bungle boy and Mirassou shone fair,
I ran across Bagshilly Plain to catch a kitchet there.
But who caught me but the vile old khoontz who terrorized the place,
With her biffle belly, monstrous arse and gibble-gobble face.
    Tinke tankle winkle wankle finkle fankle fane
    Fear and fright by pale moonlight upon Bagshilly Plain!

She seized my draps and dingles, she toyed with my emotion;
She rubbed my private enterprise with scrofulatic lotion.
She put me in a quandary and caused me deep dismay.

*She never let me out again until the dawn of
day.*
   *Tinkle tankle winkle wankle finkle fankle fade
   Stark and pale I crawled the trail which leads
to Gaggar's Shade.*

*Now that I'm a pooter bold, I wander where I
please.
I chase the kitchets back and forth with con-
descending ease.
Serene and gay I chanced to stray upon Bagshilly
Plain;
Who bounded forth but the same old khoontz
and took me once again!*
   *Tinkle tankle winkle wankle finkle fankle
foom
   Serene and bland, I walked the sand to meet
an awful doom.*

*I'll dare to slog the oozing bog; I'll risk the
frozen pole;
I'll challenge fifteen champions at Dinklestown
hadaul,
But I won't dare a promenade along Bagshilly
Plain,
In craven fear that the vile old khoontz should
take me once again.*
   *Tinkle tankle winkle wankle finkle fankle fore
   Bagshilly Plain has been my bane; I'll go there
nevermore.*

To the refrains the audience gave enthusiastic support:
stamping, yelping, belching a plangent obligato.

Gersen sidled behind the spectators toward the kitchen,
where the view was less obstructed. Certain folk present wore
ordinary Vegan garments, others the white Darsh robe and
thabbat. Two men at a table across the room attracted Gersen's attention: the first, massive and curiously still, with his
features obscured under his thabbat. The other, a smaller
man, sat with his back to Gersen and made small diffident
gestures as he spoke.

Someone thrust at Gersen and pushed him about; Gersen

looked into the sardonic face of Madame Tintle. "So isn't it you, the ardent journalist? Did you come to meet your friend?"

Gersen asked politely: "Which friend do you mean?"

Madame Tintle showed a sly malicious smile which moved her mustache more then her mouth. "I don't know as to this. Iskish* look all alike to me. But maybe you'll see him by and by. Or perhaps you came to watch Ned Ticket?"

"Not altogether. I thought perhaps to speak to you, in connection with our understanding. For instance, are these all regular patrons tonight? Who are those men sitting yonder, across the room?"

"Strangers, fresh in from Dar Sai. Could they be the acquaintances you were seeking?"

"In this dim light I can't be sure."

Madam Tintle's smile became an unpleasant grin. "Why not step across and pay your respects?"

"A good idea. I'll do so after a bit. Have you had news of Tintle? He was sent out on an errand."

"Is that correct? Tintle is becoming all the rage. He danced last night and showed nimble heels."

The singer finished his song, to belching stamping approval. Madam Tintle sniffed in displeasure. "Vile old Khoontz, is it? Never fear! On the woman's floor we eat fresh ahagaree and celebrate Tobo the Tremulous Tyrant. It works no better than a balance. What have we next? Ticket the snaveler? Watch with attention; you shall be diverted!" Madame Tintle lurched away, shouldering spectators aside with neither concern nor apology. Gersen looked back to the two men across the room. The slight man almost certainly was Ottile Panshaw. Who might be the other? . . . A drum rattled; out on the floor ran a tall thin man on long thin legs, wearing a tight costume of mustard and black. His arms were lean and corded; his long twitching nose drooped over a long pointed chin. He flourished a whip; snaps and cracks accented his recitation. "Hoy ho now, it's time for our fun! I'm Nikity Ticket; I first tasted water at Wabbers Fountain. I learned leather from Roly Tatwyn. My whip is Whirr; it's never weary, so who wants to dance? Who'll skip to leather music? Dainty and delicate! Here come our dancers!"

---

* Iskish: Darsh jargon for anyone other than a Darsh.

In fascination Gersen watched the two men across the room. One was Ottile Panshaw; the other—he hardly dared allow the name to enter his mind—might it be Lens Larque?

Madame Tintle emerged from an alcove behind the two men. Approaching from the side she stood, in a posture at once deferential and contemptuous. She leaned forward, spoke and jerked her thumb. Both men turned to look toward Gersen, who, taking warning, had sidled back into the shadows.

"—hoy, hoy, hoy!" cried Ned Ticket to the dancers. He snapped the long whip close by their feet, creating heavy succulent sounds. "Smartly now, smartly! Dance to music of leather! With a kick and a hop; that's the way of it, show us your heels, then flourish the targets!" The dancers wore tight short trousers, with scarlet disks sewn upon the seat. Two of the dancers were Darsh boys; the third was Maxel Rackrose, who danced with agility. "Hoop hap hup!" called Ned Ticket. "This is how we dance at Doodam's Shade! A touch of sweetness, the good sweet leather! The glossy leather, supple and sweet! Hey hurrah! A snap—and a snap—and a snap snap snap! Skip now, lively there! We're off for a merry reel! Around and step, twist and step, and a taste of the leather! Oh my soul, a fine smart dance! We are truly gay! Hop and skip and a snap snap snap! Pshaw, so soon? Why must you spoil the fun? A snap and a snippet, right on the target; up now, twirl like a graceful fairy. Exhaustion? A fable! Up, on with the dance; we cannot halt so soon! Up! Bend and sway; a smile and a tear, tempt with the target! . . . A moment to rest." Ned Ticket swung on his heel, bowed to the man beside Ottile Panshaw. "Sir, your whip is famous; will you join the dance?" The massive man made a negative signal. Ottile Panshaw cried out: "We need fresh dancers, keen and eager! There's one by the kitchen, the iskish spy! Thrust him out on the floor."

Gersen called: "Rackrose, this way! Quick now!"

Rackrose, glassy-eyed and panting, turned his head, hobbled toward Gersen.

"Not yet!" cried Ned Ticket. "Make ready for the dance!"

Gersen sensed a loom behind him; he looked to see Madame Tintle, arms outstretched to push. Gersen slid aside, pulled and swung her sprawling out on the floor. Snatching out his gun he fired toward the massive man's belly. His arm was jostled; the bolt went astray. A fist knocked the gun from his hand; dark shapes converged on him.

"Rackrose!" Gersen bellowed. "This way! Quick now!"

A roaring figure pressed upon Gersen; he was dealt a buffet on the back of the head. He blinked, jerked an elbow into a nearby paunch. He slipped his left hand into metal fingers, dropped a knife into his right hand. Someone struck him again; Gersen seized the arm; his assailant uttered a rattling gasp as energy jarred his body. Stabbing, slashing, Gersen reached Rackrose, hauled him into the kitchen, and even at this juncture recoiled at the oily stench. Four women bawled objurgations. Gersen seized a cauldron of bubbling sauce and threw it out into the main room, evoking cries of anguish. Through a side door which gave on the steps came Madame Tintle, eyes glaring. She seized Gersen from behind and clasped him to herself. "Women!" she bayed. "Bring the sick oil! Work the graters! We'll fry this iskish on the stove!"

Gersen touched her with metal fingers; she cried out and stumbled backward, to tumble down the stairs. Gersen toppled a rack of condiments upon the women, signaled to Rackrose. "Quick now!" They ran down the stairs, hopping over the dazed form of Madame Tintle at the bottom. The beer woman came to look in wonder. "What causes so much turmoil?"

"Madame Tintle has taken a tumble," Gersen explained. "You had best see to her. Come, Rackrose, we must be on our way."

Gersen took a last look up the stairs. At the landing the massive man stood pointing a gun. Gersen slid to the side; the bolt passed him by; he threw his knife. The angle was awkward; instead of piercing the man's neck the blade sheared away his dangling earlobe.

The man called out in rage and fired the gun again, but Gersen and Rackrose were out the door.

They ran across Pilkamp Road to the cab. Gersen called to the driver: "Quick now, back into town at top speed! The Darsh have all gone crazy!"

The cab lurched and rumbled south. There was no pursuit. Gersen slumped back into the seat. "He was there. . . . Twice I tried for his life. Twice I failed. The scheme worked well; he took the bait. Twice I failed."

"I don't know what you're talking about," snarled Rackrose. "Here and now, be notified: I can serve as your assistant no longer. The salary—" Rackrose spoke in a voice of sarcastic delicacy "—is not commensurate with my duties."

Gersen was in no mood to lavish sympathy upon Rackrose. "You came away with your life; consider yourself lucky."

Rackrose snorted and painfully shifted his position. "Easy for you to talk. You were not dancing with Ned Ticket! What a repulsive business!"

Gersen sighed. "I'll see that you're compensated. Enjoy your welts; they've earned you money."

Rackrose presently asked: "Who was that large man in the Darsh robes?"

"Lens Larque."

"You tried to kill him."

"Certainly. Why not? I failed, worse luck."

"You are a most peculiar journalist."

"No doubt you are right."

Three days later Jehan Addels made contact with Gersen by communicator. Taking note of Addels' carefully composed face, Gersen knew that significant news was in the offing.

"In regard to the *Ettilia Gargantyr*," said Addels in a voice so dry as almost to crackle, "the vessel was quite destroyed. The case at law of Cooneys' Bank versus *Ettilia Gargantyr* becomes moot."

"That is my own conclusion," said Gersen.

"One immediately begins to speculate as to insurance," said Addels. "We wonder as to the insuring agency, the coverage and, of course, the beneficiary. Some facts have now emerged, and you may wish to learn them."

"Definitely so," said Gersen. "What are these facts?"

"I find that the policy was negotiated only three weeks ago, to a total liability which approximately equals or even exceeds replacement cost of the vessel and its cargo. The insuring entity is Cooney's Fiduciary Assurance, a subsidiary of Cooney's Bank at Thrump on David Alexander's Planet. The insured party, Kotzash Mutual Syndicate of Serjeuz, Dar Sai, has presented its claim. In accordance with company policy, compensation has promptly and faithfully been rendered."

Gersen looked at Addels with a gloomy expression. "I own Cooney's Bank?"

"You do, and Cooney's Fiduciary Assurance, as well."

"Then, in effect, I have paid Lens Larque a large sum of money."

"This is the case."

Gersen, not normally given to emotional demonstration, raised his hands in the air, clenched his fists and brought them down upon his head. "He tricked me."

"He is notorious for his pranks," said Addels primly.

"Yes, so I understand."

"An ancient proverb stipulates that 'he who sups with the devil should use a long spoon.' You would seem to have attempted such a meal with a small dessert fork."

"We shall see," said Gersen. "Are you ready to leave?"

Addels' face became blank. " 'Leave?' For where?"

"Dar Sai, of course."

Addels half lowered his eyelids and tilted his head sideways. In a reedy voice he said, "Important personal affairs prevent me from joining you on this venture. Also—a side issue of course—Dar Sai is a wild and savage world, where I would surely be uncomfortable."

"Yes, possibly so."

After a cautious moment Addels asked: "When do you leave?"

"This afternoon. There is nothing to keep me here."

Addels said gruffly; "I'd waste my breath counseling you to prudence. So I will wish you luck."

"I'm as prudent as necessary," said Gersen. "I'll be in touch with you before too long."

Part II: DAR SAI

Chapter 7

From *Tourists Guide to the Coranne*, by Jane Szantho:

Dar Sai, second planet of the Coranne, cannot be considered a pleasant or propitious world; indeed, the casual observer will at once discount all possibility of human habitation. Each hemisphere may be divided into zones almost equally malignant. At the poles the winds howl around the vortex of a perpetual down-draft cyclone, to deposit incessant rain, slush and snow. The consequent ground waters drain into the Bogs, an environment of ooze, poisonous slimes, stiletto bugs, uncounted varieties of algae, some of which achieve the stature of bushes.

From the Bogs water drains south and north respectively into the equatorial Hot Zone: the so-called Wale. Some of this water evaporates, some sinks out of sight into the sand.

The Wale is pitilessly exposed to the blazing light of Cora, and seems as vicious as any other environment of Dar Sai. Gentle variable winds blow during the day, but at night all is quiet on the desert, which, at this time, becomes strangely beautiful.

A small dead star, once Cora's companion, and posthumously known as Fideske, is responsible for human habitancy upon Dar Sai. Twenty million years ago Fideske disintegrated into fragments, the largest of which, Shanitra, orbits

Methel, the third planet, as a moon. Some fragments form an asteroidal belt; others fell upon Methel and Dar Sai, bringing rare and precious elements of high atomic number, the duodecimates.* On Methel these elements are lost on the sea bottoms; on Dar Sai they have become a component of the desert sands, which the wind constantly sifts and segregates. The first men came to Dar Sai to mine duodecimate lodes; over centuries they evolved into Darsh, a folk as fierce and perverse as the world they inhabit.

These first settlers, in the main fugitives, desperadoes and ne'er-do-wells, quickly discovered that they could survive by day only with the aid of powerful air-coolers, or in more primitive circumstances, under sheds cooled by trickling water. Using riches gained from duodecimates, the Darsh erected their famous "shades": enormous parasols as much as five hundred feet high and sheltering twenty or thirty acres. Water from the underground aquifers is pumped to the top surface to flow across to the periphery and trickle down in sheets, veils and cool mists. Under these shades live the Darsh. They grow quantities of food in their garden trays, some they synthesize and the rest they import. The spices which enliven their cuisine derive from particular types of bog-algae. Some of these spices—the ahagaree, for instance—is as valuable by weight as good black duodecimate.

The Darsh are not physically appealing to outworlders, or iskish, to use Darsh jargon. They are large-boned, often bulky, and in their later years inclined to corpulence. Their features are heavy and their complexions tend to a raw roan color, occasionally with a chalky undertone. At puberty the men become entirely hairless. The women, to the contrary, are hirsute, and ten years after puberty will often grow mustaches. In that brief decade between puberty and facial mustache, the

---

* A misnomer, which nevertheless has achieved wide popular usage.

girls, or kitchets, achieve a certain degree of physical charm and are held in great esteem by Darsh men of all ages.

The Darsh ear cartilage stretches easily; the lobes hang loose and long and sometimes support dangling pendants. The men wear white robes and hoods. When they go abroad in the daylight, small air conditioners pump cold air under these robes. The women, who never leave the shade by day, wear less voluminous kirtles of maroon, orange, or mustard, which are in particularly disagreeable discord with their complexion.

Darsh children find themselves in an unsympathetic milieu. They are exploited in all manner of ways; they gain neither gratitude nor affection, and so develop a remarkable egocentricity, which is not dissimilar to pride, as if each had declaimed to Fate: "You have abused and mishandled me; you have shown me no favor, but I have survived; I have grown stubborn and strong despite all!"

This pride, in the Darsh male, expresses itself as "plambosh," a swaggering willful flamboyance, a reckless disregard for consequence, a perversity which automatically conduces to contempt for authority. If, by one means or another, such as public humiliation, this pride is fractured or destroyed, the man is "broken" and thereafter becomes almost eunuchoid.

In women, the quality is more difficult to define, and takes the form of studied inscrutability. Whoever wishes to experience human opacity need only attempt jocular intercourse with a Darsh woman. Men and women espouse each other for economic accommodation, nothing else. Procreation is accomplished by a far more adventurous process during nocturnal promenades across the desert, especially when Mirassou-shine is in the sky. The system is simple in outline but complicated in detail. Both men and women aggressively seek out young sexual partners. The men waylay girls barely adolescent; women seize

upon boys not much older. To lure the boys out
upon the desert, the women ruthlessly send out
the pubescent girls and so it goes. The system has
permutations unnecessary now to explore. In this
connection, the whipping entertainments may be
mentioned. These reach elaborate forms in the
principal towns, and the off-world visitor who
witnesses one of these strange rites will be
amazed, fascinated, and no doubt repelled. The
characteristic Darsh game *hadaul* perhaps also
should be mentioned, but this is more common
among the backland shades.

Lest the reader cultivate a negative impression
of the Darsh, their virtues must be indicated.
They are brave; there are no Darsh cowards.
They never utter falsehoods; they would thereby
compromise their pride. They are guardedly hospitable, in the sense that any stranger or off-
world wanderer arriving at a remote shade is
provided food and shelter as his natural right.
The Darsh may confiscate, pre-empt or simply
avail himself of any object for which he has an
immediate use, but he will never deign to pilfer;
the stranger's belongings are safe. However,
should this stranger discover a pocket of black
sand, he might well be confronted, robbed and
murdered. The Darsh admit such acts to be
crimes but apply no great moral indignation to
the perpetrators.

In regard to Darsh food, the less said the better. The traveler must adjust himself to a Darsh
meal as he might a natural catastrophe. It avails
nothing to pretend relish; the Darsh themselves
know that their food is repulsive, and apparently
derive a perverse pride in their ability to con-
sume it regularly.

There, my traveling friends, you have, in cap-
sule form, a sketch image of the world Dar Sai.
You may not like it, but you will never forget it.

Gersen made the passage to Dar Sai in a Fantamic Flitterwing of modest size and appearance. The course took him

into the back-regions of Argo Navis, close to the edge of Beyond: an area which he had never before visited.

Ahead burnt the white sun Cora. In the macroscope Gersen picked out the two inhabited worlds Methel and Dar Sai.

In regard to Dar Sai *Traffic Directions* made only a brief reference:

> The major settlements are, in order of importance, Serjeuz, Wabber's Fountain, Dinkelstown and Belfeser. None of these places provides other than rudimentary facilities for the repair or servicing of spaceships. There are neither entry nor departure regulations; indeed no central Darsh authority. Dar Sai is to some extent policed by Methlen agencies, for protection of their commercial interests, but away from the four main towns Methlen influence diminishes. At Serjeuz a rectangle marked out in white indicates the preferred landing site, for easiest access to the commercial warehouses.

From a height of twenty miles, Serjeuz appeared as a small mechanism lost on the gray, pink and yellow waste. As Gersen descended, details became exact in the morning light of Cora, and Serjeuz was revealed as a cluster of parasols spilling veils of water around the rims.

The fiasco at Rath Eileann had receded to the back of Gersen's memory, where it rankled like a small hidden ulcer. Looking down at Serjeuz, Gersen felt rekindled emotions: the hunter's stealth, tingling alertness, awe for the nearness of the dire beast. Lens Larque's emanations permeated the landscape. A hundred times he had cooled himself under the flowing parasols; a hundred times, in his fluttering white robes, he had crossed the desert between Serjeuz and the Bugold shades. Conceivably at this very moment he ate and drank at some favorite resort not ten minutes' time away.

In a white-bordered rectangle two dozen spacecraft of various sorts and conditions were at rest. Gersen landed the Flitterwing close beside the shimmering water-walls. The vessel became silent; the deck felt solid underfoot.

Local time was mid-morning. Gersen prepared to debark. According to the Immunological Index, wind-borne spores from the bog algae, germinating in the lungs, posed the most significant threat to human health; Gersen had already dosed himself with prophylactic counter-agents. He donned a white hooded robe, tucked money and bonded identity papers into his pouch, made sure of his weapons, stepped through the vestibule and descended to the sandy surface of Dar Sai. Heat instantly pressed against his face. He narrowed his eyes against the glare and set off toward the water-wall.

Four Darsh burst through the curtain astride dilapidated vehicles rolling on four-foot air-balls. They rode with fine *plambosh*, bouncing and bounding, white robes fluttering behind. Thabbats covered their faces except for metal hemispheres over their eyes, which gave them the look of white-robed insects. They seemed not to see Gersen and nearly ran him down; Gersen jumped to the side and shouted a curse at their retreating backs, to no effect. The four rode to the north toward the shimmer of a lone parasol at the horizon.

Gersen passed through the water-veil, into a jungle of vegetation growing from trays stacked fifty feet high. The lane passed underneath, skirted a pair of domed warehouses, and ended at a confusion of small heavy-walled concrete domes: low, high, large and small; domes piled on domes, domes impinging upon or growing out of other domes; domes in clusters of three, four, five, or six. These were the so-called "dumbles," or Darsh residences, constructed to an architecture at once heavy, vital and appropriate to the environment, like the Darsh themselves. Vegetation surrounded and overhung each dumble; in the ways and alleys wandered small children Gersen noticed a group of young boys playing a pushing, shoving, wrestling game: a child's variation of hadaul.

Gersen selected what seemed to be a principal avenue and presently passed from under the first parasol to the shelter of a second, even loftier and more expensive, enclosing an enormous volume of cool airy space.

The avenue opened into a plaza surrounded by concrete and glass domes built in a style half-Darsh, half-Interworld Galactic. The largest of these housed the Chanseth Bank, the Miner's Investment Bank, the Grand Bank of Dar Sai, and a pair of hotels: the Sferinde Select and the Traveler's Inn. Three restaurants fronted the plaza: the Sferinde Garden, the

Traveler's Inn Garden and the Olander. The Sferinde Garden catered to a clientele Gersen could not immediately identify. The Traveler's Inn Garden, spreading haphazardly under lime, persimmon and sweet anissus trees, served a variety of patrons: tourists, business travelers, miscellaneous wanderers and spacemen, a few white-robed Darsh. The Olander at the far side of the plaza catered only to the Darsh.

Of the hotels, the Sferinde Select seemed the most grand, the most expensive and presumably the most comfortable. The Traveler's Inn, while perhaps more relaxed, seemed a trifle shabby. Gersen once again inspected the folk in the Sferinde Garden. They were a handsome people, dark-haired, with clear pallid olive complexions and regular features. They wore formal garments of a style strange to Gersen; like the Sferinde Select itself they seemed incongruous to the surroundings of Dar Sai. Gersen could more easily have imagined them at a fashionable resort on a remote world at a time either in the far past or far in the future.

Intrigued, Gersen decided to take lodging at the Sferinde Select. He crossed the plaza and sauntered through the garden restaurant. The patrons, pausing in their conversations, turned to watch him with a cool curiosity he found not altogether flattering.

He entered the lobby, which under an oyster-white ceiling, occupied the entire ground floor. From a central pool grew a tree with black and orange leaves; small bird-like creatures hopped through the branches, dived into the pool, fluttered once more aloft whistling soft flute-like tones. The reception desk occupied an alcove to the side; Gersen approached. The clerk, a sallow young man with an austere visage, turned Gersen a quick sideglance, then studiously focused his attention upon the ledger in which he had been making entries.

Gersen said in a gentle voice, "At your convenience, please summon the reception clerk; I wish to engage a room, or, better, a suite."

The clerk spoke in an even monotone: "We are unable to offer accommodation; we are completely booked. Try the Traveler's Inn, or the Olander."

Gersen wordlessly turned away and departed the Sferinde Select. The folk in the garden seemed not to notice him. He crossed the plaza to the Traveler's Inn, a hostelry with a character totally different from that of the Sferinde Select.

The Traveler's Inn had been constructed in the Darsh manner, with heavy reliance upon improvisational insights. The three curving rows of parabolic arches, the eight intersecting domes, the rotundas, upper decks and balconies had been assembled in a spirit of adventure and lent the edifice a definite flavor of plambosh. The entry led through thick walls into a lobby, practical rather than sumptuous. At a circular reception desk worked a thin sandy-haired man with a thin jaw and long chin. He greeted Gersen with a courteous if perfunctory salute: "Your wishes, sir?"

"A suite, the best available. I expect to be staying several days, perhaps a week, or even longer."

"I can suit you very well, sir. I have in mind a fine airy bedroom with a sweeping view across the plaza. There is a splendid lavatory, a parlor carpeted in green frieze, and generally excellent furniture. If you wish to make an inspection, mount the staircase, turn right into the first corridor and enter the blue door trimmed in black."

Gersen visited the rooms and found them to his taste. Returning to the reception desk, he paid over a week's rent to formalize his occupancy.

The clerk was favorably impressed. "We are happy to secure your patronage, sir."

"I am reassured," said Gersen. "At the Sferinde they wanted nothing to do with me."

"No mystery there: the Sferinde is a Methlen resort; they cater to no one else."

Enlightenment came to Gersen. "So those are the Methlen. They seem quite exclusive."

" 'Exclusive' is the proper word. If Holy Symas in all his splendor came down to the Sferinde with retinue of double-winged mantics and trumpet-playing cherubs mounted on lions, they'd send the lot trooping across to the Traveler's. Expect nothing better of the Methlen."

The clerk, both voluble and alert, might prove a valuable source of information, reflected Gersen. He asked: "Why do they come to Dar Sai in the first place?"

"Some have business interests; others are sheer tourists. You'll often see a contingent out in Traveler's Garden inspecting the lower classes. Still, they're not vicious or even odious. Their wealth allows them to play at life; everything is a dramatic game. At Serjeuz they are all effete aristocrats, with the poor unwitting Darsh as clods and varlets." The clerk made a tolerant gesture. "Still, what of it all? I too am supercilious now and then."

"One would never believe it," said Gersen graciously.

"Oh, I have become easier over the years. Remember, I must deal with every lout and mooncalf who chooses to show me his face, just as I am doing now. For many years my nerves were like electric wires. Then I discovered the first axiom of human accord: I accept each person on his own terms. I keep a close tongue in my head; I offer opinions only when so solicited. What a remarkable change! Dissension vanishes, novel facts emerge, digestion flows like a wide river."

"Your ideas are interesting," said Gersen. "I would like to discuss them later, but now I think I will try your restaurant."

"Very good, sir. I wish you a pleasant meal."

Gersen stepped into the garden, and selected a table with a view across the plaza. He touched a button and the tabletop became an illuminated display of the food and drink on order. A waiter stepped forward. Gersen pointed to one of the depicted items. "What is this?"

"That is our 'Sunday Punch.' It is enlivened with three tots of Black Gadroon rum and a half-gil of Secret Elixir."

"The day is still somewhat young. What is this?"

"That is a simple swizzle, prepared from fruits and pale elixirs."

"That sounds more practical. What is this?"

"That is 'Tourist Ahagaree,' especially modified to suit the off-world taste."

"And this?"

"Those are parboiled night-fish, fresh from the bogs."

"I will have simple swizzle, ahagaree and a salad."

"At your order."

Gersen sat back in his chair and contemplated the surroundings. The plaza extended to a bank of trees with leaves of a rich nutmeg-brown; beyond rose the shafts of distant parasols. In certain areas veils of falling water obscured the view; in others he could see to the far edges of Serjeuz. Cosmopolitan architects, using standard materials and Darsh motifs, had created most of the structures around the plaza, with the notable exception of the Traveler's Inn, which seemed authentically Darsh.

The waiter wheeled up a trolley loaded with covered salvers. The ahagaree was placed on the table with flanking side dishes. To the left went the salad, to the right a beaker of "Simple Swizzle." The waiter withdrew. Gersen tasted with caution and found "Tourist Ahagaree" definitely more palatable than that served by Madame Tintle.

Gersen ate a leisurely meal, then sat musing over a pot of tea. From his pocket he brought a memorandum prepared by Jehan Addels and submitted to him immediately before his departure from Aloysius. It started off briskly:

> Kotzash Mutual is an operation formulated by an ingenious trickster with considerable financial expertise. Also evident is a cruel impudence and the utter absence of scruples one might expect in a deep-sea monster. The two gentlemen of our recent acquaintance, taken in tandem, are reflected in the Kotzash charter as in a mirror.
>
> The charter reads, in part:
>
> *To ensure efficient and expenditious management the executive directorship shall be vested in that person or entity holding the largest number of shares. The second directorship shall be vested in that person or entity holding the second largest number of shares. The third directorship shall be vested in that person holding the third largest number of shares. In all cases, the minimum qualification shall be ownership of at least twenty-five percent of shares outstanding. Other shareholders shall vote in proportion to their holdings to elect an advisory council, whose duty shall be to advise and inform the directorship in regard to efficient and profitable operation.*
>
> *The directors, or their nominees, and the advisory council, shall meet at such time and place as may be designated by the executive director, to consult and to direct the management of the syndicate. At such meetings each director shall vote in proportion to his number of shares. If any*

director or his nominee is absent from the meeting, the directors, or director, present shall constitute a quorum.

You will observe that the executive director effectually controls the company, inasmuch as he can call meetings at the time and place of his choosing, no matter how inconvenient to the other directors and the advisory council.

4,820 shares are in circulation; 2,411 shares constitutes a voting majority. The largest stockholder of record, according to the Interworld Agency is:

> Ottile Panshaw
> The Dindar House
> Serjeuz, Dar Sai

holding 1,250 shares. Chanseth Bank, (headquarters at Twanish, Methel, with a branch at Serjeuz) holds 1,000 shares. A certain Nihel Cahous, of Inkin's Shade, Dar Sai, holds 600 shares. I attach a list of small holders, more or less complete."

The price per share, as currently listed by the IAES is one centim per share. In short, the shares are worthless. The shares I have mentioned total 2,850. You currently hold 92. The remaining 1,878 shares are scattered among a hundred or more individuals, at almost every shade of Dar Sai.

Despite the almost negligible value of the shares, it is interesting to note that Kotzash now possesses substantial assets, including control of a pair of subsidiaries: Hector Transit (which has recently collected a handsome insurance payment); and Didroxus Mining and Exploration. Kotzash would seem underpriced except for the fact that the executive (and single) director is Ottile Panshaw.

The situation has its interesting aspects, but I would not care to explore them at close range. I

wish you good health and longevity, and urge
caution upon you, both out of personal esteem
and consideration of self-interest, since I would
have to look long and far to find work as remu-
nerative.

With my very best respects:

JA

Gersen put away the letter, leaned back in his chair and
sat in profound cogitation. The way to Lens Larque led
through Ottile Panshaw, perhaps via Kotzash Mutual. At this
moment the stuation was even and serene, like a pond on a
windless day. The great fish lurked hidden beneath glassy reflections. To force him to move, to lunge, to display himself,
the water must be disturbed.

Out into the garden stepped the receptionist, to stand blinking this way and that. Gersen raised his hand; the receptionist approached: a wiry little man, sandy-haired, with a thin
face and wise heavy-lidded brown eyes, either bow-legged or
lame, so that he walked with a swaggering hop.

"Sit down," said Gersen. "May I offer you a 'Sunday
Punch'? Or would you prefer something less conspicuous?"

"Thank you." The receptionist turned to the waiter. "I'll
take a gill of that good Engelman Yellow." He turned back
to Gersen. "You enjoyed your meal?"

"Yes indeed. The management seems to understand out-
world tastes."

"They ought to, by this time. They've been at it for years."

"What of yourself? You're not native to Dar Sai."

"Certainly not. I was born at Svengay, on Caph IV. A
lively little world; have you ever visited there?"

"No. My closest approach would be the Mizar system, or
perhaps Dubhe. I'm not certain of the distances."

"I see you've had your share of wandering among the stars.
Where is your home, may I ask? Usually I can make a guess,
but in your case I am baffled."

"I was born in a world you have never heard of. As a boy
I was taken to Earth by my uncle."

"And where did you live on Earth?"

"We never stayed long in one place. I know London well,
and San Francisco, Noumea, Melbourne—wherever my uncle
chose to educate me." Gersen smiled faintly as he remem-

bered the style of his uncle's instruction. "I am also well acquainted with Alphanor, and the Concourse in general. May I inquire your name? I am Kirth Gersen, as you know."

"I am Daswell Tippin, at your service: a person of no pretensions."

"Speaking of pretensions, I was interested to hear you speak of the Methlen. They are a people unfamiliar to me."

"They are a group of over-wealthy bashaws and not particularly interesting," said Tippin. "I seldom have dealings with them. Their money comes from duodecimates, and they are here principally to look after their interests. For all I know they are indeed glorious, superb and exquisitely sensitive. Had I these attributes I might also avoid tourists, Darsh and other vulgarians."

"Do the Methlen themselves mine duodecimates?"

"Certainly not. Show one a shovel, he'd call it an implement. They buy, sell, deal in options, leases, futures and all mining finance, and of course they all have vast investments."

"What of Kotzash Mutual? Was that a Methlen operation?"

Daswell Tippin darted Gersen a swift sharp glance, then gave a snort of disgust. "To the contrary. Kotzash Mutual was advertised as a counter to the Methlen: a way to beat them at their own game. It cost me six hundred good svu."

"Then you must know Ottile Panshaw."

"By sight, no more," said Tippin with a prim sniff. "He still keeps his office yonder under Skansel Shade."

"He's not considered a swindler and a scoundrel?"

"I've heard hard talk, but what can be proved? Nothing." Tippin drained his goblet and set it down with a thoughtful clink. Gersen raised his finger to the waiter. "Two more of the same, please."

"Thank you," said Tippin. "I seldom take drink but today I find myself in the mood."

"I enjoy your conversation," said Gersen. "The Kotzash affair is intriguing in itself. Is the name of the robber generally known?"

Tippin looked right and left. "People use a dreadful name: Lens Larque, one of the famous 'Demon Princes.'"

Gersen nodded. "I know his reputation. He's Darsh, so I'm told."

Tippin again glanced right and left. "Apparently so: a

Bugold rachepol.* I don't like to use his name; it falters on my tongue. He is a trickster, with a humor like that of the devil Sclamoth, who puts the heads of sons in their mother's ovens."

"Come now," said Gersen lightly. "A name is no more than a word. Words are without substance."

"Wrong!" declared Tippin with intense fervor. "Words are what magic is made of! Have you not read *Farsakar's Cantrip Mechanisms*? No? Then you know nothing of words!"

Gersen, who lacked any large interest in the subject, made an offhand gesture. "We live in a world of solidities. I fear the man and his whip. Not the words 'Lens Larque' and 'Panak.'"

Tippin frowned down into his goblet. "Well, no great matter, one way or the other. He is human and a Darsh. How the Methlen would love to take him! He is their bugbear; he in turn bears the Methlen a grudge. Have you visited Methel?"

"Not yet."

"Twanish is their spaceport and first city. The Methlen can't abide the odor of ahagaree and Darsh must keep to a special downwind quarter. Isn't this a strange and wonderful universe? I believe that I might enjoy another half-gill of this excellent liquor."

Gersen gave an appropriate order to the waiter. "The Methlen lost nothing in the Kotzash calamity?"

"Nothing whatever. The Darsh and small speculators such as myself: we are the victims!"

"And Ottile Panshaw neither lost nor gained?"

"I wouldn't know. He disappeared for months but now he is back in Serjeuz; I saw him only yesterday. He appears wan and unhealthy."

"Understandable, after such a catastrophe. What might be the value of your own Kotzash holdings?"

"I own twenty shares. Twenty times zero is still zero."

Gersen leaned back in his chair, frowned up at the underside of the parasol. He reached in his pouch and brought out twenty svu. "I have a foolish habit of speculation. I'll buy your shares, for an svu apiece."

---

* Rachepol: a person driven away from his native shade; an outcast; a homeless wanderer, more often than not a criminal.

Tippin's thin jaw slackened. He frowned down at the certificates, then turned a suspicious side-glance toward Gersen. "Speculation usually has a basis of hope."

"Mine is based on caprice."

"You do not seem a capricious man."

"Suppose Lens Larque indemnified Kotzash: I would profit."

"That is forlorn thinking, if ever I heard any."

"No doubt you're right." Gersen reached out to reclaim the money, but Tippin's skinny hand was there first. "Not so fast. Why shouldn't you enjoy your whims?"

"No reason whatever. Where are your shares?"

"Up in my rooms. I'll bring them to you at once." He hurried away and presently returned with the shares; money changed hands. "I have access to other Kotzash shares," said Tippin. "I'm not quite sure how many, but I'll also sell them at this price."

Gersen leaned back with a sour grin. "Be absolutely discreet! Don't tell anyone that an off-worlder is buying Kotzash shares. They'll suspect a swindle and raise their price. I won't buy and there'll be profit for no one. Do you understand this chain of events?"

"In every detail except one, which is why you are buying the shares—aside from caprice, of course."

"Caprice and, let us say, altruism."

Tippin leaned back with a morose sneer. "One is as plausible as the other. Please advance me some working capital. A hundred SVU will suffice for today. You will surely take all and any Kotzash shares at one SVU apiece?"

"Surely and definitely." Gersen produced the money. "One final stipulation: under no circumstances approach Ottile Panshaw!"

Tippin's eyes shifted. "His shares are as good as any."

"He owns more shares than I care to buy. Discretion is absolutely necessary. Do you agree to this?"

"Well, yes, of necessity. Still, I fail to understand—"

"Caprice."

" 'Caprice' is a blanket which cannot cover every bed. I took you for a man fixed upon grim fact."

Gersen held up a packet of SVU notes. "These are my facts; call them 'grim' if you like."

"You have made your point." Tippin rose to his feet. "I'll

report back later today." He departed the garden, and at skipping trot set off across the plaza. Summoning the waiter, Gersen paid his account. "Where is Dindar House?"

"Yonder, sir, under Skansel Shade. Notice the great dome just left of the shaft? That's Dindar House."

Tippin had gone toward Skansel Shade. Gersen decided to follow.

Chapter 8

From *The Darsh Habitat,* by Stuart Sobek, in *Cosmopolis:*

Dar Sai, hard by the sun Cora, is hot and arid around the equatorial band where the sands are rich with duodecimates. Over the centuries a race of hardy men and women have learned tricks to defeat Cora's heat while mining wealth from the sands. These are the Darsh: a race of ten thousand oddities. By day they enjoy the shelter of vast metal umbrellas which spill veils of water from their brims: the famous "shades " of Dar Sai. Unprotected out on the Wale a man will die of heat and sun-blister in minutes; under his "shade" he enjoys cool greenery and icy sherbets.

The Darsh are not a merry folk, nor prone to philosophic insight; still they concentrate on the essence of every instant, and display a curious propensity for enjoying that particular quality by experiencing its antithesis. Their food is seasoned with vile condiments, so that they may better savor cool pure water; they drink offensive teas and beers if only to exemplify this typical perversity, which they value for its own sake.

Their erotic relationships are of a quality to alarm placid dispositions, and apparently are based upon hatred and contempt, rather than mutual regard.

Gersen passed under the water veil which separated Central Shade from Skansel Shade. The flow, a drizzle of misty droplets, felt cool on his face and no more than dampened his garments. He proceeded to the Skansel plaza, under trees and foliage, past structures age-worn and shabby, in contrast to the cosmopolitan modernity under Central Shade. The folk peering from the dumbles were urban Darsh, distinguished from desert Darsh by soft slippers, light robes and a sallow undertone to their complexions, still with heavy noses, anvil jaws and dangling jeweled earlobes.

Gersen halted at the edge of Skansel Plaza, Tippin was nowhere visible. A few assiduous tourists wandered among the shops and booths, buying curios from Darsh women with wooden faces and black mustaches, or doggedly drinking Darsh beer at outdoor places of refreshment. All in all, thought Gersen, a quaint and picturesque scene, tainted only by the psychic proximity of Lens Larque.

To the right rose Dindar House: a massive pile of low flat domes, intersecting in curving slanting arcades. Across the second level a large sign read:

THE MINING JOURNAL
Serjeuz, Dar Sai
Comprehensive news of desert, mine and shade.

Ottile Panshaw maintained an office at Dindar House. Daswell Tippin had set off in this direction, while Gersen had no wish to confront Ottile Panshaw at this particular instant; it might be wise to check upon Tippin's reliability. He sauntered up a ramp and into Dindar House. The foyer, paved with liver-colored tile and rank with a smoky odor, gave upon a pair of dim corridors.

A flight of steps ascended to the upper levels.

Gersen consulted the directory; *Ottile Panshaw, Mining Securities and Leases*, was designated as the occupant of Suite 103.

At random Gersen chose one of the corridors and found a set of tall green doors numbered 100, 101, 102. At the door numbered 103, Gersen paused to listen. He thought to hear a murmur of voices. He put his ear to the panel. Either the occupants had stopped speaking or the chamber was vacant.

Gersen moved away, fearful of discovery. Adjoining offices, so he noticed, were separated by foot-thick concrete walls. There would be no eavesdropping into Ottile Panshaw's office, except through door or window.

Gersen departed Dindar House. At a nearby kiosk, almost concealed by the foliage of a kumquat tree, a squat old lady, with a bush of black hair and a remarkable mustache, sold sweetmeats, journals, maps and general oddments. Gersen bought a copy of the Mining Journal and stood leaning negligently against the kiosk. To the wall were pasted advertising placards, one over the other, an accretion of years. The most recent read:

EXTRAVAGANZA OF TRICKS AND DANCERS

1. Panko Wapshot;
   He dances a duel against
   the Four Armed Snaveler.
2. Bungles and Chelts:
   A merry farce.
3. The Four Scorpions and the
   Drunken Snaveler:
   See them at their tricks
   and pranks.
4. Miffet and his Wonderful
   Sand-machine.
   A notable invention!
5. Other farces and displays. At
   Twinkner's Plaza, under
   Twinkner's Shade, on the 20th
   day of Dirdolio.

Another placard, tattered and faded announced:

REMARKABLE DISPLAY OF SNAVELRY!

Presenting:

Whippity Ticket and the Inept Bungles
Jumping Jipsum and the Unwilling Chelts
Caliogo and Offish
The mad khoontz catches an imbecile snaveler.
with other amusing tricks, poses
and acrobatic feats.

Toward the front a glossy new placard, printed in green and yellow, announced:

GRAND HADAUL
at Dinkelstown
Daffleday,
the 10th day of Mirmone.

Gersen's attention was distracted by the appearance of a
Methlen girl coming from the direction of Central Shade.
Gersen watched her first with detachment, then interest, then
fascination. Loose black curls framed her face which at the
moment was intent and preoccupied, but which on other oc-
casions would seem to be a vivacious instrument of expression.

She wore a knee-length gown of a dark green stuff, and
carried a large gray envelope. She moved with a jaunty care-
lessness which, with her pale faintly dusky skin, short straight
nose and delicate chin, suggested a background of heedless
privilege. To Gersen she exactly represented that existence
from which his circumstances excluded him and which occasionally stirred bittersweet longings in his consciousness. . . .
Passing the kiosk, the girl turned Gersen an incurious glance,
then ran up the ramp and into Dindar House.

Gersen watched her out of sight; her figure slender and
shapely, without soft adiposity, was most appealing. He
heaved a heartfelt sigh and gave his attention to the *Mining
Journal*.

Ten minutes passed. The Methlen girl emerged from Dindar House and marched down the ramp. Meeting Gersen's
gaze, she turned him a cool stare, elevated her chin a trifle
and set off in the direction of Central Shade.

Gersen smiled his crooked smile, folded the journal and
once more entered Dindar House. Again he approached Suite
103; as before he seemed to hear subdued voices, and then
the scrape of furniture. Gersen retreated quickly down the
hall and took refuge in the shadows behind a buttress. From
Suite 103 came two men. One was Daswell Tippin, the other
a tall Darsh with a square hard-featured face, a strong
physique and long earlobes. Instead of robe and thabbat he
wore a conventional nutmeg-brown tunic with pale blue
breeches and black ankle boots.

The two departed Dindar House. After a moment Gersen
followed out into Skansel Plaza, but they had entered one of
the tree-shrouded byways and could not be seen.

Gersen returned the way he had come: back through the veil of mist and out upon Central Plaza. He crossed to the Traveler's Inn and glanced into the lobby. Daswell Tippin was not at the desk.

Gersen went out into the garden. The time was now middle afternoon. The air felt warm and heavy; falling water created a soporific murmur. Those folk still abroad moved at a languid pace, and these were for the most part tourists. Gersen seated himself at a table beside the plaza. Suddenly, there was much to think about. He brought out Addels' letter, referred to the text, and copied off a list:

> Ottile Penshaw 1250
> Chanseth Bank 1000
> Nihel Cahouse 600
> Others 1970

Gersen performed a few calculations. Were he to acquire all the Chanseth Bank stock and all that owned by Nihel Cahouse, he could claim the executive directorship of Kotzash, although he would still fall short of a majority holding.

Jehan Addels' candid avowals of cowardice amused Gersen. Smiling, he looked up and once again met the eyes of the Methlen girl, by chance passing in front of the Traveler's Garden. Gersen could not fail to notice her look of cleanliness and perfect health. She also seemed self-willed and haughty. Compressing her mouth, she darted Gersen a sidewise glance of annoyance and continued on her way. Gersen's smile became a lame grimace. Glumly he looked after her. Delightful and superb, thought Gersen, if somewhat irascible. Through whim or curiosity she looked back over her shoulder; noting Gersen's continued attention she tossed her head in contempt and marched off across the plaza. "My status, in this case, is not at all in doubt," reflected Gersen.

Looking beyond the girl he saw the façade of the Chanseth Bank: one of the more splendid structures of Central Plaza. The girl entered the bank and was gone from view, but Gersen already had refocused his mind. The Chanseth Bank held 1000 shares of Kotzash Mutual stock. Time might well be of the essence, now that Daswell Tippin, for better or worse, had become his associate. Gersen rose to his feet and set off across the plaza.

A formal garden flanked the approach to the Chanseth Bank; four tall pointane trees, each a perfect tear-drop, stood surrounded by a low hedge of russet crackleberry. Gersen passed under an arch into a large cool area paved with blue tile. To his right a balustrade of carved alabaster enclosed the working area; to the left spiral columns supported a screen set with crystal lenses. The far end of the chamber was a lounge area, where sat half a dozen Methlen of various ages, including the girl Gersen previously had noted, now in company with an older man. Observing Gersen, her jaw dropped in surprise; she turned quickly away and spoke earnestly to her companion.

Gersen smiled sourly and went to the counter. A minute passed, then another. Gersen became restless. He spoke to a clerk. "This is the Chanseth Bank, I presume."

The clerk responded in a neutral voice. "Quite so."

"Who is the managing director?"

"May I inquire your business?"

"I want to discuss a financial transaction."

"Our business is almost wholly commercial. Since we are affiliated with no other bank we cash neither checks nor credit vouchers."

"My business is of some importance. Be so good as to summon your managing director."

"He is that grandee* yonder, the Gentle Adario Chanseth. At the moment you will notice that he is importantly occupied."

"Oh? That young lady is a person of distinction?"

"That is his daughter, the Gentle Jerdian Chanseth. You may take up your business as soon as he is disengaged."

"My business transcends idle chatter with a girl," declared Gersen. He left the counter and approached the lounge. Two

---

* The Methlen term *averroi* signifies a status considerably more elevated than that connoted by the term "gentleman." *Averroi* implies dignity, punctilio, exclusivity, social poise and an unthinking mastery of Methlen etiquette. The Methlen give lip service to the fiction that any Methlen ranks on even terms with any other; hence they use a single honorific, here rendered by "the Gentle." In actual fact social distinctions are very real, reflecting factors far too numerous and subtle to be considered here.

Parenthetically, it may be noted that the Methlen are highly susceptible to ridicule and humiliation. Their civil and criminal penalties reflect this sensitivity.

tall men, displaying identical bristling mustaches, came to meet him. Each seized one of his arms and marched him swiftly toward the entrance.

"Here, here!" Gersen complained. "What are you up to?"

"Get out and stay out," said one of the men.

"Never molest a Methlen lady; it will go poorly with you!" said the other.

"I have molested no one!" Gersen protested. "You are making a mistake." He pulled back and resisted their impetus, but they seized him by the back of the trousers, frog-marched him to the entrance and sent him flying into one of the crackleberry hedges.

Gersen rose to his feet, brushed leaves and trash from his garments and returned into the bank.

The two gentlemen, astonished by his persistence, stepped forward. Gersen said crossly, "Please stand back. My business is with the Gentle Adario Chanseth, not yourselves." He sidestepped the two men and approached Chanseth, who had turned away from the Gentle Jerdian.

"Well then, what is the meaning of this affair?"

Gersen produced a business card, which he gave to Chanseth. "At your convenience, I would like to discuss some business with you."

" 'The Honorable Kirth Gersen,' " read Chanseth. "President, Cooney's Bank, Rath Eileann, Aloysius.' " He gave a dubious grunt. "What is your business with me?"

"Must we discuss it here? Things go differently at Cooney's Bank. If you came to discuss a business matter with me I would not have you thrown into the hedge."

"There has obviously been a mistake," said Chanseth in a frosty voice. "If you will be good enough to elucidate even an inkling of your business, I can at least inform you as to whether I am the proper person to consult."

"As you wish," said Gersen. "Frankly, I am here to solicit your advice. My bank has substantial interests in the metallurgical field and we are hoping to establish branches both here and at Twanish. We are interested in duodecimes and duodecimate stock."

"Let us discuss this matter privately." Chanseth led him through a plasmatic film into an office. He indicated a chair of bent whitewood. "Sit, if you will." Chanseth himself remained standing.

Ignoring Chanseth's rather pointed rigidity, Gersen relaxed into the chair. In a casual voice he said, "The Methlen method of greeting a business associate is definitely unique."

Chanseth responded in a measured tones. "My daughter reported that you had eyed her in an impudent manner, 'grinning and leering,' so she put it, not once but several times, after following her to Skansel Shade and back, then here to the bank. I therefore ordered you ejected."

"If anyone other than your daughter had made the complaint," said Gersen, "I would think her vain and giddy."

Chanseth, clearly uninterested in Gersen's opinions, gave a grim nod. "This is a barbaric world, never doubt it. The Darsh are an indescribably vulgar race; they are brutal and violent as well. You may consider Serjeuz peaceful and orderly; so it is, but only because the Methlen tolerate nothing else. We are on the alert for impudence, and your conduct, whatever its nature, incurred a quick rebuke. There let the matter rest. Please explain your reasons for consulting me."

"Certainly. The collecting and marketing of Dar Sai duodecimates is evidently an inefficient process. I suspect that these operations could be rationalized, perhaps through a central agency, to the benefit of everyone."

"Your assessment is correct," said Chanseth. "The duodecimate business is unstructured and disorderly. But the miners are Darsh, and not disposed to disciplined conduct."

"Still," said Gersen, "they would appreciate the convenience of a single stable agency. Perhaps a cooperative system could be evolved."

Chanseth gave a bark of humorless laughter. "If you wish to be assaulted, broach this topic to a Darsh miner. Kotzash Mutual was just such a snydicate. The Darsh miners took stock certificates for their ore, the warehouse was robbed and the certificates are now worthless."

"I've heard something of this," said Gersen. "If Kotzash were revived and in some way made good outstanding claims—"

"A very expensive procedure."

"Still I may take up a few shares of Kotzash. At the very least I would gain a presence in the community."

Chanseth nodded thoughtfully. Walking behind his desk he

seated himself. "Possibly so. I hold a few shares—a thousand in fact—which I'll sell at a fraction of their face value."

Gersen gave an indifferent shrug. "I'd have no need for more than a few hundred, if that many. What is the board price on these shares?"

"I'm not sure. Rather low, I daresay."

"No doubt. Well, I'll take up your shares at a strictly nominal price. Fifty SVU should be adequate."

Chanseth raised his eyebrows. "Are you serious? For a thousand shares, each on the face worth ten ounces of duodecimate?"

"Ten ounces of nonexistent duodecimate. Each is worth exactly nothing."

"Quite so, unless someone undertook to indemnify shareholders. Yourself, for instance."

"You must evaluate that possibility for yourself."

"Still, fifty SVU is a trifling sum."

Gersen heaved a sad sigh. "I will pay a hundred SVU and no more."

Chanseth went to a cabinet, brought out a folder which he placed before Gersen. "There are your shares. They are to the interest of the bearer; no transfer document is necessary."

Gersen paid over a hundred SVU. "Money thrown away, of course."

"I agree."

"How did you come into their possession?"

Chanseth grinned. "They cost me nothing whatever. I traded them for an item equally worthless: shares in a defunct mining corporation."

"That would of course be Didroxus Mining and Exploration?"

Chanseth eyed him sharply. "How did you know?"

"The IAES lists Didroxus Mining as a Kotzash subsidiary, but indicates no Didroxus assets."

"Correct. The only asset is mining rights on Shanitra, the Methel moon."

"That would seem a valuable concession."

Chanseth showed his cool smile. "Shanitra has been explored a hundred times over; it is no more than a lump of pumice. I traded nothing for nothing."

"Your trade brought you a hundred SVU. You're a clever man."

Chanseth again showed a brief wintry smile. "I'll offer you some free advice worth considerably more. If you envision a branch of your bank here—or anywhere else on Dar Sai, for that matter—reject the notion. There is no business for you. Our trade is almost entirely Methlen; you'd get none of that and the Darsh rarely use banks."

"I'll keep your advice in mind." Gersen rose to his feet. "Convey my respects to your daughter; a pity that she suffered distress on my account. On the first occasion I'll personally make amends."

"Please do not trouble yourself," said Chanseth. "She has already forgotten the incident. In any event we very shortly return to Methel." He performed a curt bow. "Good day to you, sir."

Gersen departed the office. In the lounge the Gentle Jerdian sat with a friend, nibbling confections. Gersen nodded politely but he stared unseeingly past him.

Gersen went out upon the plaza. Not far away a dusty blue dendron, spiked with white and red blossoms, arched over an outdoor café. Gersen found a table in a shadowed niche and was served a pot of tea.

He sat considering the possible phases of the future. They made a bewildering tangle: a maze, in fact, at whose center crouched a sinister figure. Gersen smiled at the extravagance of the image. Lens Larque crouched somewhere, certainly. He might be that bulky man munching a custard-bun across the café; Gersen had no way of knowing. Like all the Demon Princes, Lens Larque concealed his public identity. Through the maze led a single thread, of several strands: Kotzash Mutual Syndicate, Ottile Panshaw, Didroxus Mining and the Shanitra exploration and development leases (why had Panshaw troubled to make the trade?) and now, conceivably, Daswell Tippin (why had Tippin, almost instantly and despite Gersen's admonitions, gone directly to the offices of Ottile Panshaw? Who was that quasi-Darsh Tippin had met there?)

The next twist along the "Kotzash" strand would seem to lead to Nihel Cahouse of Inkin's Shade, who owned 600 Kotzash shares. How had Cahouse gained so large an interest, equivalent to three tons of black sand? No matter what his methods, it would be wise to reach him in advance of

Daswell Tippin, or anyone else. . . . At the thought of Tippin, Gersen made a restless movement. The enlistment of Tippin might well have been a serious mistake. Originally, he had seemed a useful agent for the collection of small holdings, but Tippin might now have his sights set on larger transactions.

Who then was Cahouse and where was Inkin's Shade?

A shop sign nearby caught his eye:

THE DESERT TRADING POST

Equipment for the Tourist
Travel Information
Expeditions and Excursions,
arranged and conducted,
Witness an authentic hadaul
in safety and comfort.

Gersen went to look into the front window. The display featured articles designed to expedite desert travel: motor bubbles, skimmers, Darsh-type robes, insulated boots and undersuits, air-conditioning packs, and like merchandise. A rack of books, maps and pamphlets was flanked by a pair of easels. The first supported a poster entitled:

NOTICE TO TOURISTS

with an appended text. The second displayed a poster printed in dramatic green and yellow:

GRAND HADAUL

at Dinkelstown
Daffleday,
the 10th day of Mirmone.

One of the great games of the year!
An event not to be missed!

Travel in comfort with our experienced guide,
and witness this typical Darsh spectacle.

Gersen entered the shop and bought a book entitled: *The Clans of Dar Sai,* a folio of maps and a pamphlet: *Guide to the Shades.*

He took his purchases back to the table under the tree. He spread out the map: a strip three feet long by a foot wide, tinted various colors over an underlying base tone of sandy yellow. The limiting areas, at top and bottom, tinted green, were labeled BOG and were otherwise featureless. The four principal towns: Serjeuz, Wabber's Fountain, Dinkelstown and Belfeser, were indicated by black stars, smaller settlements by large black dots, isolated shades by small dots. Places of historical interest, tourist spectacles and the like— "Strangler's Gantry," "The Tournaline Towers," "Scorpion Farm," "Bagshilly Plain," "The Skutch"—were marked by crosses or dotted outlines. Tinted areas, some large, some small, indicated clan domains. Gersen located "Bugold Region" and "Bugold Shade" somewhat to the north and two thousand miles east of Serjeuz. . . . Looking up from the map Gersen noticed Daswell Tippin hopping and trotting across the plaza with a look of worried concentration on his face. His eyes darted right and left, but he failed to notice Gersen in the shadows. With interest and amusement Gersen saw him enter the Chanseth Bank. The interview between Tippin and Adario Chanseth would gratify neither. Keeping half an eye on the bank, Gersen folded the map and looked into *The Clans of Dar Sai.* The first chapter outlined the early history of Dar Sai: the building of the shades, the formation of the clans. The second, third and fourth chapters described the typical circumstances of a clan, its interpersonal relationships, procreative habits, caste distinctions and recreations. In the fifth chapter, the game *hadaul* was analyzed at length, the author tending to the belief that the games of any specific society could be viewed as a microcosm of the society itself. . . . From the bank came Daswell Tippin, his gait perceptibly less brisk. He looked nervously in all directions, walked listlessly to the café and seated himself with his back to Gersen, not ten yards away.

A waiter approached; Tippin gave a terse order, and was served a small glass of carbonated punch, which he sipped as if it were a medicinal draught. With a nervous gesture he reached into the pocket of his jacket and brought out a sheaf of papers; Gersen saw them to be certificates very like those he had bought from Chanseth. Tippin counted through the sheaf with fidgeting fingers.

Gersen rose to his feet, walked up behind Tippin, reached over his shoulder and took the certificates from Tippin's suddenly palsied hand.

"Good work," said Gersen. "I'll take these now and pay you tonight. Carry on." He returned to his seat.

Tippin uttered a small choked protest. He half-rose from his seat, then slowly subsided.

Gersen counted the certificates: six of twenty shares, five of ten shares and eight singles: 178 in all.

Tippin watched him wordlessly a moment, then slowly turned and hunched over his drink, the curve of his back eloquent of angry reproach.

Gersen added up his shares: 1,112 plus 178: 1,290. He now commanded sufficient shares to qualify as a director: even executive director if Ottile Panshaw continued to hold only 1,250 shares: not a realistic hope. . . . At Tippin's table, appearing as if from nowhere, stood the tall Darsh Gersen had noticed at Dindar House. He dropped into a seat beside Tippin, who spoke a single terse sentence. The Darsh uttered a disgusted expletive and glanced in contempt toward the bank. He put a brusque question to Tippin, who gave his head a helpless shake and offered a placatory explanation, which prompted the Darsh to another curse. Tippin made a meek comment which failed to ameliorate the situation. The Darsh jumped to his feet and strode off across the plaza. Tippin watched him go, then looked sidewise toward Gersen, who returned a cold stare. Tippin hopped over to Gersen's table. Attempting a sedate and business-like manner he settled into a chair. "Those shares were not intended for you."

"Who were they intended for?"

"No matter. You must return them."

"Small chance of that. I'll pay you your money if you want it."

"I want the shares. I had taken them in trust for that Darsh gentleman."

"Who is he? What his sudden interest in Kotzash shares?"

"His name is Bel Ruk. I don't know why you want the shares, and I don't know why he does."

"He wants them only because you told him that I wanted them—exactly contrary to my instructions."

Tippin twisted his mouth in a wincing grimace. "No matter. Those shares are mine and I want them back."

"You bought them for me and I'm keeping them. Do you want your money?" Gersen counted out a hundred and eighty svu. "There it is."

Tippin picked up the money with indecisive fingers. "This imposes a great inconvenience upon me.

"You shouldn't have gone to Dindar House. You made the inconvenience for yourself."

Tippin grunted. "I was at one time Panshaw's associate; that's the truth of the matter. I have no choice in what I do."

"Bel Ruk also works with Ottile Panshaw?"

"I suppose that's the way of it."

" 'With' or 'for?' "

" 'For.' That's my guess."

"How many more shares can you locate?"

"None! I am finished with this business!" Tippin jumped to his feet. Like a nervous bird he peered through the foliage as a party of young Methlen settled at a nearby table. He looked down at Gersen. "Do you know what the Darsh mean by 'rachepol?' "

"I've heard the word."

"It means 'crop-ear'—that's the same as 'outcast.' Bel Ruk is a rachepol. He has no conscience. He is a skillful killer. If you value your life, leave Serjeuz." Tippin departed the café, and limped at best speed across the plaza.

Gersen returned to his reading. A few minutes later one of the Methlen at the nearby table jumped erect and approached Gersen: a tall young man with fine black eyebrows, a long nose, and a spare patrician cast of countenance. "Sir! A moment of your time!"

"Certainly," said Gersen. "What do you want?"

"I am puzzled by your conduct. I request an explanation."

"There is little to explain. My conduct is as you see. I sit here drinking tea and reading this book, which I bought at the shop yonder. It describes the habits of the Darsh."

"That is not the conduct I had in mind."

"Please explain."

"I refer, in essence, to your traffic in Kotzash shares."

"The basic principle is: 'Buy low, sell high'. Why not make

inquiries of the Gentle Adario Chanseth? He is skilled in these affairs and can give you far more information than I."

The young man seemed not to hear. "I am concerned with your acts of misrepresentation and to the suspicions which you have generally aroused."

Gersen, smiling, shook his head. "I can't go into such vague matters. We would sit for hours defining our terms, and I for one have not so much time to spare."

The young man's voice rose in pitch. "You have instigated an odd series of events. I want to know what more you intend."

"For a fact, I don't know. And now, please excuse me." Gersen returned to his reading. The Methlen took a half-step forward. Gersen sighed and began to gather his books.

A second person approached the table. "Aldo, the matter is really of no consequence. Come, we want to discuss the excursion."

Looking sidewise Gersen saw a lower torso clad in soft dark green; raising his eyes, he discovered the upper parts and face of Jerdian Chanseth.

Aldo, never taking his eyes from Gersen, said crisply: "This man is devious for a fact! I find him barely civil."

"Well what of that? Things are as they are; do you hope to alter his nature?"

"Even andropes can be guided; perhaps I should have a word with the constables. A prod with the truncheon might do wonders for this fellow's disposition."

"Or it might make him more surly than ever. Leave him to crouch in his lair: why concern yourself?"

"It is not so simple. His manipulations already are a source of trouble to your father."

"Well then, let me talk to him. Perhaps he will conduct himself gracefully."

"I think not. This is a gentleman's affair."

Jerdian's voice took on an edge. "Aldo, stand aside, or better, go back to the table."

"I will wait here," said Aldo with glacial dignity.

Gersen had followed the conversation with only mild interest. As Jerdian dropped into the seat vacated by Tippin, he rose politely, once more seated himself. "This is an unexpected pleasure. May I offer you tea? I am Kirth Gersen, by the way."

"No tea, thank you. Why are you here at Serjeuz?"

"I could give you a dozen answers," said Gersen. "I travel a great deal. I like to explore odd corners of the galaxy. I am interested in exotic peoples like the Darsh and the Methlen; I consider them picturesque."

The Gentle Jerdian's lips curled. Gersen could not decide whether she was irked or amused. "You are evading me."

"Not at all. There is far too much to tell. Send this fellow away and we will spend the rest of the day together, and perhaps the evening as well."

Aldo stiffened and drew back. "I have never heard such astounding nonsense! Jerdian, come along; this man's impertinence is tiresome."

Jerdian turned him an expressionless glance and Aldo became abruptly silent. Jerdian spoke to Gersen in a silken voice: "You have represented yourself as a banker."

"True."

"You are like no banker I have ever known."

"Your instincts are sound. The usual banker is diffident and ruthless only when the odds are on his side. What, in fact, is your opinion of me?"

"If anything, I think of you as the man who has just swindled my father."

Gersen raised his eyebrows. "Odd! Your father was sure that he had exploited my innocence."

Aldo cried out: "These remarks verge upon slander! They will bring you to grief!"

Gersen said to Jerdian: "Why not ask this gentleman to leave us? He is like a raven at the feast."

Jerdian looked thoughtfully toward Aldo, then returned to Gersen. "Unless you care to speak candidly, our conversation has come to an end."

Gersen made a contrite gesture. "Perhaps I've been evasive, but I stand in awe of Aldo. His threats and interjections inhibit me."

Jerdian turned suddenly. "Aldo, please go back to the table. For a fact, it is hard to think with you looming over my shoulder."

"As you wish." Aldo stalked away. Gersen signaled the waiter. "Bring us a new pot of tea, or better, a flask of Spondent Flux and two glasses."

Jerdian drew back, disassociating herself from Gersen's

conviviality. "I don't care for anything. In a moment I must get back to my friends."

"Why bother to come at all? You evidently find me detestable."

The remark amused Jerdian; she laughed and became more winsome then ever. Gersen felt a sudden throb. To love Jerdian Chanseth, and with her correspondingly in love, would be a fascinating circumstance.

Jerdian, perhaps sensing something of Gersen's mood, spoke in a carefully neutral voice. "I will explain my interest; it is perfectly simple. The Kotzash scandal involved the notorious Lens Larque. When we hear the word 'Kotzash' we are instantly on edge."

"Understandable."

"Then why are you buying Kotzash shares?"

"It's a tactical matter, and not at all discreditable. If I explained to you, you'd tell your father, who would tell a dozen others, and I would be inconvenienced."

Jerdian looked off across the plaza. Then she said: "And you are not connected with Lens Larque?"

"Definitely not. If I were, I'd hardly advertise the fact."

Jerdian gave her shoulders a half-frivolous half-disdainful shrug. "You seem very much aware of him."

"So do you."

"For good reason. He is our local bugbear. In fact, we have had an unpleasant little adventure involving Lens Larque. Of course he is Darsh of the deepest dye and rachepol to boot. Do you know that word?"

"It means 'outcast.' "

"Something of the sort. The Darsh make a great ceremony and cut off one of the culprit's ears."

"I cut off the other," said Gersen.

Jerdian jerked her head around. "What did you say?"

"What was the offense that cost Lens Larque his ear?"

Jerdian put on a face of cool dignity. Lens Larque's offense evidently was one which polite Methlen girls considered either unimaginable or unspeakable. "I am not acquainted with the details. And still you have given me no information."

Gersen picked up his goblet and squinted through the facets of the crystal. "With the representative of Chanseth Bank, I am close-mouthed and evasive. With someone whose personality could be considered charming, stimulating, even endearing, I'd have many things indeed to tell."

Jerdian again gave her frivolous shrug. "You are definitely impertinent, and very forward."

Her voice, Gersen noted, seemed neither peremptory nor biting. She added thoughtfully: "I had reason to complain of you earlier today."

"You misunderstood everything. I looked up from a letter which amused me, and saw you, but I neither 'grimaced' nor 'leered.' Then I saw the Chanseth Bank and went there to transact business, but instead was ejected."

Jerdian's dignity had almost evaporated. "Well then, what of Dindar House? Surely you followed me?"

"How is that possible? I was there before you arrived."

"Well—true. But even now you are expressing yourself in personal terms."

"I can't help but notice that you are fascinating to look at, and pleasant to talk to. Shall I go on?"

"Please do not trouble yourself." Jerdian rose to her feet. "You are indeed a strange man. I can't decide what to make of you."

Gersen stood erect. "On better acquaintance you may be less skeptical."

"Our acquaintance has no prospects. If you are interfering with Lens Larque, he will have you killed."

"He is not yet aware of me. There is still time."

"Not really. I'm returning to Methel directly after the Dinkelstown hadaul. Are you still likely to be alive?"

"I hope so. Will I see you before then?"

"I don't know."

Jerdian went back to her table. Aldo and her other friends had been covertly watching; at once they put questions, to which Jerdian gave absent-minded responses. Presently the group went off toward the Sferinde Select Hotel.

Cora slid down Dar Sai's chalky blue sky, trembled on the horizon, became red and oblate, then quickly disappeared, leaving a lemon-yellow afterglow. Hundreds of miles to the north and south, high flakes of cirrus glinted vermilion, then purple, then faded from sight. With the coming of dusk the desert air cooled. The Serjeuz water veils dwindled to random drops and the evening breeze moved through the domes without impediment. With the cessation of falling water, Serjeuz seemed oddly silent, and the white-robed Darsh moving across the plaza were altered into mysterious creatures of intrigue.

One of the white-robed shapes was Gersen, carrying a soft bag containing what might be considered the tools of his trade. As he passed from Central Shade into the even dimmer precincts of Skansel Shade, he reflected that if Jerdian Chanseth could be with him now, and know his various accoutrements, she would consider him a strange man indeed.

Just as well that Jerdian was somewhere else, thought Gersen, presumably safe in the polite environs of the Sferinde Select Hotel. Just as well, or even better, if he could put her definitely out of his mind. By no reach of the imagination could she ever become part of his precarious life, for which she herself predicted a sudden end.

The idea at once saddened him and keyed him to his highest level of competence. He approached Dindar House alert as a hunting beast, with all his faculties, conscious and subconscious, monitoring the environment.

He halted in the shadows beside the vendor's kiosk. The proprietress had gone home, leaving her wares and coin-dish exposed for the convenience of anyone who might choose to serve himself.*

---

* The Darsh are not prone to petty theft; indeed, away from the towns, thievery is virtually unknown. Murder face-to-face and robbery, especially in connection with duodecimates, is rather more common, but still considered a vile crime. The perpetrator, when apprehended, is first whipped raw, then chained out among the rocks where he becomes prey to the lancilark, gnaw-bugs and scorpions. The crime considered most vile by the Darsh is the theft either of another's desert-roller, or his water supply. The penalties entail flogging, then staking out at the bottom of the town's cesspit.

As a note of possible interest, the offense which occasioned Lens Larque's ejection from Bugold Shade was the theft of an air-conditioner from the corpse of a man who had drunkenly fallen into poisonous cactus. The crime was considered repulsive but not superlatively heinous. Husse Bugold, as he was then known, suffered the loss of an earlobe and was whipped away from Bugold Shade.

As another sidelight it might be noted that Jerdian Chanseth, lacking exact information as to the nature of Husse Bugold's transgression, automatically imputed to him that sin regarded most reprehensible by the Methlen: i.e., unnatural sexual conduct, activity which the Darsh take for granted: hence her reaction to Gersen's question.

The full scope of comparative criminology is morbidly fascinating,

Gersen waited. Five minutes passed; Dindar House showed only three lights, on spikes atop the three highest domes. Through the night air sounds arrived from far distances, clear as the small voices issuing from an earphone. He heard a distant raucous outcry, quickly stilled, and somewhat closer the electronic din of Darsh music: a mindless thumping, twanging and wailing. These sounds only emphasized the quiet of Dindar House.

Gersen left the deep shadow. Quiet and soft as a wisp of smoke he slid up the ramp and into the entrance hall. Here again he paused to listen, but now the outside sounds were muffled, and nothing could be heard but dead silence.

He flicked on a flashlight, swept it up the hall, and saw, as before, mouldy concrete, heavy archways, old varnished wood. He dimmed the light to a glimmer, walked on long soft strides down the hall to the tall green door opening into the offices of Ottile Panshaw.

Carefully he examined doorway, door, lock and latch in a tendril of light but found no sign of alarm or monitor. He tested the door; unlike most Darsh doors this was securely bolted, with a lock proof against manipulation. Significant, thought Gersen. Locks were discovered only in conjunction with objects of value.

He retreated to the entry ramp, and once again appraised the surroundings. Across the plaza a pair of beer gardens, shrouded under foliage, showed clusters of green and white lamps. No one walked the plaza. Gersen jumped up on the slanting face of a buttress, edged over a dome and down upon another curved surface which extended past a line of windows. Gauging distances, Gersen identified that window opening into Ottile Panshaw's office, and approached along a convenient slope of the dome. Unlike other windows of the row, a grating of vondaloy tubing guarded the opening, which was additionally closed off by a pane of heavy glass.

There would be no easy entry here.

---

and is discussed not only in Book VII of Baron Bodissey's monumental exegesis of the human condition, but also in more specialized works, such as Karen Miller's *Interplanetary Crime: Causes and Consequences*, or Theodore Pedersen's *Peccant Souls*. Richard Pelto, in *Peoples of the Coranne* discusses the almost polar sociologies of Methel and Dar Sai at length.

The room was dark within. Gersen tried to illuminate the interior with his flashlight, but was baffled by reflections.

He retreated a few steps to the next window: this open to the night, careless whether someone might or might not intrude. Gersen flashed his light within, discovering what might be the headquarters of an import agent. This office and that of Ottile Panshaw at one time had functioned as a suite. A case of books, pamphlets and samples blocked off the interconnecting door.

Gersen stepped into the office, slid aside the case and examined the door. It hung on hinges and opened toward Gersen. He turned the knob and pulled. The door held firm, secured by a bolt in Ottile Panshaw's office.

Gersen gave his attention to the hinges. They were interlocking and semi-concealed, impossible to disassemble without destroying the door.

Gersen examined the door itself. Lock-picking was not one of his special skills; still he felt a modest confidence in his abilities. But there might be an easier way.

The door opened toward him. The bolt or latch therefore was only as secure as the fastening holding it to the door. Gersen put his knee to the wall, gripped the doorknob, turned, pulled, exerting leg-force with his knee.

A slight splintering sound, and the door opened. Gersen allowed it to move only a few inches. He ran his torch around the slit, seeking broken alarm wires. None were visible, which meant little: Gersen knew a dozen invisible methods to guard a door. He also had encountered chambers charged with lethal gas, to smother the unwary intruder. Gersen sniffed the air but discovered only the rancid scent of long human occupancy. Unlikely, in any event, that Ottile Panshaw as a regular precaution would poison the air of his office. He eased open the door and flashed his light around the room. He saw only what he had expected: greenish-brown walls, a desk, table, three chairs, cabinet and an incongruously expensive communicator.

Gersen worked deftly and quickly. He inserted a trifle of receptor tape into the angle between door-molding and wall, where it became for all practical purposes invisible. Using a pressure canister he sprayed a trail of conductive film from the tape around the door casing into the adjoining office and around the walls to the window. Returning to Panshaw's office he repaired the bolt he had broken loose as best he could, reinserting the fasteners into their sockets. To casual inspection the bolt and its socket were once more securely attached.

Gersen now turned his attention to the desk. On the top lay a folder marked: *Important, Confidential*, which seemed to contain a sheaf of papers. Gersen thought it a somewhat ostentatious invitation, and by extension of logic, a generalized danger signal. Prudent withdrawal became instantly necessary. Gersen's sensory apparatus, tensioned to an almost painful level, at this same instant received a signal. Gersen paused not a second to analyze the warning. He slid through the door, held the bolt back against its spring tension, closed the door, whereupon the bolt struck into its socket, and the door was apparently secure. Gersen pushed the display cases back into place, then went to the door into the hall. He placed his ear against the panel: no sound. He eased the unlocked door open and at once he heard the shuffle of footsteps along the hall. He closed the door, shot home the latch-bolt and ran to the window. Standing in the shadows he peered out, and there, at the back of the dim area below, stood a man in a dark cape and a soft slouch hat. Gersen thought to recognize the posture and dimensions of Ottile Panshaw.

Gersen drew back out of range of Panshaw's vision, should he be wearing night-glasses. He touched his detector to the conductive trail he had sprayed upon the wall and turned high the volume. For a moment he heard nothing. Then: the sound of moving hardware, the creak of the opening door. Again silence, as the room was surveyed. Next footsteps and then a soft voice, apparently speaking into a transceiver: "Nothing. No one here."

Soft and faint in response came Panshaw's voice: "Has there been disturbance?"

"Apparently nothing."

"Perhaps a false alarm. I'm coming up."

Watching through the window Gersen saw Panshaw move off toward the front.

Gersen immediately stepped through the window and out upon the surface of the dome. Again he touched the detector to the conductive trail. Presently he heard Panshaw's voice: "What caused the alarm?"

"Lumen impact, brief and low-intensity."

Silence. Then again Panshaw's voice, cautious and thoughtful. "Nothing seems disturbed. . . . Peculiar. I wonder about that man. Still I am often over-subtle. He may be exactly as he represents himself."

"That in itself is an over-subtle idea."

"Possibly true. . . . We have a mystery on our hands, which will annoy Big Bird. But first things first, which I measure by what is likely to cause Bird the least vexation. In this case, Cahouse comes first. The fellow at Travelers' Inn must wait his turn."

A grunt, then: "Cahouse is not at Inkin's Shade. I may be out several days looking for him."

"Go your best speed, but get the work done. It will be at your own initiative: I am leaving at once for Twanish."

"So soon? You had better stay here and collect shares."

"I do as I am told. Well, so much for a false alarm. I see nothing to keep us here. . . . A moment! The door into Litto's. I believe it has been forced. The paint is broken. . . ." A mumble of words which Gersen could not distinguish; then the shuffle of hurried footsteps.

Gersen ran back across the dome, dropped down upon the entrance ramp, gained the shadows of the kiosk before turning. The windows of both offices showed light; as Gersen watched a dark shape appeared briefly at Litto's window, then disappeared.

Gersen returned the way he had come. Crossing Central Plaza he noticed a troupe of musicians in the Sferinde Gardens. They played for a large group of Methlen all wearing an evening costume of yellow and white, the men with pale blue sashes.

Gersen watched a moment, then smiling a trifle wistfully he continued to the Traveler's Inn.

Behind the reception counter stood Daswell Tippin. The sight of Gersen brought a curious expression of surprise and concern to his face. Gersen approached the desk. "Why do you look at me like that?"

Tippin blurted, "Someone called asking for you, not five minutes ago. I thought you were in your room, and said as much."

"Who called?"

"Well—he gave no name."

"Panshaw? No? Ruk? I see. Well, no great affair. I am go-

ing to my room now, so you were only five minutes wrong—
a trivial period. Do you agree?"

"I agree absolutely!"

"Where will I find Nihel Cahouse?"

"At Inkin's Shade; he's Fogle Clan; many Fogles live at Inkin's Shade."

"What if he is not at Inkin's Shade?"

Tippin threw out his hands. "He might be anywhere."

"Do not mention my interest in Cahouse to anyone."

"Your interest in Cahouse is taken for granted," growled
Tippin. "I'd be telling nothing new."

"Still—keep a quiet tongue in your head."

"Indeed, indeed, indeed! My tongue is as secret as if it
had been torn out!"

Gersen went up to his chambers, which he inspected carefully. Then, installing alarms of his own across doors and
windows, he bathed, went to his couch and slept.

Chapter 9

From *Peoples of the Coranne,* by Richard Pelto:

The Darsh espouse each other only through calculation. The women judge the weight of the man's duodecimates; the men taste the woman's cooking and test the comfort of her dumble: so are Darsh marriages made. The two probably will not engage in sexual congress; both will surely go out on the moonlit desert to pursue their amatory affairs.

The marital relationship is formal and cool. Each party knows what is expected of him or her and, even more keenly, what he or she expects. If thwarted, the woman retaliates with rancid ahagaree or scorched pourrian; the man in his turn will throw less duodecimate upon the table, and spend his time at the beer gardens.

In the morning, an hour before Cora-rise, the woman awakes the man who sullenly dons his day-clothes and goes to look at the sky. He utters a phrase of rather hollow optimism, in loose translation: "It will be good!" and sets off to his sift. The woman looks after him with a dark phrase of her own: "Go to it, fool!"

Late in the day the man returns. As he steps under the shade he takes a final glance around the sky and says, again in rather hollow tones: *"Asi achih!"* which means, "And so it went!" The woman, watching from the shadow of her dumble, merely chuckles quietly to herself.

Gersen awoke at dawn. Rays of Cora-light flashing across the desert nearly parallel to the surface cast long black shadows across the plaza. Looking from his window, Gersen thought of Rigel-light, also white and brilliant. At the distance of Alphanor Rigel-light seemed cool, brittle, crackling with overtones of violet. Cora-light, received at closer range, sizzled and stung.

Gersen dressed in loose gray trousers, a striped blue and white singlet, air-pad sandals: conventional hot-weather garments across the human universe. Using the communicator, he called the Mining Journal, and learned that the offices would not be open for yet another hour.

Descending into the empty lobby, Gersen went out into the garden where he found only a few conscientious tourists. He breakfasted upon tea, fruit, pastries and cheese imported across unknown distances. As he left the garden, water began first to drip, then to fall in veils, from the parasol rims. Day had started in earnest; Cora's assault must be thwarted.

Gersen went directly to Dindar House. Ignoring the fusty halls of the first floor, he ascended to the premises of the Mining Journal: a room long and wide, dominated by an enormous relief map of the Wale along one wall. The front counter showed a checkerboard surface of jasper and jade and supported to the right a rack of glass vials containing the various fractions of black sand, with small disks of the corresponding metals below; and to the left a faultless cube of pyrite a foot and a half on the side.

A man of middle years, grave, deliberate and wearing an urbane gray beard, came to the counter. "Sir, your needs?"

"I represent *Cosmopolis*," said Gersen. "I've been sent out to do a short series on Dar Sai and the Darsh. My budget allows for the hiring of a local aide, hopefully someone from your staff."

"My staff consists mostly of myself. But I'll be glad to assist you, as a hireling or otherwise."

"Excellent. My name, incidentally, is Kirth Gersen."

"I am Evelden Hoe. What sort of thing are you doing?"

"Perhaps a set of biographical sketches. I've been told to look up a certain Nihel Cahouse, possibly resident at Inkin's Shade."

Hoe pulled at his beard. "I know the name. Hmm . . . I can't quite recall the connection. Let's check the index. Come along; this way, if you will."

Hoe took Gersen into a back room. "This is our library, so to speak. Our index is in fair shape; if it's appeared in the

Journal we'll find it." Hoe seated himself before a button-board and screen. "Nihel Cahouse. Here he is. I remember the story now. Shall I give you the gist of it? Or do you care to read the news piece?"

"I'd just as soon hear it from you."

"Cahouse is a Fogle, out of Inkin's Shade, and a sand-miner. At a place called Jamile Wallow he located a rich sift and won over a thousand ounces of sand. He went back to Inkin's Shade and found a hadaul in progress—or maybe he simply went back for the hadaul, which is more likely. He bet like a man inspired and when the day was over he'd won five thousand ounces—a princely fortune. At this time Kotzash Mutual was a going enterprise. The Kotzash comptroller, a certain Ottile Panshaw, happened to be on hand. Cahouse converted his sand into six hundred Kotzash vouchers.

"Two days later the Kotzash warehouse was looted. Nihel Cahouse lost everything and became the topic of a sad news item."

"Where is he now? Still at Inkin's Shade?"

Hoe touched buttons. "Here's a followup."

On the screen appeared a brief paragraph:

> "Nihel Cahouse, the erstwhile millionaire, has returned to the desert. He'll go back to Jamile Wallow and seek another sift."

"That's a fairly recent item," said Hoe. "About three months old."

"How will I find Jamile Wallow?"

"It's west and southerly. I'll show you on the map."

"Good, but first another topic: Lens Larque, who stole Cahouse's sand."

Hoe's face became still and guarded. "That is a name we mention very quietly at Serjeuz."

"Still, he is Dar Sai's most famous citizen, and he'd certainly be the subject of one of my stories."

Hoe showed an uneasy smile. "Understandable. He is an amazing man. Incidentally, he dislikes unfavorable publicity, and he has far connections. In short, he is not a man to be trifled with."

"So I am told. Have you ever met him?"

"Not to my knowledge. I hope never to do so."

"What about photographs? Are any in your files?"

Hoe hesitated, then muttered: "Probably not. Nothing useful."

"'Our conversation is naturally confidential," said Gersen. "The Mining Journal will not be quoted, nor named as a source; still *Cosmopolis* needs a picture. In fact, it would be worth fifty, or even a hundred svu." Gersen placed down a certificate. Hoe touched it with tentative fingertips, then regretfully drew his hand away. "I have no recent photographs. But only a few days ago I happened to notice something in an old picture . . . I don't know whether or not it's what you want."

"Show me the picture."

With a glance over his shoulder, Hoe pushed buttons. He spoke in a suddenly brassy voice: "What I am about to show you is a collection of quaint old clan-pictures, recorded over many years. Where would you like to start?"

"With the Bugold Clan."

"Certainly. This is the oldest photograph on file. It was recorded almost two hundred years ago. Look at those people! Aren't they a picturesque sight? In those days the Bugolds were something of an outlaw clan; perhaps they show us their most ferocious expressions. . . . Here is something more recent, possibly thirty years old. The Bugolds again, and almost demure by comparison. On this side stand the 'bungle boys;' over here are the 'kitchets,' as they are called. During these fleeting transitory months, the Darsh women are at their best. Look at this girl with her straight body and flashing eyes! She is really quite handsome. Now these are the young bucks, no longer 'bungles' but not yet fleshed out into the full reek of Darsh manhood. Look at this one in particular! I don't know his name, but I am told that he later committed a theft and became what the Darsh call rachepol. Who knows what has happened to him? . . . Do you care to look at other photographs?"

"Later, by all means. I'd certainly like copies of these two; they make a most interesting study."

Hoe depressed a toggle and facsimiles fell into a tray. "There you are, sir."

"Thank you." Gersen tucked the photographs into his pocket; Hoe did likewise with the money.

"I'm in something of a rush just now," said Gersen. "Show

me Jamile Wallow, or better, give me the coordinates, and I'll be on my way."

Hoe touched buttons and handed the print-out to Gersen. "Will you be returning soon?"

"In a day or so."

"Our conversation is of course confidential."

"That goes without saying. In both directions."

"Naturally." Hoe escorted Gersen to the door. "Until our next meeting, my good wishes."

At the tourist shop Gersen rented a late-model skimmer and desert-wear: a process which, undertaken through the instrumentality of a languid clerk, took an extended period. Gersen envisioned Bel Ruk fleeting through the stars toward Jamile Wallow, and became agonized with nervous frustration, which he managed to dissemble. At·last he was given freedom of the vehicle. He jumped into the cockpit, pulled up the cowl, arranged the sun-screen over his head, then took the craft aloft. He swept through the veil of water, up at a slant, away from the clustered parasols of Serjeuz, away to the west.

He fixed the auto-pilot to the coordinates of Jamile Wallow, pulled the speed control far back and relaxed into the seat. Below slid the desert in a thousand subtle variations: a gravel-plain, sand dunes breaking against outcrops of black tuff, an area of wind-scoured canyons, a plain of pale sand heaving in mounds and swales around a settlement of three parasols: Fotheringay Shade according to the map. On the northern horizon stood a solitary parasol: Dugg's Shade.

An hour passed and another. Cora kept pace with the skimmer, bearing gradually to the north as the skimmer slanted south.

Below, another lonely shade, uninhabited and derelict: Gannet's Shade, according to the map. No water flowed over the parasol; the vacant dumbles hunched under a tangle of seared brambles and skeleton trees. On the map, a red circle indicated its dead condition. Gersen looked along the course to Jamile Wallow, which was marked by a small red asterisk: still an hour away.

Gersen's mood grew taut. Depending upon Cahouse's whereabouts, Gersen calculated that he had either an hour's advantage over Bel Ruk, or a disadvantage of two or three hours. If Bel Ruk had preceded him to Jamile Wallow his mission became dangerous.

At the horizon appeared a low plateau, and, where a low ravine cut down to the desert floor, Jamile Wallow. Gersen saw a makeshift parasol, fabricated of arafin tubing and metal-coated membrane. The structure had been damaged; the parasol tilted drunkenly to the side, dripping random gouts and spatters of water. The parasol shaded three shacks. One had partially collapsed; two were in little better condition. Fifty yards south, in full Cora-light, beside a corroded clutter of mining equipment stood a tool-shed built of algaic planks.*

Gersen lowered the skimmer and drifted around the shade, perceiving no signs of life. He made a second circle, then landed the skimmer behind the cluster of huts. He lowered the cowl and was instantly struck by a waft of hot desert air. He listened. . . . A forlorn plash of dripping water, a sighing of wind in the trusswork of the parasol; otherwise, silence.

The heat began to prickle at Gersen's skin. He pulled the hood up over his head and activated the air-cooler. Over his eyes he fitted translucent metal hemispheres and slipped his feet into desert shoes. Alighting from the skimmer he surveyed the landscape. To one side the desert spread stark and far; to the other, a hopper, a rickety conveyor and a heap of dun sand indicated the site of Cahouse's workings. Overhead the sagging parasol spilled an irregular trickle of water. Nihel Cahouse was nowhere to be seen, and Gersen felt a hollow sense of defeat.

He went to peer into the stone huts, to discover only trash and a few trifles of dilapidated furniture. The fourth shed, fifty yards south, evidently housed the power module, the well-head and the water pump. Gersen started across the open space to investigate. A moving glint in the sky caught his attention. He froze to a standstill and instantly identified the object as an approaching aircraft: apparently a skimmer similar to his own.

Gersen ran back under the parasol in excitement and exhilaration: if Bel Ruk were aboard the skimmer, he evidently had not yet found Nihel Cahouse. Gersen jumped aboard his

* Certain types of bog algae, when compressed and heated, liberate a gum, which upon cooling binds the matrix into a waterproof mat.

own skimmer, jerked at the controls and slid it behind the pile of tailings. He threw several broken sheets of arafin roofing over the skimmer, achieving a reasonable camouflage. He armed himself with his projac and hand gun and dodged behind the tailings pile. Here he alarmed three scorpion-like creatures, each a foot long, mottled white and tan with orange underbodies. They erected rows of glinting scales, glared from hooded emerald eyes, waved whip-stings, and began a purposeful sidelong encirclement. Gersen destroyed them with quick pulses from his hand gun, creating three small tinkling explosions.

Gersen looked up into the sky. The approaching skimmer was hidden behind the parasol. His place of concealment, he decided, was short of satisfactory; crouching and trying to merge into the hillside he ran out to the plank shed. Ducking around to the back, he hopped high and twisted in mid-air, and barely avoided stepping into a hollow crowded with a dozen basking scorpions. The stings jerked erect; emerald eyes flashed and blinked. Gersen killed them with a single pulse of power, then dodged behind the shed.

Overhead hung the skimmer: a craft enameled green and black, somewhat larger than Gersen's rented vehicle. It slid under the parasol and dropped to the surface. Two men in Darsh desert gear alighted. Their faces, hooded and disguised by metal eye-guards, were unrecognizable. So, too, however, was Ottile Panshaw, whose frame was distinctively slight. The two men stood looking glumly about the shade, much as Gersen had done.

Swinging close their hoods to maximize the effect of the cold air,* they walked to the huts. After a glance within, they stood pointing here and there and discussing their findings. Gersen wondered what could interest them. They clearly had no expectation of finding Nihel Cahouse. What then? The Kotzash shares?

At the third hut the two men became intent. One pointed with an air of satisfaction. He entered, and emerged with a metal box obviously of great weight. He set it down, threw back the lid, touched the contents, gave his head a shake which could indicate almost anything. The other man closed the lid, carried the box to the skimmer. His comrade looked

---

* A typical Darsh mannerism constantly repeated.

toward the planked shed. He gave a peremptory signal; the two crossed the sunlit area to the shed. One flung open the door, looked within, and jumped back with a startled exclamation. Gersen, at the rear, put his eye to a crack. By the light entering through the doorway he glimpsed the interior.

The second man approached. "What's here?"

The man first on the scene waved his hand. "As you see."

"*Asi achih!*"*

"The place stinks. It swarms with the devils."

"They create their own stink. Ah, how putrid! Well, there are no papers here."

"Not so fast. The shrig** wants twelve hundred vouchers, six hundred from here. We had best be diligent."

"Give him the hundred you have already gained and the news that no more are to be found."

"It may come to that. Bah, Cahouse would never keep the paper out here, if he troubled to keep it at all."

"Ha, ha! Cahouse the mad reveler! He probably threw it high into the sansuun*** with a curse. He was noted for his noble curses, so I'm told."

"He'll utter his great curses never again."

"Let's be away from this squalid place. We've got the sand to share; there's profit to the day after all!"

"The shrig wants his vouchers and he speaks with a heavy voice. I am Bel Ruk, but I am not without fear."

"Even fear cannot force the appearance of nonexistent vouchers."

"True. . . . Let's look once more in the huts."

The two turned away and walked toward the shade.

Behind them a voice spoke: "Gentlemen, stop in your tracks. Do not look around; death is close at your backs."

---

* A Darsh expletive of fatalistic acceptance: "So be it!" or "That's the way it goes!" The Darsh do not gracefully or philosophically accept misfortune; they are good grumblers. '*Asi achih*' indicates the final recognition of defeat, or, as in this case, the inexorable force of destiny.

** Larva of a bog animal, notable for its sinuous dancing gait upon a pair of caudal feet. The shrig stands four to five feet high and emits a yellow phosphorescence. At night the shrig dance by the hundreds across the bog to create an eerie and fascinating effect. Here the word is used in a deprecatory sense to typify a dilettantish impractical fellow, out of touch with reality.

*** Sansuum: the evening breeze which follows the sun around the planet.

The two men jerked quivering to a halt.

"Slowly raise your hands. . . . Higher. Walk forward, toward the base of the parasol. Do not look around."

Ten minutes later Gersen had arranged matters to his satisfaction. The two men had declared their names to be Bel Ruk and Cleander. They stood with faces to the trusswork, hoods pulled over their eyes and bound tight by bands of cloth. Similar bands of cloth, but from their own garments, secured their arms to the trusswork. When, to Gersen's critical eye, both men were helpless, he made an inspection of their persons, removing their hand guns, and Bel Ruk's dagger. At their skimmer he investigated the box they had taken from the hut; it contained black sand to the weight of perhaps fifty pounds. On the seat of the skimmer rested Bel Ruk's pouch. Within Gersen discovered Kotzash certificates to the aggregate of 110 shares, which he took into his own possession.

He returned to his two captives, both of whom had been surreptitiously twisting at their bonds. "I hope that you are taking a good-natured view of this situation," said Gersen. "In a sense this is your lucky day. I am taking some Kotzash shares which I found in a pouch yonder. In exchange I have left ten svu. Since the shares are totally worthless, you actually have reason to rejoice. I am also taking Cahouse's black sand."

Neither Cleander nor Bel Ruk had comment to make.

"I prefer that you do not struggle against your bonds," said Gersen. "If you broke loose I might be forced to kill you."

Cleander's shoulders sagged; Bel Ruk stood rigid and unforgiving. Gersen watched them a moment, then returned across bright sand to the toolshed. Bel Ruk and Cleander had left the door ajar; sunlight shone on a rumpled heap of gristle and dry bones among shreds of white cloth. Nihel Cahouse apparently had died while attempting to repair his pump, perhaps by electric shock. Scorpions by the dozens ranged in a circle. They had cut away Cahouse's garments to feast upon his corpse.

As Bel Ruk and Cleander had remarked, the stench within the shed transcended all ordinary degrees of fetor.

Gersen went to the hopper, found a shovel, returned to the shed and half-dragged, half-scraped the remains of Nihel Cahouse out upon the sand. The Scorpions, tinkling in rage, made sorties with emerald eyes glaring. Gersen killed them with the flat of the shovel.

Eventually both corpse and scorpions had been removed. Gersen strolled back under the shade, and examined his captives. Bel Ruk asked in a flat voice: "How long do you intend to keep us here?"

"Not long now. Be patient."

Gersen returned to the shed. The stench had eased somewhat, and the scorpions were gone. Gersen gingerly entered. First he threw the master switch on the power panel, then turned to look at what he had seen through the crack.

Nihel Cahouse had used his Kotzash shares to paper the walls of the tool shed. The adhesive had deteriorated in the heat to a granular crumble; the certificates peeled away without difficulty.

Gersen took the salvaged documents back under the shade and counted them: 600 shares. With the 110 shares taken from Bel Ruk, his holdings now totaled an even 2000.

Gersen returned to his prisoners. Bel Ruk, chafing his bonds against the metal, had almost won free. Without comment Gersen made the bonds once more secure.

"Gentlemen," said Gersen, "I am about to depart. Bel Ruk has demonstrated that the effort of an hour or so will break you loose."

Bel Ruk blurted a question: "Why do you take my Kotzash shares? They are worthless."

"In that case, why do you carry them?"

Bel Ruk said in a rough voice: "At Serjeuz a crazy iskish pays money for trash."

"Kotzash shares are suddenly in demand," said Gersen. "Perhaps that earless rogue Lens Larque is about to bring back the money he stole."*

Bel Ruk and Cleander maintained an uneasy silence.

Gersen watched them a moment, then, carrying the chest of black sand to his skimmer, he departed Jamile Wallow.

At Serjeuz, with Cora half below the horizon, Gersen dropped the skimmer down upon the sand beside his Fantamic Flitterwing. He transferred the coffer of black sand and

---

* Words like "steal," "theft," "pilfer" have a most biting connotation in the Darsh context.

his Kotzash shares aboard, then slid the skimmer through the water veil and back to the rental agency.

Crossing the plaza to the Traveler's Inn, Gersen waited until Tippin's attention was diverted, then slipped past and up to his room. He bathed, changed into fresh garments and returned to the lobby. He allowed himself to be noticed by Tippin, who signaled him to the desk. "Good evening," said Gersen.

"Yes, no doubt. Where have you been all day?"

Gersen fixed Tippin with a long level stare, Tippin's gaze shifted. Gersen asked: "Why are you interested?"

"Inquiries have been made," said Tippin peevishly.

"By whom?"

"By Bel Ruk, if you must know, and not ten minutes ago. He thinks that you robbed him out in the desert."

Gersen asked in a flat voice. "How could I rob Bel Ruk if I was in my room all day?"

"I don't know. Were you in your room?"

"Do you know differently?"

"I don't know one way or another."

"This is the first time you've seen me today?"

"Yes, of course."

"And I just came down from my room?"

"That is true."

"Then tell Bel Ruk that to your knowledge I never left my room all day."

"But are these the facts?" cried Tippin fretfully.

"To the best of your knowledge, they are indeed." Gersen turned away and went out into the garden. He settled himself at a shadowed table, and dined without haste.

From the lobby came Daswell Tippin. He searched the garden, saw Gersen, and approached at an agitated trot. Flinging himself into a chair he said in a tragic voice: "Bel Ruk has threatened my very existence. He claims that I conspired with you; he calls me 'robber.' He says that he will take me out to Sangwy Shade.* Do you know what that means?"

"Nothing good, apparently."

---

* Sangwy Shade: an isolated settlement on the Sheol Barrens, inhabited by ruffians, rachepols and fugitives. At Sangwy Shade, the purchasing agent "Sudo Nonimus" met with Lens Larque, an episode he chronicled in *Reminiscences of a Peripatetic Purchase Agent.*

"It means those cursed Darsh whips, and don't sneer; such affairs occur, to my certain knowledge!"

"When did Bel Ruk make his threat?"

"Not five minutes ago! I spoke with him by telephone; I told him that so far as I knew you had not been gone from Serjeuz. He became furiously angry."

"Where is he now?"

"I don't know. Here at Serjeuz, so I suppose."

"Look here a moment." Gersen produced the list furnished by Jehan Addels. "When you took up those shares for me, who did you buy from? Mark off their names."'

Tippin glanced along the list without any great interest. He marked with a stylus: "This one. This one. This one." With a gesture of revulsion he threw down the stylus. "This is madness! If Bel Ruk sees me, he'll take off my skin."

"Today he had a hundred shares on his person; where did he get them?"

Tippin stared at him aghast. "So you did indeed rob him?"

"I took up property to which he had no right. After all, Lens Larque looted the Kotzash warehouse."

"But that is not Darsh logic," whispered Tippin. "At Sangwy Shade we shall dance together." He turned sideways and searched the plaza. "I'll have to leave Serjeuz; I can live here no longer."

"Where do you want to go?"

"Home. To Svengay. I had a bit of trouble long ago, but surely it's forgotten now."

"Then there is no problem. Take the next ship out."

Tippin held out his hands. "What shall I use for money? I've been keeping a woman; she's bled me dry."

Gersen scribbled a note on a piece of paper, brought out a hundred svu, and handed both to Tippin. "Take this letter to Jehan Addels at New Wexford, on Aloysius. He'll pay you a thousand svu, and find a job for you at New Wexford, if you so choose. I advise you not to tell the woman you are going, although it's none of my affair. If she bled you dry here she'll do it again elsewhere."

With numb fingers Tippin took the money and the note. "Thank you. . . Your advice is sound. . . . Yes, very sound. I'll leave tomorrow; there's an outbound packet."

"Don't tell anyone you're going," said Gersen. "Just go."

"Yes, exactly. Won't there be a great surprise when they find me gone?"

"Back to the Kotzash shares; where did Bel Ruk get his hundred shares?"

"Well—twenty he got from me. He picked up the others along Melby Sift."

"Mark them off this list."

Tippin studied the schedule and made a number of marks. "I can't be sure of these. What's left is out along the Deep Wale, and a few along Scumby Barren. You won't find anyone at home now. They'll all be up to Dinklestown for the Grand Hadauls. And that's where Bel Ruk will be, if he wants more Kotzash."

"What does Panshaw want with Kotzash?"

"When you say 'Panshaw,' you are saying 'Lens Larque.' "

"Then why does Lens Larque want Kotzash?"

Tippin searched the plaza. "I have no idea. Panshaw thinks Lens Larque is crazy. He had trouble with the Methlen and now he wants his own back. Of all men alive he is most to be feared. Imagine an insect in human form. . . . Look now! Here comes Bel Ruk!"

"Sit quiet! He won't harm you. He's only interested in me."

"He'll take me away!"

"Refuse to go. Say nothing; obey none of his orders!"

Tippin made an asthmatic whimpering noise. Gersen looked at him in digust. "Control yourself."

Bel Ruk entered the garden and marched at a stately pace to Gersen's table. With exaggerated delicacy he drew back a chair and seated himself. "I intrude on no private conversation?"

"None whatever," said Tippin in a quavering voice. "I must introduce you: Kirth Gersen, this is Bel Ruk, an important man of Dar Sai." With a wild attempt at facetiousness he added: "You have much in common; you both are interested in finance."

"Oh we have much more in common than that," said Bel Ruk. He shrugged back his hood, to reveal his bony bronze face, massive cheek-bones and cropped ears. Noting Gersen's gaze he said, "Yes, it's true: I am rachepol. My clan dealt harshly with me. Still, I took vengeance and I cannot complain." He signaled the waiter. "Bring me a quart of beer, and these gentlemen to their taste."

"Nothing for me," said Gersen.

Tippin said cautiously: "I'll have a tot of Tivol."

Bel Ruk examined Gersen with a deliberation almost insulting. "Kirth Gersen, eh? And where is your home-world?"

"Alphanor, along the Concourse."

"And you are taking up Kotzash shares?"

"When I can get them cheaply. Are you selling?"

"I have none to sell, after suffering robbery and shame at your hands today."

"Surely you are mistaken," said Gersen. "Tippin has hinted something to his effect, I'm not sure whether or not I have convinced him."

"If he is convinced, he is more of a fool than I take him for. Let us discuss our business one item at a time." He held out his hand. "First, return my shares."

Gersen smilingly shook his head. "Impossible."

Bel Ruk withdrew his arm and turned to Tippin. "You have strained our bonds of friendship."

"Not at all!" Tippin protested. "By no means! Never!"

"We shall discuss the matter again." Bel Ruk lifted his tankard of beer and swallowed half at a gulp. The remainder of the beer he threw casually at Gersen's face. From vast experience, Gersen had recognized the pattern of events. Bending to the side, he avoided most of the beer. In the same motion he lifted the table, thrust it at Bel Ruk's chest and toppled him backwards. Bel Ruk fell sprawling across the garden.

The waiter gingerly approached. "Gentlemen, what is the matter?"

"Bel Ruk has had a bit too much to drink," said Gersen. "Take him away before he injures himself."

The waiter helped Bel Ruk to his feet, then picked up the table and set it into its place.

Gersen stonily watched Bel Ruk, who stood considering his options. Finding no obviously profitable course, Bel Ruk turned and departed the garden.

Tippin said in a sick voice: "He's going for his gun."

"No. He's got other concerns."

"There's no way back for me now," gloomed Tippin. "It's either Sangwy Shade or go and never return."

Gersen gave Tippin a certificate for fifty svu. "Settle my account here, through tomorrow. I may also be leaving."

Tippin asked in dull confusion: "Where are you going?"

"I'm not quite sure." Gersen jumped to his feet. "Excuse me; now I'm in a hurry."

He ran up to his room, picked up items of equipment. Returning below, he left the hotel and ran off across the plaza and under Skansel Shade. In Skansel Plaza he halted to look up at Dindar House. Lights showed from the windows of Panshaws' office; there was no time to be wasted. He climbed up over the entrance, scaled the sloping roof and sidled to the window giving on Litto's office. He brought out his detector, touched the controls to the conductive trail he had sprayed only two nights before. Bel Ruk's guttural voice sounded immediately in the earphone: "—not all so easy. They're scattered here and there around the Wale."

"They'll be at the Dinkelstown for the hadaul, most of them."

"But that's not necessarily to the good," growled Bel Ruk. "These sifters aren't fools. They'll sniff a plot and go for full recovery."

"That may well be. Here's an idea. Cry out a hadaul and post a stake. The challenge can be a hundred Kotzash shares. Let the roblers collect the shares for us."

Bel Ruk grunted. "And then when there's a winner?"

Panshaw's voice dripped sarcasm. "Must I plan out every detail?"

"You were glib enough in regard to Gersen, or whatever his name."

"That is a different tale. Gersen will not be at the hadaul."

Bel Ruk vented a gusty snort. "So you say. And if he is?"

"That again is at your discretion. The Bird would like a word with Gersen."

"Tell the Bird to come out to the hadaul. Let him show his famous techniques."

"Maybe he'll come over without my instructions, to comment upon your work."

Bel Ruk's voice was suddenly dubious. "Do you really think so?"

"No. I do not. He is obsessed with his wonderful scheme."

Bel Ruk's voice came somewhat easier. "So long as he works his tricks he diverts his energies."

"They'll not be diverted if he loses Kotzash."

"I can only do my best. Gersen is not inexperienced. Still, he neglected to kill me when he had the chance."

Panshaw chuckled. "He regards you as no great threat."

Bel Ruck said nothing.

"Well then," said Panshaw, "do your best. From here I cannot guide your feet while you walk. You are reputedly skillful in the robles.* Fight in your own hadaul and come away with the post-pot.**

"The idea already had occurred to me."

"One way or another, collect at least seven hundred shares. Then, whether or not Gersen took Cahouse's shares, we'll be secure. Now I will go back to my couch; Twanish time is a taskmaster. The cursed Methlen start the day at sunrise, just when good thieves like you and me are ending it. Oh why must I pay the price for the Bird's social yearnings? If it were not so funny I could cry for grief."

"All this is beyond my understanding," grumbled Bel Ruk. "It's nothing to do with me."

"Just as well! You'd be less effective than ever."

"Some day, Panshaw, in one hand I will squeeze your neck into a thin stalk."

"Some day, Bel Ruk, I will poison your vile beer. Unless, of course, we lost Kotzash and the Bird gives us both to Panak."

Bel Ruk made a dull sound, and the conversation was over.

Gersen waited a moment on the chance that Bel Ruk might make other communications, but the office remained silent, and Gersen presently went back the way he had come.

---

* Robles: the hadaul field.
** The post-pot: the accumulation of challenge moneys; the victor's prize.

Chapter 10

Gersen flew eastward in the Fantamic Flitterwing. The desert below, in the blaze of Cora-light, showed swaths and smears of color: pink, ochre, a whitish yellow like talc mixed with sulfur; toward the horizon the colors stratified like sediments into pencilings of cinnamon brown, gray-green, plum, with occasional harsh scratches where ledges of black rock broke through the surface.

Gersen crossed a region of low dunes, a line of rose-red buttes. Beyond extended a plateau overgrown with desert flora; silky coral, jutting ears of honeycomb, yellow sandtripe, tinkleweed, purple magmold.

At far intervals parasols spilled water over lonely communities where old Darsh custom persisted in the purest form. Bunter's Shade, Ruph Shade, Itchy Nola's Shade: so read the names on the map. Then, where Terwig Waste began, the shades were seen no more.

Terwig Waste, a smouldering basin of liver-red pumice, once described by an impressionable travel-writer as "the floor of Hell exposed to daylight," ended against a bone-white palisade. Beyond, the ground lay twisted and gashed in a vast badlands of wind-eroded sandstone, and then once again the desert spread away to north, south and east. Finally, the five parasols of Dinkelstown appeared on the horizon.

Gersen approached and circled the town. On the landing area, at the western periphery, rested an assortment of vessels: two small cargo ships, five space-yachts of various quality, scores of desert-skimmers, air-cars and carryalls.

Gersen landed close behind the water-wall. He changed into Darsh robes, armed himself and disembarked. Heat struck his face; he made haste to penetrate the water-veil, and found himself in a cluster of dumbles, from which issued pungent odors and loud voices. By crooked ways he came to a plaza far less grand than Central Plaza at Serjeuz. A single hotel-restaurant offered modest hospitality to the offworld visitor.

Around the edge of the plaza, beer gardens under flip-flap trees served the needs of Darsh holiday-makers. In front of the hotel workmen made final arrangements for the hadaul. Circles had been painted upon the paving. Two small grandstands and several sets of serried benches offered seats of vantage to spectators.

Gersen crossed the plaza to the hotel. In the garden sat a dozen Methlen; Jerdian Chanseth was not among them.

The hotel could offer Garsen no accommodation. "These are the days of the clan meetings!" said the clerk in a curt voice. "Sleep out in the bushes like everyone else!"

Gersen returned to the garden. Not ten feet distant stood Bel Ruk in conversation with a fox-faced young Darsh. Bel Ruk wore iskish clothes, with a white sash around his head to hide his mutilated ears. His back was half-turned; Gersen moved past without attracting his notice. He halted behind a sprawling nephar tree and watched through the black-green foliage.

Bel Ruk spoke with force and urgency. He brought a packet of svu from his inside pocket and slapped it against his hand in cadence with his words. The young man nodded with earnest attention. Finally Bel Ruk gave the young man the packet and made a curt gesture. The young man flicked his fingers in the Darsh signal of assent, and departed across the plaza. Gersen paused five seconds, then followed at a discreet distance.

The young Darsh marched at the striding "plambosh" gait; across the plaza, through a jungle of vegetation, past a dozen dumbles, under the veil of a second parasol, finally into a second plaza, where he joined a group who sat drinking from iron pots. He spoke, and presently money changed hands. Iron pots were tilted and emptied and all departed, leaving only the young Darsh Gersen had followed.

Gersen seated himself on a hummock in the shade of a plantain bush. An insect crawled up his leg; slapping and shaking, Gersen dislodged the creature and took himself to one of the beer gardens. He settled into an inconspicuous seat, was served beer in an iron pot.

An hour passed; then one of the group returned with a sheaf of what Gersen thought to identify as Kotzash shares.

Gersen rose to his feet, walked out into the plaza, made a show of looking around the tables, then advanced upon the table which he had been watching. Without formality he seated himself. "My name is Jaide; Bel Ruk will have mentioned me. There is a change in plan. Enemies are watching him and he wishes to dissemble. You must now work through me. How many shares have you taken up?"

"Sixteen, so far." This was the man whom Gersen had followed.

"Your name?"

"I am Delfin." He indicated the man who had brought in the shares. "This is Bartleman."

"Very good, Bartleman," said Gersen. "Go out again; find more shares for us."

Bartleman showed no haste to obey. "It is not so easy. Folk consider me either a fool or a sharper. I have my dignity to consider."

"What is undignified about paying good money for worthless paper?"

"It's not worthless if someone wants to pay for it. This is the general feeling, especially in connection with Kotzash."

"Well then, offer more money. Delfin, give him money to work with."

Delfin grudgingly counted out twenty svu. Gersen took the shares, folded them and tucked them into his pocket.

"Money is draining away," Delfin grumbled. "Ruk told me to bring him shares and he'd give me more money."

"I'll handle that end of things," said Gersen. He brought out the list which Jehan Addels had prepared. "A certain Lampeter controls eighty-nine shares. Find him at once and buy his shares, as cheaply as possible."

Bartleman said sullenly, "I won't get them for twenty svu, and where is my commission?"

Gersen paid over ten svu of his own money. "Bring me the eighty-nine shares, and you'll make sure of a commission."

Bartleman gave a skeptical shrug and moved away.

Gersen said to Delfin, "Remember, you will be working through me. Under no circumstances approach Bel Ruk! It could bring the wrath of a certain bird down on your head. Do you understand?"

"Perfectly."

"If you so much as see Bel Ruk, give him a wide berth. Do all your business with me."

"This is clear."

Another of Delfin's couriers appeared, with nine shares. Delfin gave him another ten svu of Bel Ruk's money and sent him out again. Gersen added the nine shares to the first sixteen. 2025 in grand total; 386 to go.

One by one the couriers returned, bringing back a total of forty-nine shares. Bartleman returned a second time, somewhat crestfallen. He spoke in a morose voice, "The rumor is out. Everyone has become suspicious; no one wants to sell. Those people who already sold are now angry. They call me a sharper; they want their shares back."

"Not possible," said Gersen. "What of Lampeter?"

"There he sits in Valt's Arbor drinking beer." Bartleman pointed across the plaza. "That old man with the crooked nose. He says he'll sell for full value, no less."

"Full value? We don't pay that kind of money for worthless paper."

"Explain that to Lampeter."

"I'll do exactly that." Gersen once more considered his list. "Do you know Feodor Diamant?"

"He is well known."

"He controls twenty shares. Find him, buy his shares if possible. If not, bring him here."

"As you say." Bartleman once more moved away.

Gersen stepped across the plaza to Valt's Arbor and approached the old man with the crooked nose. "You are Lampeter?"

"I am that man. Who are you, if not an iskish?"

"I am iskish, certainly. As an idle pastime I collect worthless securities: really no more than a whim. Do you have any use for your Kotzash shares?"

"None whatever."

"In that case, perhaps you will give them to me. If you prefer I can make a token payment: say, ten svu for the batch."

Lampeter pulled at his nose and turned Gersen a broad gap-toothed grin. "It is my experience that when someone wants to buy, the merchandise has value. I will sell at what they cost me, no less."

Gersen exhibited astonishment. "That is totally unreasonable."

"We shall see. If I collect, I am vindicated. If not, I am no worse off than before."

"Do you carry these shares on your person?"

"Naturally not; I considered them worthless until now."

"Where are they?"

"In my dumble, just yonder."

"Let us go for them. If you guarantee to say nothing of the transaction, I'll pay you eighty-nine svu."

"Eighty-nine svu? That offer is almost insulting! You are trying to cheat me of two thousand svu!"

"Lampeter, observe me closely. What do you see?"

Lampeter, who had already taken several pots of beer, inspected Gersen with an unsteady vision. "I see a green-eyed iskish, who is either a sharper or else crazy."

"I prefer that you think of me as crazy. Now ask yourself: how many times in the few scant years left to you will a crazy iskish offer you money for worthless trash?"

"Never again, I have no doubt. That is why I must exploit this particular occasion."

"On this particlar occasion, two svu a share is the limit."

"Full value or nothing!"

Gersen made a signal of defeat. "I'll pay quarter value, and that is my best offer. I am running low on cash."

Lampeter drank beer, then put down the iron pot and rose to his feet. "Come along with me. I am being defrauded, but I can waste no more time." He lurched off along a path which led through the jungle and halted beside the dark entrance into a dumble. "One moment." He entered, to emerge with a greasy envelope. "Here are the shares. Where is the money?"

Gersen took the envelope, withdrew the certificates and counted: eighty-nine shares. "Good enough; come with me. I don't carry so much money on my person."

He led the way to the water well, along the boundary lane, then out through the water to his Fantamic Flitterwing. He unlocked the port, motioned Lampeter up the ladder. Lampeter looked at him in suspicion: "Where are you taking me?"

"Nowhere. I can't pay you out here in the hot sun."

"Well, be swift. My beer is going flat."

Gersen brought out the box of black sand he had taken from Bel Ruk at Jamile Wallow. "Eighty-nine shares at a quarter value is 223 ounces."

In a grumbling voice Lampeter declared a preference for cash, to which Gersen paid no heed. He weighed out 223 ounces of black sand, which he poured into a canister and gave to Lampeter. "Consider yourself a lucky man."

"I can't avoid curiosity. Why do you pay good black sand for worthless trash that I was about to throw away?"

Gersen calculated. "I need at least 248 more shares. Find them for me and I'll explain why I want them."

"You'll pay in black sand?"

"Not at quarter value. I don't have so much sand."

"I doubt if so many shares can be had at Dinkelstown. Still, let's go back to Valt's Arbor. Bring the box. We'll see what can be done. My friend Jeus owns ten or twenty shares. Maybe he'll agree to sell."

"Bring your friend Jeus to the beer garden across the plaza, where I now must return." Gersen took leave of Lampeter, and rejoined Delfin. His couriers, between them, had taken up only thirty-one additional shares which Gersen took in hand. Bartleman, however, had with him a short fat man with round black eyes and a parrot-beak nose. "This is Fat Odo," said Bartleman. "He carries fifteen shares of Kotzash."

"Well, sir, what is your price?" asked Gersen. "I have about all I need for my purposes. Still I'll listen to your offer."

"The price is printed on the certificates," said Odo.

"So is the signature of Ottile Panshaw. Both are a waste of ink."

"I won't sell; why should I be hoodwinked by an iskish? I am no worse off than an hour ago; good-bye."

"Just a moment. Fifteen shares? I'll pay a quarter value, no more."

"Impossible."

"Good-bye; these are my terms."

"Oh well; pay half value. Today I will be generous."

Gersen finally settled for forty ounces of black sand, just as Lampeter brought up his friend Jeus, as old, gaunt and drunk as Lampeter himself. Lampeter pointed out Gersen with a grand flourish: "There he sits, the crazy iskish who pays black sand for Kotzash."

"Here are my shares," cried out Jeus. "There are eighteen only, but pay me a hundred ounces, in all generosity!"

"The rate is somewhat less," said Gersen. "Twenty ounces for the lot."

The bargaining attracted attention; soon Gersen was surrounded with persons who either held a share or two and wanted full redemption, or persons, now angry, who had already sold at lesser prices. Gersen scraped the box clean of black sand, but acquired only another forty-three shares. His total holdings now were 2270 shares, with another 141 shares needed. The Darsh now stood around him eagerly flourishing their shares, but Gersen could only shake his head. "I have no more sand and no more money, until I cash a bank draught."

The asking prices began to descend. Gersen, now so near to his goal, became correspondingly anxious. He turned to Delfin. "Give me what money you have left."

"It is only five svu," said Delfin. "In view of the large sums being thrown about, this is scanty payment for the day's work."

"Bartleman has thirty svu for which he has not accounted."

"Nor will he ever. Go back to Bel Ruk for more money."

"I hardly dare. Already I have spent too much. . . . But that gives me an idea. Write out this note: 'Prices are very high. Return another two hundred svu by the bearer. . . . Delfin.' "

Delfin somewhat dubiously wrote the note. The circumstances were puzzling, but who was he to question the mad iskish?

"Now," said Gersen, "send it off to Bel Ruk, who will surely send back the money."

"Hardous! Here a moment!" Delfin gave Hardous the note. "Go to the hotel garden; there you will find a rachepol wearing a white head sash with an emerald clasp. Give him this note. He will pay over money which you are to bring here. Hurry!"

Gersen, now on tenterhooks, ran around the circle of those who had been offering shares. He took as many of them as he could reach. "Give me yours, and yours, and yours. Collect from Delfin or meet me tonight at the hotel. Delfin knows me well; he will vouch for me. Tomorrow you will be paid, or perhaps even tonight if Bel Ruk provides the money."

Some of the shareholders numbly surrendered their shares; others jerked back. Gersen could waste no more time. He beckoned to Delfin. "Come along to the plaza; let us make sure that Bel Ruk is on hand to pay the money."

They halted under the foliage, looked across to the hotel garden, into which Hardous was just now entering. Bel Ruk sat in obvious impatience at a central table. Hardous tendered him the note; Bel Ruk snatched it open and read. For a moment he sat silent, then heaved himself to his feet. He spoke to Hardous; the two left the garden and set off across the plaza.

Gersn spoke soberly to Delfin: "I suspect that events are not going well for Bel Ruk. He seems out of sorts. Avoid him. If he sees you he will demand an accounting and what could you tell him? Nothing. Keep your distance, and we'll all be the easier for it."

Delfin said in a concerned voice: "There is a great deal here which I don't understand."

"No doubt. But do as I say, and as soon as I cash a bank draught you will profit."

Delfin again became moderately sanguine. "That is a gratifying prospect, at least."

"Good. Then I am assured of your cooperation?"

"At every point of the circle."

The metaphor, so Gersen recognized, was abstracted from the language of hadaul and was not altogether reassuring. "I need—let me count—another 120 shares, at least. Tonight I want you to go everywhere. The news will be out; shares will certainly be offered to you: perhaps the entire 120."

"Tonight? Not possible. Mirassou floats high; kitchets run the desert and I run close behind."

"And who runs behind you?" asked Gersen.

"Ha ha! I've been chased by some fast ones! Tonight is a night to beware! Are you going out? Let me advise you. The kitchets romp among the Chailles, but every shadow conceals a khoontz. The less agile man, who is usually not quite so discriminating, goes out on Differy Downs, but he often comes home stiff and surly, because the kitchets have the upper hand and make their own choices."

"I'll keep your advice in mind," said Gersen. "What of tomorrow?"

"Tomorrow it's hadaul and that will occupy the day. Kotzash must wait."

"Still, don't stand aside if Kotzash shares are offered. Take them up on my account, and keep well clear of Bel Ruk; at the moment he may well be annoyed with all of us."

Delfin again became subdued. "Behind your words I divine a larger meaning. I will certainly avoid Bel Ruk. And now I wish you good evening and a happy night on the desert."

Gersen went out to his Fantamic Flitterwing where he counted his shares and locked them into a cabinet. He changed from the Darsh robes into loose gray trousers and a blouse striped in dark green and black. He made sure of his weapons and sauntered back under the parasol. The time was dusk; the water-flow was quiet and Dinkelstown lay open to the desert.

Gersen approached the hotel garden, and halted in the shadows to take stock of those who sat at the tables: a dozen tourists, as many Darsh of evident substance, a group of young Methlen, with two older women of refinement and dignity.

From the hotel came Jerdian Chanseth wearing a soft white gown. She passed close to where Gersen stood. He called out in a quiet voice: "Jerdian! Jerdian Chanseth!"

Jerdian halted, looked wonderingly to where Gersen stood half-lounging against a tree. She paused, turned a quick glance toward the Methlen group, then approached. "What are you doing here?"

"I'm looking at you, and grateful for the opportunity."

Jerdian made a mocking sound between her teeth. "Sss-ssss! You are gallant in your phrases." She looked him up and down. "You are more relaxed, more easy than the grim banker-swindler-space wanderer of Serjeuz. You seem almost a young man."

"That can't be. I'm at least six years older than Aldo. Still, at this moment, I don't feel at all grim."

"Why, at this moment?"

"Must I explain? I am standing here with you and I find you bewitching."

"More gallantry!" Jerdian, despite a cool little laugh,

seemed not displeased. "Words are cheap. You already have a spouse and a large family."

"Nothing of that sort whatever. I have no one but myself."

"How did you become a banker?"

"I bought the bank for a special purpose."

"But a bank costs money! Are you a wealthy criminal?"

"I'm certainly not a criminal. At least, not altogether."

"Then what are you, in all truth and candor?"

"A space-wanderer is really the best description."

"Kirth Gersen, you take pleasure mystifying me, and I detest secrets!" Then Jerdian added, in a voice dictated by her Methlen training: "Still, your secrets are no concern of mine."

"Quite right." Gersen looked away across the plaza, out upon the dusky desert. "In fact, I should not so much as talk to you. I succeed only in tantalizing myself."

Jerdian stared at him a minute, then uttered a sudden laugh. "What marvelous dramas you enact! The picaresque adventurer, the banker who outswindles my father, the patrician in languid garments, and now the love-lorn boy, wistful and noble, renouncing his love."

Gersen's own amusement was somewhat more constrained. "I don't recognize myself in any of these roles." A reckless mood came over him, almost an intoxication. "Come over here, where we'll be secluded." He took her arm and led her to a table at the far dark side of the garden. She walked stiffly, half-resisting, and seated herself in a posture tentative and prim. She looked at Gersen coldly, now all disdainful Methlen. "I can only stay an instant; we are making an excursion out on the desert, and I must help with the arrangements."

"The desert is said to be beautiful by night. Especially by moonlight. Are you walking?"

"Indeed not. We have hired a charabanc. Now I must go. My interest in your affairs is really most casual."

"Our feelings complement each other, since I didn't want to tell you anything."

Jerdian made no move to rise. "And why not?"

"You might tell someone else and cause me no end of trouble.

Jerdian scowled. "So you think I prattle of everything I know to my friends."

"Not necessarily. But as you yourself point out, our interest is casual; you might easily make an idle comment which eventually would reach the wrong ears. I'll take you to your friends." He rose to his feet.

Jerdian perversely refused to move. "Be so good as to sit down. In effect you are asking me to leave, which is far from flattering. Where is your vaunted gallantry now?"

Gersen slowly resumed his seat. "I vaunted no gallantry. I just spoke impulsively."

"You show very little concern for my vanity," said Jerdian crossly.

"Your vanity is quite safe in my hands," said Gersen. "May I express myself frankly?"

Jerdian pondered a moment. "Well—there is no one here to stop you."

Gersen leaned forward, took her two hands in his. "The truth is this: I have a spaceship outside; I would like nothing better than to take you away with me and make love to you across all the constellations of the universe. But I can't indulge myself even in the speculation."

"Indeed? And—again from idle curiosity—why not?"

"Because I have work to do which is urgent and dangerous."

Jerdian asked mischievously: "Would you give up your work if I agreed to come with you?"

"Don't even suggest such things; my heart stops beating when I hear you."

"The gallantry is now back in full force."

Gersen bent forward across the table; Jerdian made no move to draw back. With their faces only inches apart, Gersen halted, then drew abruptly back. He felt Jerdian's hands twitch in his.

After a moment Gersen said, "If you recall, at Serjeuz we spoke of Lens Larque."

Jerdian regarded him with pupils dilated. "He is the most evil man alive!"

"You mentioned an unpleasant episode. What happened?"

"It was nothing important, simply an incident. We live in a district known as Llalarkno. One day a Darsh wanted to buy the house next to ours. My father is not partial to the Darsh; he hates the smell of their food; he can't tolerate their music. He cried out in a passion: 'Go away; leave this land! You may not buy the house. Do you think I want to look up ev-

ery day to find your great Darsh face hanging over my wall?
Be off with you!'

"The Darsh walked away. Later we learned that it was
Lens Larque himself."

"What did he look like?"

"I hardly noticed. I have the impression of a large man,
with long arms. He had a big smooth head with a black
mustache. His skin was brownish pink, pale Darsh color."

"You haven't seen him since?"

"Not to my knowledge."

"He never forgets a harm—so goes the Lens Larque
legend—and he is famous for clever tricks."

"He can trick as he pleases. We maintain a careful security, because we are so close to Beyond. But why are you
interested in Lens Larque?"

"I hope to destroy him. First I must find him. So I buy
Kotzash to attract his attention."

Jerdian stared at Gersen in awe and wonder. She started to
speak but a tall shape loomed over them: Aldo, his head
tilted somewhat back, mouth set in an austere droop. He
bowed jerkily to Jerdian: "If you please, your aunt, the Excellent Mayness, is anxious that you should join her."

"Very well, I'll come at once."

Gersen spoke to Aldo. "You are planning an excursion out
on the desert."

"That is correct."

"Where are you planning to go?"

"We are visiting the Chailles." Aldo's tone was now icy.
"Come, if you will, Jerdian."

Gersen said: "The Darsh, both male and female, will be
out in force."

"That is no concern to us, so long as they stay out of our
sight."

"They may even cause you annoyance."

"We have hired a charabanc; the driver declares that there
will be no slightest inconvenience. In any event, we are Methlen; the Darsh will keep their distance." He went to stand by
Jerdian. Slowly she rose to her feet and walked away like a
somnambulist.

Gersen sat brooding for a time, then went out to his
space-boat. He paused beside the boarding ladder; he stood
looking to the east across the desert, where the rising moon

already illuminated the sky. Small groups of people slipped out from under the shade, riding vehicles, or going afoot, women and girls apart from the youths and men. On a dilapidated air-buggy came Delfin with three of his comrades, wearing light robes and gay head-sashes. They passed close beside Gersen, who hailed them. Delfin brought the air-buggy to a bouncing halt. Gersen moved forward. "How goes the evening?"

"So far very well."

"Have you located any more shares?"

"No. As you suggested, Bel Ruk is unhappy with today's events. He intends to whip both you and me."

"First he must catch us," said Gersen. "Then he must raise his whip."

"True. In any event, you will find no more Kotzash in Dinkelstown. Bel Ruk has ordained a great hadaul, to a prize of a thousand svu. The roblers* must challenge with either a hundred svu or twenty shares of Kotzash. Needless to say all remaining Kotzash will go to finance the challenges."

"A pity," said Gersen.

"Still you did your best and cleverly; you are a trickish man. But why do you keep us talking? The kitchets are drinking moonlight!"

One of his comrades added: "Along with every old swag-bottom of the Wale, as well."

"Look yonder!" cried Delfin in a voice of mirthful amazement. "There go the constipated Methlen out to enjoy the moonlight! Notice the man who drives the charabanc? That is Nobius, a trickster as sly as yourself!"

Gersen acknowledged the compliment. "Do you expect that Nobius will trick the Methlen?"

Delfin made a jocular sign. "There is a tender kitchet named Farrero; she is guarded by three enormous khoontzes. Nobius vows that tonight he will take Farrero. How he will do this while driving the Methlen charabanc remains to be seen! We must be off! There rises the Mirassou. Kitchets are running the sand and dreaming delicious dreams! Hoy! Off we go! Cambousse* give us power!"

---

* Roblers: participants at a hadaul. The "robles" are the concentric rings of a hadaul field, painted yellow, green and blue.
* The satyr Cambousse, Pittaugh the Sand-sprite and Leino the Grandmother are elementals of the Darsh mythology.

The buggy trundled off on soft wheels. Gersen turned to look after the charabanc, already a dark blur far across the sand.

Uneasy and fretful, annoyed by his own conflicting urges, Gersen watched the charabanc disappear. Methlen affairs were none of his concern—except the comfort and dignity of a certain Jerdian Chanseth, toward whom he felt a whole range of emotions, protective and otherwise.

Well, there was no help for it. With a muttered curse, Gersen climbed into the vessel, opened a side-port, swung out davits and grounded the utility boat. He pulled a helmet over his head and clamped a night-seeing panoptic to the visor. Into the side-rack he stowed a pair of weapons, then, stepping aboard, he took the boat into the sky.

Mirassou floated free of the horizon: a great silver-white disk, subtle and serene, which nevertheless projected an ardent force. The Wale became a place where events otherwise unthinkable became not only conceivable but reasonable. Gersen, as always, aware of at least two levels of consciousness within his mind, was amused to find himself no less susceptible to Mirassou than Delfin. . . . He slanted his boat somewhat to the south of the charabanc and drew abreast at an altitude of a thousand feet. Pulling the panoptic down over his eyes, he switched on the nocturnal phase, turned up the magnification; the charabanc with its passengers seemed only yards away. With splendid garments and moonlight-pale faces the Methlen seemed a company unreal: a troupe of pierrots on a frivolous escapade. Gersen watched in fascination, half-sardonic, half-envious. In all, ten Methlen rode the charabanc. Three young men sat along the stern seat. Four girls, a pair of older women and Aldo occupied the side seats. Jerdian, frail and wan-seeming, sat far forward, turned somewhat away from the others. Influenced, perhaps by Mirassou, Gersen felt a swelling of exhilaration for his own escapade on this moonlit night.

High in the front, on the coachman's bench, Nobius rode in a comfortable slouch, occasionally glancing back at his passengers in easy condescension. The older ladies, whenever they chanced to notice him, became annoyed by what they conceived to be insolence and made haughty gestures, signaling Nobius to mind his driving; commands which Nobius totally ignored, to augment the antic mood of the expedition.

Over the silken sands moved the charabanc. Ahead and somewhat to the side stood the Chailles: a decayed volcanic crag rising from a shoal of ledges and outcrops. One of the older ladies gave Nobius new instructions, signaling him to veer away from the Chailles. Nobius gave obsequious acquiescence, twitching the controls to change course, but as soon as the lady's attention was diverted, he swung the charabanc back toward the rocks. Scanning the Chailles Gersen detected the flicker of white Darsh robes; other folk had gone out to enjoy Mirassou.

The Methlen ladies once again noticed the proximity of the Chailles, instantly and with vehemence they ordered Nobius to bear away, and again Nobius politely complied with the order, only after a moment cunningly veering the craft back to its original direction. His destination seemed to be a rocky hummock perhaps twenty feet high, standing free a few yards from the principal ledges. On top of the hummock stood a kitchet, quiet and pensive, looking south across the sands.

Nobius suddenly curved the charabanc smartly about, accelerated and drove it into the sandy avenue between the hummock and the main ledges of the Chailles. The ladies expostulated sharply; Nobius blandly paid them no heed, then suddenly pretended to hear. Bringing the charabanc to a halt just under the hummock, he turned in his seat as if the better to hear instructions.

The ladies spoke briskly and made agitated gesticulations, which Nobius attentively acknowledged. He turned in his seat, but now something had gone wrong with the machinery. The charabanc lurched forward a few yards, then halted even while Nobius diligently worked switches and levers. At the stern of the charabanc the three young men rose questioningly up in their seats. Nobius desisted from his efforts and sat warily watching to the side.

Out from the shadows lurched three heavy figures in black gowns. They jumped forward; each seized one of the young Methlen men on the rear seat about his middle and carried him flailing and squirming off into the darkness.

Nobius crouched and became tense. From the shadows under the hummock came a fourth figure, even more massive than the others. She jumped aboard the charabanc, seized Aldo, and despite his shouts, carried him away.

Instantly Nobius bounded from the charabanc and up to

the top of the hummock. He seized the kitchet, led her down the far side and off into the dunes.

Stunned by events, the Methlen ladies rose dumbfounded in their seats. In the shadows and on the ledges was further motion; the swirl of white robes, then a sudden rush to the charabanc and aboard. The first to arrive seized the girls, and the next, less enthusiastically, possessed themselves of the chaperones, and all retreated to their preferred places.

The man who had seized Jerdian carried her out into the desert, ignoring both her outcries and her blows. A hundred yards out among the dunes he halted and lowered her to the sand. A flying platform landed beside them. Gersen stepped off. Jerdian made a sound of incredulous joy and relief.

The Darsh assumed an attitude of menace. "Be off with you; I am about to entertain this kitchet."

Speaking no words, Gersen pointed a hand gun at the man's feet and burnt the sand into a molten puddle. The Darsh jumped back in fear and fury. Gersen lifted Jerdian to her feet and put her aboard the boat; an instant later they were in the air, leaving the disconsolate Darsh staring after them.

At no great altitude the boat drifted southward over the dunes, Jerdian from time to time looking askance at Gersen. Presently she said in a husky voice: "I'm grateful to you. . . . I don't know what else to say. . . . How did you happen to be so promptly to hand?"

"I saw you on the charabanc. The driver is notorious; I came out to protect you from his tricks—even though you had not asked me to watch over you."

"I'm glad that you did." Jerdian drew a deep sigh. She looked back toward the black rocks, and made an odd sound, something between a sob and a laugh. "My aunt Mayness and my aunt Eustacia are back there. Can't we help them somehow?" Then by implication she answered her own question: "I suppose nothing too dreadful will happen."

"Whatever may happen, it's already in progress." Gersen removed his helmet and placed it in a locker. He allowed the boat to drift low, only thirty feet above the dunes. Jerdian leaned back in the seat and looked off across the sand. She showed neither anxiety nor any urgent desperation to be elsewhere. In a soft thoughtful voice she said: "The desert is a very strange place by moonlight. It gives off an enchantment like a dream-place. . . . No surprise that it works so much mischief."

"I'm very conscious of this," said Gersen. He put his arm around her shoulders and drew her close. She looked up and went limp against him; he kissed her, again and again.

The boat drifted low and grounded upon a sand dune. The two sat quietly, looking out over the moonlit sand. Presently Jerdian said, "I am unutterably surprised to find myself here with you. . . . And yet, perhaps not really surprised. . . . I can't help thinking of everyone's outrage. What will they say tomorrow? Will I be the only one returning with my virtue intact?"

Gersen kissed her again. "Not necessarily."

Ten seconds passed. Then jerdian said in a husky whisper: "But I do have the option?"

"Yes indeed," said Gersen. "You have the option.'"

Jerdian stepped from the boat and walked a few feet out along the dune. Gersen came to stand beside her. Presently she turned to face him; again they embraced. Gersen spread the white Darsh cloak down upon the sand, and on the ancient dunes of the Wale, in the light of Mirassou, they became lovers.

The moon reached the zenith, and sank beyond. The night was becoming old; slowly the magic was dying. Gersen took Jerdian back to Dinkelstown, then returned to the charabanc. The four young men, sullen and disheveled, stood to the side. One of the chaperones and one of the girls sat silently in the charabanc. As Gersen approached, the other chaperone appeared through a cleft in the rocks. Wordlessly she climbed aboard the charabanc.

Gersen came forward; they looked at him with suspicious stares. "I happened past and was able to help Jerdian Chanseth," said Gersen. "She is back at the hotel, and you need not worry about her."

One of the older women, Aunt Mayness, said grimly: "We are sufficiently worried about ourselves; we all have had beastly experiences."

Aunt Eustacia said in a voice somewhat more moderate: "I suppose that we must be philosophical. We have suffered outrage, but no irreparable damage; let us be grateful at least to this extent."

"That is hardly my present emotion," snapped Aunt Mayness. "I was set upon time after time by a gross beast smelling of beer and that intolerable food."

"The man who attacked me also smelled poorly. Otherwise he was almost courteous, if the word is at all appropriate."

"Eustacia, you are far too bland!"

"I am, most of all, tired. If Jerdian is back at Dinkelstown that leaves only Millicent and Helen to be accounted for. Here they come now, together. Let us leave this awful place."

"And what of our reputations?" cried Aunt Mayness in a brassy voice. "We'll be the laughing-stock of all Llalarkno!"

"Not if we bind ourselves to secrecy."

"How can we have these bestial Darsh punished if we hold our tongues?"

Gersen interposed a remark. "I doubt if you will be able to punish the Darsh. They assume that if you go out on the desert by night, your purpose is procreation. The guilty party is your driver; he played you a merry trick."

Aunt Eustacia said, "This is the sad truth, so we might as well accept it. Let us just pretend nothing happened."

"This man knows! The Darsh know!"

"I'll say nothing," said Gersen. "The Darsh may make a few jokes among themselves, but probably that's as far as it will go. One of you men show some spirit! Drive the charabanc back to Dinkelstown!"

Aldo grumbled: "If you'd been through what I have, you'd lack spirit too. I'll not go into details."

"None of us is happy with the night's events," snapped Aunt Mayness. "Now get up into the driver's seat and be brisk about it! I am more than anxious for a bath."

Chapter 11

From *Games of the Galaxy,* by Everett Wright: the chapter entitled *"Hadaul."*

Hadaul like all good games is characterized by complexity and the multiple levels upon which the game is played.

The basic apparatus is simple: a field suitably delineated and a certain number of players. The field is most often painted upon the pavement of a plaza; occasionally it will be constructed of carpet. There are many variations, but here is a typical arrangement. A pedestal stands at the center of a maroon disk. The pedestal can be of any configuration, and customarily supports the prize money. The diameter of the disk ranges from four to eight feet. Three concentric rings, each ten feet in width, surround the disk. These are known as "robles" and are painted (from in to out) yellow, green and blue. The area beyond the blue ring is known as "limbo."

Any number of contestants, or "roblers," may participate, but usually the game starts with a maximum of twelve and a minimum of four. Any more creates excessive congestion; any less reduces the scope of that trickery which is an essential element.

The rules are simple. The roblers take up positions around the yellow roble. All now are "yellow roblers." As the game starts they attempt to eject the other yellow roblers into the green roble. Once thrust or thrown into the green, a robler becomes "green" and may not return to yellow. He will now attempt to eject other green roblers into the blue. A yellow robler may venture into the green and return into yellow as a sanctuary; similarly a green robler may enter blue and return to the green, unless he is ejected from blue by a blue robler.

A game will sometimes end with one yellow robler, one green robler and one blue robler. Yellow may be disinclined to attack green or blue; green disinclined to attack blue. At this stage no further play is possible. The game halts and the three roblers share the prize in a 3-2-1 ratio. Yellow receiving the "3" or half share. Green, or blue, may wager new sums equal to the yellow prize, and by this means once again become yellow, a process which may continue until a single robler remains to claim the entire prize. Rules in this regard vary from hadaul to hadaul. At times a challenger may now propose a sum equal to the prize; the previous winner may or may not decline the challenge, according to local rules. Often the challenger may propose a sum double the prize, which challenge must be accepted, unless the winner has suffered broken bones, or other serious disability. These challenge matches are often fought with knives, staves, or, on occasion, whips. Not infrequently a friendly hadaul ends with a corpse being carried off on a litter. Referees monitor the play assisted by electronic devices which signal crossings of the roble boundaries.

Conspiracy is an integral part of the game. Before the game starts the various roblers form alliances of offense or defense, which may or may not be honored. Tricks, crafty betrayal, duplicity are considered natural adjuncts to the game; it is surprising, therefore, to note how often the tricked robler becomes indignant, even though he himself might have been intending the same treachery.

Hadaul is a game of constant flux, constant surprise; no one game is ever like another. Sometimes the contests are jovial and good-natured, with everyone enjoying the tricks; sometimes tempers are ignited by some flagrant act of falsity, and blood is wont to flow. The spectators wager among themselves, or, at major hadauls, against mutualization agencies. Each major shade stages several hadauls each year, on the occasion of their festivals, and these hadauls are considered among the prime tourist spectacles of Dar Sai.

Gersen slept in his space vessel and awoke to find Cora halfway up the sky. He lay still a few moments. Already the events of last night had lost reality. What of Jerdian? No longer intoxicated by the moonlight nor emotionally vulnerable by reason of her rescue: how would she feel?

Gersen bathed and dressed, today in ordinary spaceman's gear. He armed himself with care: not knowing what the day might bring.

He ran through the heat, under the water-veil, and went to the hotel garden. The Methlen were already at their table. Jerdian turned him a quick half-smile, and gave her fingers a secret flutter. Gersen was reassured: she felt no regrets. The other Methlen paid him no notice.

As Gersen made his breakfast, he watched the Methlen. The young men were surly and taciturn. The women seemed more serene, but spoke in measured voices. Only Jerdian showed good spirits, for which she received reproachful glances.

At last the group finished their meal. Jerdian crossed to Gersen's table. He jumped to his feet. "Sit down with me."

"I don't dare. Everyone is a bit edgy, and Aunt Mayness has her suspicions. I'm not worried, since with her they are automatic."

"When can I see you? Tonight?"

Jerdian shook her head. "We're staying for the hadaul, because that's why we came; then we'll fly back to Serjeuz and tomorrow over to Llalarkno."

"Then I'll visit you at Llalarkno."

Jerdian smiled wistfully and gave her head a shake. "Everything is so different in Llalarkno."

"Will you feel differently?"

"I don't know. It would be better if I did. Right now I'm

in love with you; I've thought of you all night and all this morning."

After a moment Gersen said: "I notice that you say 'I'm in love with you,' rather than 'I love you.'"

Jerdian laughed. "You are very perceptive. There is a distinction. I love something; I'm sure of that. Perhaps it's you; perhaps—who knows what?" She searched his face. "Are you offended?"

"It's not exactly what I'd like to hear. Still—I often wonder about myself. Am I a man? Or a motivated mechanism? Or an absurd distorted idea?"

Jerdian laughed again. "There's no question in my mind; you are quite definitely a man."

"Jerdian!" called Aunt Mayness in a cold voice. "Come along; we are going to the grandstand."

Jerdian gave Gersen a wan smile and walked away. Gersen watched her go, an ache at the base of his throat. Foolishness, he told himself; sophomoric nonsense! He was languishing like a schoolboy! He could allow himself no emotional attachments until the work which obsessed his life was done! . . . He followed the Methlen to the center of the plaza, where now a crowd milled around the robles.

The hadaul was about to start: the most characteristic of all Darsh spectacles, an activity somewhere between a game and a gang fight, given savor by tricks, broken faith and opportunism: in short, a microcosm of Darsh society.

To make convenient provision for spectators was a concept foreign to Darsh philosophy. Those who cared to watch were forced either to use the makeshift grandstands, to perch upon the surrounding structures, or to crowd close to the fence which surrounded the robles.

On a post hung a set of boards listing participants in the various hadauls. Gersen could not read the looping Darsh script. He approached the registration booth and attracted the clerk's attention. "Which is Bel Ruk's hadaul?"

"That would be the third round." The official tapped one of the placards. "The challenge is a hundred svu, or twenty-five Kotzash shares."

"How many challenges have been made?"

"So far nine."

"How much Kotzash?"

"A hundred shares."

Not enough, thought Gersen. He needed at least 120 shares. He looked in distaste toward the robles and the grandstands crowded with white-robed Darsh. Fastidiously aloof, in a section reserved for tourists, sat the Methlen. Gersen gave a fatalistic shrug. The game was strange to him; the Darsh would be quick to take advantage of an iskish. Still, a hundred shares would bring him close to control of the company. He paid over the last of his money: a single hundred svu certificate. "Here is my challenge; for Bel Ruk's hadaul."

The clerk drew back incredulously. "You intend to compete in the robles? Sir, you are iskish and I only tell you for good nature, but you are risking broken bones; there are strong and notorious trickers going into Bel Ruk's hadaul."

"It will be an interesting experience. Does Bel Ruk himself take part?"

"He has guaranteed a thousand svu prize, but he will not fight. If the challenges exceed a thousand svu he will profit."

"But the Kotzash shares are part of the prize?"

"Exactly so; the challenges, including the shares, go on the prize board."

"Then put my name on the placard."

"As you wish. The bone-setters sit under yonder red flag."

Gersen found a vantage where he could look over the field. The roblers for the first turn had now appeared: twelve young men wearing correct hadaul attire: short trousers of white canvas, a singlet of brown, gray or pale red, cloth slippers, a head-cloth, tied so as to gather up dangling earlobes. The roblers walked around the periphery of the blue, pausing to talk together, sometimes confidentially, mouth to ear; sometimes exchanging no more than a jocular word. Occasionally small groups formed to listen while tactical theories were expounded. Another robler might join such a group to hear plots not to his liking, whereupon angry words would be exchanged, and on one occasion a small scuffle.

From a nearby dumble came the referees: four old men wearing embroidered red and black vests. Each carried a six-foot wand terminating in a puff-ejector. The chief referee additionally bore a glass bowl containing the prize—in this case, a sheaf of svu certificates. He went to the central disk and placed the prize upon the pedestal.

The referees took up their positions. The chief referee struck upon his chest-gong with a heavy metal thimble; the contestants desisted from their conversations and ranged themselves around the yellow roble.

The chief referee spoke: "I now command an ordinary hadaul of craft and force, a ban upon all wields and weapons, and a prize of one hundred svu vouchsafed by the trustworthy Luke Lamaras. I now ring the seventeen-second bell." He rapped his chest-gong; the players began a restless shuffling motion, sidling to positions from which they hoped to gain advantage.

Again the chief struck a tone from his chest-gong. "Six seconds."

The players crouched, darted glances right and left, extended their arms in formalized postures.

Two sharp tones from the chest-gong. "Play!"

The players moved to the contest, some fast, some deliberate. Some would attempt pre-agreed stratagems; others would betray the same. Three converged on one massive man to hurtle him into the green. In a rage he dragged one with him and swung him dancing across and into the blue. The referees at once used their wands to mark the two with colored fluffs.

Wrestling, butting, tripping, hurdling: one by one the players were ejected from yellow into green, from green into blue, from blue into limbo and away from the game. Some players used agility, others massive strength. A favorite ploy, running around the robles to attack an adversary from the back, kept the game in constant motion. In general the game seemed good-humored; the players chortled at a clever thrust or a particularly stealthy attack from the rear, but as fewer and fewer players remained in the robles, and the prospect of winning the prize became ever more possible, the mood became more intense. Faces became strained and corded; lunges verged on the ferocious; two players in the blue began to exchange blows. As they struck out at each other a third player darted out of the green and thrust both into limbo. The combatants continued to flail away at each other—not too skillfully, so Gersen noticed—until a referee ordered cessation, on the grounds that they distracted attention from the hadaul.

Finally there remained a single player in the green and a larger, heavier player in the blue. Green ran along the boundary, feinting and dodging, while blue limped back and forth pretending pain, fatigue and despair. Green, however, thought better of venturing into the blue, preferring a certain three-fifths of the prize to the strong possibility of none. Blue at last began to hurl taunts, hoping to infuriate green into recklessness. Green stood stock-still, considered a careful moment, then turned to the chief referee as if about to request termination of play. Blue turned away in disgust; instantly green lunged at his back, to thrust him into limbo. The chief referee struck three tones on his gong, terminating the game, and the entire prize went to that resourceful robler who had deceived his opponent.

The basic theory of the game was simple, Gersen decided. Flexibility, vigilance and a wide field of vision were almost as important as strength and weight. The thrusts, twists, throws and pushes showed him nothing new; if he could avoid the concerted effort of four or five adversaries he felt that his chances were at least fair. He went to the referees' hut where he discovered that his costume, while eccentric and sub-standard, could not be judged illegal, except for his boots. One of the referees, rummaging in a box, discovered a pair of dirty old slippers which Gersen fatalistically strapped to his feet.

Returning outside, Gersen saw Bel Ruk at the registration desk. He seemed angry and agitated; Gersen deduced that he had looked down the list of roblers and there had seen the name Kirth Gersen.

Bel Ruk moved aside and spoke to a tall strong man in robler's costume: a conversation, reflected Gersen, which undoubtedly concerned himself.

The second game, for a prize of two thousand svu, went with considerably more zeal and less joviality than the first. The victor was a certain Dadexis: a middle-aged man, thin, sinewy and wickedly clever. He was immediately challenged by a frustrated young robler who had been ejected early in the bout. Dadexis, now with the option of weapons, chose *afflocks,* that implement with the pronged ball at the end of an elastic thong, which pleased the challenger not at all, but which he must now use or forfeit his challenge stake.

The spectators rose to their feet and pressed so close to the robles that the referees decreed an empty periphery around the field of play. The chief referee rang his gong; the contestants took up their positions and the challenge match proceeded. The bout was short and devoid of either blood, pain or drama, to the annoyance of the spectators. The canny Dadexis, in a practice flourish, swung his *afflock* with such frightening skill that the challenger became suddenly gloomy. The contest started; Dadexis sidled and dodged, easily avoiding the effect of his opponent's weapon, then snapped out his own thong. The ball curled around the haft of the other's *afflock;* Dadexis jerked and the challenger was bereft. Dadexis grinned, flourished his *afflock* around the field and at four gong tones from the referee went to pick up his now augmented prize, while the challenger walked away.

Gersen looked toward the grandstand, and discovered Jerdian. She had risen to her feet with the others, the better to observe the challenge bout; now she settled in her seat between her aunt Mayness and Aldo. What would she think to see him thrusting and bumping, slinking, sliding and lunging, in the robles with the Darsh?

At the very least, mused Gersen, she would be perplexed.

The contestants for the third hadaul gathered around the field, among them, so Gersen noted, that man whom he had noticed with Bel Ruk.

The chief referee spoke into his microphone. "A hadaul of one thousand svu guaranteed by the generous Bel Ruk! Eleven contestants have challenged with six hundred svu and 125 shares of Kotzash. They include experts from several clans and even an iskish."

Feeling slightly ridiculous Gersen went out to join the others around the robles. One hundred twenty-five shares! If he won the hadaul he won Kotzash Mutual Syndicate.

At once a stocky round-faced man came to consult with him. "Have you ever played hadaul before?"

"No," said Gersen. "I expect I have a lot to learn."

"Too true. Well; let's arrange a compact. I am Rudo. You, I and Skish yonder are undoubtedly the three weakest players here. If we work together we can cut down the odds."

"Good idea," said Gersen. "Who is the strongest?"

"Throngarro yonder——" this was Bel Ruk's confidant "—— and Mize, the great heavy man."

"Let's first eject Throngarro, then Mize."

"Agreed! Easier said than done, of course. Our pact holds until these two are ejected."

Gersen, now entering into the spirit of the game, looked around for other possible allies. He was again approached, by a stalwart young man who exuded that reckless swaggering manner known as plambosh. "You are Gersen? I am Chalcone. You won't win, of course, nor will I, but let's ally ourselves against Furbil yonder. He's rude and vicious and best ejected early."

"Why not?" said Gersen. "I'd also like to eject Throngarro; I'm told he's dangerous."

"True enough. Furbil, then Throngarro, and we guard each other at least until the green, or even blue; agreed?"

"Agreed."

"Then here's how we thrust Furbil. You feint him from the side; when he turns to deal with you I'll leg him from the rear, you push and he's tumbled."

"Sound tactics," said Gersen. "I'll do my best."

A moment or two later Furbil came to confer with Gersen. "You're the iskish? Well, good luck to you. But you'll want more than luck. I suggest that we work in duo."

"I'm agreeable to anything that will keep me in the game."

"Good. See that young chap yonder? That's Chalcone, an insolent rascal, but quick and deft. Here's how we'll ditch him. From opposite sides we'll close on him; you drop in front of him, I'll swing him and away he goes, halfway into the stands."

"First, Throngarro," said Gersen. "He's the most threatening of the group."

"Oh very well, Throngarro first, with the same tactics, then Chalcone."

"If we're still in the robles."

"No fear there. So long as we work together!"

Three more contestants approached Gersen, suggesting ploys and cooperations of various kinds, to which Gersen gave a general acquiescence, on the theory that any advantage was better than no advantage whatever.

Among the spectators he glimpsed Bel Ruk, and for an instant met his baleful glare. Gersen also took occasion to glance toward the Methlen, to find Jerdian watching him in total bewilderment.

The chief referee marched to the central pedestal and there arranged the challenges: packets of svu certificates and folded Kotzash shares.

The chief referee pounded his chest-gong. "Contestants: assume your positions!"

The eleven men moved into the yellow roble.

A gong. "I call thirty-one seconds!"

The contestants began to move here and there, hoping to achieve favorable angles of attack against those adversaries they considered the most critically dangerous.

Another gong. "I call seventeen seconds!"

The contestants crouched, looked right and left, hopped warily away from obvious thrusts.

"Six seconds!"

Then: "Play hadaul!"

Eleven men created a swirl of motion. Gersen, noticing Throngarro sidling purposefully toward him, moved away. Behind Throngarro appeared Chalcone. He caught Gersen's eye, made a sign and thrust at Throngarro who turned to fend off the attack. Gersen moved in, thrust and Throngarro was greened. "Now Furbil!" exclaimed Chalcone. "Remember our compact! You make the feint. There he is; quick now!"

Gersen obligingly feinted at Furbil, who recoiled against Chalcone, who seized his arm and attempted to swing him into green. Furbil deftly retained his footing, and using their joint movement greened Chalcone. Gersen came behind, thrust and Furbil also stumbled into the green. At the same instant a massive force struck Gersen from the side: the vast bulk of Mize, whose methods were brutally simple; he merely walked around the yellow, shouldering everyone he met into green. By sheer luck Gersen chanced to catch hold of Skish backing away from another adversary; by greening Skish, Gersen retained his balance and remained in the yellow. Gersen signaled to Rudo and indicated Mize. Sensing the joint attack, Mize put his back to the center table, swung his great arms in menacing circles. "Come at me then, if you dare!"

Gersen seized one of the arms and was almost jerked from his feet. At the same time Rudo, his erstwhile ally, seized him around the waist from behind and attempted to hustle him from the yellow. Gersen jerked his head back into Rudo's nose. He broke the grip and dived behind the great bulk of Mize. Here he put his back to the pedestal, raised his feet, thrust and sent Mize lurching toward the green, into which he was assisted by Rudo, his nose streaming red. Furious and roaring Mize charged at Throngarro, who nimbly gave way. Four of the green roblers seized on various parts of Mize: lurching, dancing, cursing, roaring he was thrust through blue toward limbo, but threw himself backward, kicked, and so escaped.

Gersen stood back to assess the situation. Throngarro and Mize, the two most formidable adversaries, had been ejected from yellow, where he remained with four others. Each of the five, with Throngarro and Mize ejected, could now realistically envision victory, and so became correspondingly more cautious. There were no more alliances either to be honored or betrayed; each man was reluctant to commit himself for fear of attack from the rear.

Gersen noticed that the other roblers were regarding him with wary respect. An iskish who had survived so long must be a man to take seriously.

From the corner of his eye Gersen saw Rudo and a certain Hement exchange a few words, then Rudo sidled toward Gersen. "Does our compact still hold?"

"Of course," said Gersen.

"Then Dexter is next, the tall squint-eyed man. You come at him from the side, I'll pass him and catch him in a crotch constrictor, and out he goes. On the ready!"

Gersen, as instructed, sidled toward Dexter, at the same time watching Hement. Just as he came within arm's length of Dexter, Hement lunged toward him, as did Dexter, and smartly from behind, his erstwhile ally Rudo. Gersen had been expecting the ploy. He pulled Dexter into Hement, threw Rudo head over heels into the green, then seizing Dexter's leg, heaved him into the green just as a flying body struck him from behind. Gersen bent, reached over his head, jerked and his assailant toppled on top of Dexter in the green. As they staggered erect, both were seized and blued. Hement somewhat tentatively seized Gersen's arm and tried to swing him; Gersen hacked, feinted, reached, heaved. Hement hurtled into the green, and Gersen was now left alone in the yellow save for a single other: a bulky young man who had retained yellow principally by staying out of everyone else's way. Gersen advanced upon him; he retreated. Gersen stalked him around the ring once, then twice, whereupon the young robler could retreat no further: to be chased three times around the ring meant automatic ejection into the next roble. Warily the two came together. Gersen extended his arm; the other gingerly took his wrist, essayed a pull. Gersen fell forward, applied an arm lock, swung the young man around and marched him hopping and squirming to the green.

Gersen was now alone in the yellow. He might, if he chose, venture into green, or even blue, and still return to yellow—unless in the green he were forcibly ejected into blue, or, in the blue, thrust into limbo. But he felt no interest in participating in green or blue contests, where the roblers, now anxious and angry, had abandoned temperate conduct. They struck, kicked, butted and kneed with gasping, roaring, cursing abandon. Gersen leaned against the pedestal and watched the activity. Throngarro, in blue, had come to grips with Rudo. Gersen watched Throngarro's tactics with interest; he was undoubtedly a skillful fighter: quick, strong and resourceful. He was still no match for Mize, whose sheer bulk made him almost impregnable. At the thought of facing Mize one to one, Gersen grimaced. He probably would win, by striking and hacking, and attempting to close Mize's eye, but he would surely suffer sprains and bruises, possibly broken bones, or even a broken neck.

Throngarro had ejected Rudo; he now gave his attention to Mize. Forming a cabal with a pair of other blues, he attacked Mize. The three men were jerked around like ants on a beetle. Finally, more by luck than design, they caused Mize to stumble into limbo, where he flung himself prone and beat the ground with his fists. Throngarro meanwhile took advantage of the situation to thrust out the two who had assisted him with Mize.

Gersen glanced around the ring of spectators. He encountered Bel Ruk's baleful glare, and let his gaze swing past. He looked toward the Methlen and for a flickering instant caught Jerdian's eye; he could not read her expression. Her aunt Mayness called to her and Jerdian looked away.

The hadaul reached a static level. In blue stood Throngarro, in the green Chalcone and in the yellow Gersen. If the hadaul, as of now, terminated the prize would be divided 3-2-1.

Gersen spoke to Throngarro and Chalcone: "I'll take the Kotzash shares; you two can divide the money: six hundred svu. Is this agreeable to you both?"

Chalcone calculated. "I agree."

Throngarro started to speak, then looked back at Bel Ruk,

who gave his head a stern shake. Throngarro reluctantly said, "No; the whole prize must be shared out."

Gersen signaled Chalcone up close to the yellow-green boundary. "Let's make a compact, which I guarantee to honor, if you will make the same guarantee."

"What do you have in mind?"

"Let us both go into blue and eject Throngarro, then I will return to yellow and you to green. I will take the Kotzash and you can take the money, all 600 svu."

"I agree to this compact."

"Mind you," said Gersen, "this is a contract of honor, not a hadaul ploy. If you break your promise I will take the matter most seriously. You can trust me; can I trust you?"

"For this single occasion, yes."

"Very well. You go in on the left, I on the right, with an arm's length between us and we will push him out backwards."

"Agreed."

With no more ado Gersen stepped into the green, then into blue, with Chalcone beside him. Throngarro waited in a crouch. Conceiving his best hope lay in attack, he sprang out at Chalcone, hoping to tackle him around the middle and hurl him around and run him out into limbo. Gersen hooked his arm, whereupon Chalcone seized the other arm. Gersen kicked the back of Throngarro's knees; Throngarro collapsed, but as he did so kicked Chalcone in the groin and Chalcone went down, bent double. Throngarro kicked at Gersen, who siezed Throngarro's ankle and twisted; Throngarro screamed as the ligaments tore. He struggled to roll over and away; Gersen turned the ankle again. Throngarro was forced to roll one again, up to the very edge of limbo, where in a frenzy he struggled and lurched. Lashing out with his free foot he kicked Gersen in the side. Gersen turned the ankle again; Throngbarro, screaming in despair, rolled out into limbo.

Gersen stood back panting. Chalcone had gained his feet but stood crouched in pain, pressing at his lower abdomen. The two considered each other, Chalcone with glazed eyes. Gersen returned into yellow and Chalcone hobbled back into green. Gersen called to the chief referee. "Give me the Kotzash shares; give Chalcone the money, and the hadaul is ended."

The chief referee asked Chalcone: "Are you agreed to this division?"

"Yes. I am more than satisfied."

"So, let it be." He spoke into his microphone. "For the first time in my recollection and perhaps in all the annals of our glorious game, an iskish has won at a major game, in combat against the best of Dar Sai. I now call out for challenges; does anyone challenge the victory of this redoubtable iskish?"

Bel Ruk stood talking furiously to Throngarro, who sat on a bench, his sprained ankle already swollen. Throngarro merely shook his head. Bel Ruk savagely turned away. "I challenge!" he shouted hoarsely. "It is I, Bel Ruk, and we shall fight with whips."

"Weapons are at the option of the challenged, as well you know," said the chief referee. "Do you challenge both Chalcone and Gersen?"

"No; I challenge Gersen alone."

The chief referee gave the svu certificates to Chalcone. "Go in pride from this hadaul!"

"I do so, and I give honor to Gersen, who plays with great skill." Chalcone took the money and hobbled gratefully off the field.

Bel Ruk marched forward. He gave the referee two svu. "Here is double the value of 125 shares of Kotzash, which are known to be worthless."

The referee stood back in disapproval. "You yourself placed a value upon these shares of four svu each!"

"By no means! I guaranteed a prize of a thousand svu; I agreed to allow twenty-five shares to represent a hundred svu. If Gersen wishes to surrender the 125 shares to me, I will pay him 500 svu. Otherwise he will lose his life, as I will kill him if he opposes me."

"You take a stern attitude," said the referee. "Well, Gersen, what is it to be? Bel Ruk is challenging your Kotzash and your life and all it costs him is a miserly two svu. If you wish to withdraw, evidently Bel Ruk will pay you 500 svu for your Kotzash, and you will have spent a profitable day. I must inform you that Bel Ruk is notoriously skillfull with his whips and weapons; your chances are not at all good. Still, you may specify which weapons, if any, are to be used."

Gersen shrugged. "If I must fight him, I will use either knives or bare hands, as he wishes."

"Knives!" cried Bel Ruk. "I will undertake to cut him apart."

One of the referees tendered a tray in which rested a pair of daggers, with black wooden grips and double-edged blades almost a foot long.

Gersen took one of the knives and hefted it. The blade, a long thin triangle, broad at the grip, made for a lack of that balance which Gersen preferred; still, he decided, it would do well enough; certainly it was not a weapon designed to be thrown, which implied the absence of such skill among the Darsh. He looked up in the stands, to find an expression of fascinated horror on Jerdian's face.

The chief referee spoke: "The bout will be fought within the robles, and will continue until one of the parties in contention indicates surrender, either by throwing up his hands, or by crying out, or by vacating the robles, or until he is unable to proceed, or until I cry a halt. The bout will be free; there are neither regulations nor limitations. You may take up positions in the yellow, on opposite sides of the pedestal. The bout will begin at the fourth gong-strike and continue until I intervene, when it must come to an instant halt, on pain of three days in the cess-pit. So guard your ardor and stop fighting at my command, since I will have no leisurely carving up of a disabled man." These words were accompanied by a meaningful glance toward Bel Ruk. "Three retreating or pursued circuits of the pedestal also constitute surrender. I now sound the thirty-one second gong. Take your places."

Gersen and Bel Ruk faced each other across the pedestal.

"Seventeen seconds."

Bel Ruk waved his blade back and forth, enjoying the feel of death. "I have been waiting for this occasion."

"I am not averse to it," said Gersen. "Tell me, did you go out on the Mount Pleasant raid?"

"Mount Pleasant? That was long ago."

"So you were there."

Bel Ruk's only response was a cold grin.

"I can now kill you without compunction," said Gersen.

"Six seconds! Gentlemen, flourish your weapons! At the next gong-strike, make your engagement!"

The seconds marched past, traversing that mysterious boundary which separates future from past.

The gong sounded.

Bel Ruk advanced around the pedestal, knife low and held as if it were a sword. Gersen waited in a slouch, then threw the knife at Bel Ruk's heart. The blade skimmed fair to its target, struck with metallic *clink*, rebounded and fell to the ground. Bel Ruk evidently wore a vest of dympnet sequins under his singlet. The referee made no protest; apparently the vest was considered a legal accessory.

As soon as the knife struck the ground, Bel Ruk kicked it toward limbo; simultaneously Gersen sprang forward and Bel Ruk's attention was diverted. The knife slid to a halt just inches inside the blue.

Bel Ruk thrust; Gersen ducked sideways to the left and hacked with his hand at the side of the burly neck and punched at Bel Ruk's left eye. Bel Ruk hacked at Gersen's ribs: the blade cut through his blouse and laid open six inches of skin; blood oozed forth.

In a rage Gersen caught Bel Ruk's arm, applied a lock, tripped Bel Ruk, and using Bel Ruk's own momentum broke the elbow joint.

Bel Ruk gave a grunt; the knife dropped from his limp fingers. But he groped with his left hand, seized the haft and cut up backwards, plunging the knife into Gersen's thigh. Gersen stood back aghast. Had he become so clumsy? He now bled from two wounds; he would soon go limp and weak, and then he would be killed . . . Not yet! He hacked at Bel Ruk's neck once again. As Bel Ruk attempted to break away and stab, Gersen caught Bel Ruk's left arm, but could not apply a lock. Bel Ruk jerked away, to stand panting, his right arm limp, his left eye almost closed.

Bleeding from ribs and thigh, Gersen limped over to his knife. Bel Ruk rushed after, dagger held high for a downward thrust. Gersen caught the upraised arm, then reached down to catch Bel Ruk's knee as it jerked up toward his crotch. He heaved; Bel Ruk tottered back, and Gersen retrieved his knife. Bel Ruk, mouth open, nostrils distended, eyes bruised, came staggering forward. Gersen threw the knife a second time. it plunged almost to the hilt into Bel Ruk's corded neck. Bel Ruk fell to his knees, and with a final effort, almost a reflex, threw his knife at Gersen. The point dropped; the edge cut Gersen's hip. Bel Ruk sagged forward and the weight of his body drove the dagger entirely through his neck, and the point issued six inches from the nape.

"I declare the hadaul ended!" called the referee. "Gersen is the winner, his prize is 125 shares of Kotzash and two svu."

Gersen took the certificates and staggered from the robles. A surgeon led him to a nearby dumble and attended to his wounds.

One hundred twenty-five shares of Kotzash! Gersen now owned 2,416 shares, six over half. He controlled Kotzash Mutual.

Gersen emerged from the dumble to find that Bel Ruk's corpse had been carried away. He looked up into the stands. The Methlen had departed, apparently having seen enough.

Gersen limped away from the area, and out to his spaceship. He climbed aboard, secured the hatches, took the vessel into the air and east toward Serjeuz.

Gersen spent the night in his spaceship, drifting over the desert. In the morning he landed beside the Serjeuz water-veils. Impelled by caprice he dressed in loose trousers of black twill, a white linen blouse, and a dark green sash: the costume that a wealthy young aristocrat of Avente on Alphanor might wear on a promenade. He hobbled through the morning sunlight, under the water-veils, then out upon the plaza. The garden at the Sferinde Select was almost untenanted. At the Travelers' Inn a few early tourists sat at breakfast.

Gersen went into the lobby. At a telephone he called the Sferinde Select and asked to be connected to Mistress Jerdian Chanseth. Presently her soft voice came from the speaker. "Yes? Who is it?"

"Kirth Gersen."

"Wait a moment, while I close the door. . . . Kirth Gersen! Why did you do what you did? Everyone believes you insane!"

"I needed a hundred and twenty more shares of Kotzash. Now I control the company."

"But the risks you took!"

"I couldn't avoid them. Were you worried for me?"

"Of course! My heart was in my throat. I didn't want to watch, but I couldn't not watch. Everyone says that Bel Ruk was a notorious assassin, extremely skilled with weapons. They think that you must be the same."

"That's not the case. Can I see you?"

"I don't know how. We're leaving for Llalarkno at once and Aunt Mayness is with me every moment. She's certain already that something is wrong with me. . . . Where are you? At the Travelers' Inn?"

"Yes."

"I'll come across; I can risk fifteen minutes."

"I'll meet you in the garden, where we sat before."

"Where I first decided that I was in love with you. Do you remember?"

"I remember."

"I'll be right there."

Gersen went out to the garden. Two minutes later Jerdian appeared. She wore the same dark green gown in which he first had seen her. He rose to his feet; she came into his arms and they kissed: once, twice, three times. "This is so pointless," said Jerdian. "This is the last time I'll ever see you."

"So I tell myself. But I find it hard to make myself believe it."

"Somehow you must find a way." Jerdian looked over her shoulder. "I'd be in disgrace if I were found here with you."

Gersen was a trifle nettled by the remark. "Would you mind so very much?"

"Well—yes. At Llalarkno we maintain very exact images."

"What if I came to Llalarkno?"

Jerdian shook her head. "Our world is small. Everyone knows everyone else, and we must live up to expectations. It makes for a happy existence—usually."

For a long minute Gersen looked at her. Then he said: "If I could offer you a happy serene life I wouldn't listen. But I can't assure you of anything but anxiety, travel to strange uncomfortable places, and perhaps danger. . . . Not in the foreseeable future. . . . So, good-bye."

Tears welled up in Jerdian's eyes. "I can't abide that word; it's like death. . . . Sometimes I wish you'd just carry me to your ship and fly away with me. I'd not resist, or cry out; I'd be thrilled with happiness!"

"It would be wonderful for a while. But I can't do it. I'd only bring you grief."

Jeridan rose to her feet, blinking against the tears. "I must go."

Gersen stood up but made no move toward her. She hesitated, then came to him and kissed his cheek. "I'll never forget you." She turned and walked from the garden.

Gersen sat back in his chair. The episode was finished. He would forget Jerdian Chanseth as quickly and as thoroughly as possible. He was now in a hurry. Panshaw still would not know of Bel Ruk's death, nor of Gersen's new status as Kotzash majority stockholder. He used one of the two svu he had won from Bel Ruk to buy his breakfast, then returned to his ship. Into a case he packed a set of tools, then limped hurriedly to Dindar House, under Skansel Shade. He went directly to Panshaw's office.

As before the door was locked. Gersen brought tools from his bag, cut the lock free and thrust open the door, careless of any alarm which might be set off. With Ottile Panshaw off-planet and Bel Ruk dead, there might be no one to heed such an alarm. He entered the room which as before smelled stale and rancid.

He heard hurrying footsteps in the hall. Two men looked through the door. Gersen gave them a cool inspection. "Who are you and what do you want here?"

One of the men said sharply: "I am manager of this building. Mr. Bel Ruk has asked me to keep a lookout against intruders. How dare you break into this office?"

"I control Kotzash Mutual. This office is my responsibility; it is my right to enter and do as I like, with or without a key."

"Bel Ruk said nothing to me of this."

"Nor will he ever. Bel Ruk is dead."

The manager's face became grave. "That is sad news."

"Not for any honest man. Bel Ruk was a scoundrel. He deserved worse than he got. Now please go away; I intend to examine the Kotzash records. If you care to inquire about me, I refer you to Adario Chanseth, at the Chanseth Bank."

"As you say, sir." The two men withdrew and after a whispered consultation in the hall, withdrew.

Gersen started with the file cabinets, then went to the shelves, then explored the desk. He found records of Kotzash dealings; of ore acquisition and the corresponding distribution of share vouchers, information which at one time he would gladly have possessed. Now it meant nothing. He discovered copies of leases, licenses and mineral exploration rights granted to Kotzash: all worthless, so he had been assured. He made a parcel of these and set them aside.

The desk yielded nothing of interest whatever.

Gersen looked around the office one last time. It had harbored Ottile Panshaw, Bel Ruk and, almost certainly, Lens Larque; the air still seemed tainted.

Gersen departed Dindar House. He went directly to his Fantamic Flitterwing, and a few minutes later was gone into space.

Part III: Methel

Chapter 12

From *Peoples of the Coranne,* by Richard Pelto.

Methel! the enchanted planet where a folk superb, handsome, proud and splendidly dressed live in privilege, ostentatious privacy and the often irritating conviction of their own superiority.

"Arrogance," a word functionally apt when applied to the Methlen, carries far too many incorrect connotations, and quite misrepresents the ingenuous charm of this people. Even their servitors and functionaries—the so-called "Mongrels"—regard the Methlen with an amused and even appreciative tolerance, which, while often wry, is seldom bitter.

For the student of the human condition and its infinite permutations, the Methlen are a fascinating case. Their history is relatively uneventful. Methel was located for and chartered to the membership of Aretioi, an exclusive club of Zangelberg on Stanislas. Tracts of land were allocated among the membership; the remainder of the planet was designated a wilderness reserve. Many Aretioi who came from Zangelberg to visit remained in residence, and all enormously augmented their wealth by dealing in duodecimates.

With great dedication the Methlen have kept their world private and remote. A space-port at the service city Twanish is the single depot of ingress or egress. The population of Methel is

small. Twenty thousand Methlen inhabit Llalarkno; perhaps as many more keep to their
country estates. Twanish is, in effect, an enclave
inhabited by fifty thousand "Mongrels," off-
worlders of many varieties: a mixed race indeed,
which includes the occasional result of a Meth-
len/non-Methlen liaison, and a large colony of
Darsh, who undertake menial tasks.

Llalarkno is more like an outsized village than
a town. The wonderful Methlen homes are
sacred to the families who inhabit them. Each is
named; each owns a reputation, or an atmosphere, or a mood, which is unique and well-
known. In these houses the Methlen perform
their rituals, play their games and undertake the
pageants which provide variety and color for
their lives. Tournaments of a hundred sorts, the-
atricals, opera cycles, pavannes, classical panto-
mime; the spectacles progress in their seasons;
there are roles for everyone.

Drama is the grand motif of Methlen existence. Part of the game is to pretend that all
other folk of the Oikumene are primitive or at
best uncouth. The more perceptive Methlen
recognize the game for what it is: a fantasy or
frivolity to be enjoyed for its own sake. Others
hold the concept to be a fundamental truth. The
Methlen in general lack awareness of their
propensities. They tend to overstate, to make
grand gestures, to adopt flamboyant postures. Every instant becomes a new tableau where they arrange themselves to best advantage. However and
withal, the Methlen are a hardheaded people who
make few mistakes, and will not allow an extravagance to proceed to where it becomes inconvenient.

Eight forts orbited Methel at a distance of half a million
miles. Following procedures specified in *Space Pilot and
Gazeteer*, Gersen declared himself to one of these forts. He
was boarded and examined by a Methlen lieutenant and a
pair of cadets, and presently cleared for entry. He was as-

signed a landing plat at Twanish Space-port and a traffic channel for the guidance of his auto-pilot.

The fortress authorities departed; the Fantamic Flitterwing dropped away toward Methel: a globe solemn and magnificent, showing like mottled velvet, dark blue and green, in the Cora-light. To the side drifted the moon Shanitra, an angular lump of sinter the color of ash, an object to which Gersen controlled exclusive rights of mineral exploitation, for whatever these were worth.

The traffic control drew him down to Twanish, the single city of Methel, and landed him on that plat assigned to him at Twanish Space-port.

The time was mid-afternoon. Through the ports came Cora-light, clear and lucid, but lacking the brutal impact of Dar' Sai Cora-light. Gersen stepped out upon the soil of Methel: Jerdian Chanseth's world.

In the west Twanish showed a set of glass and concrete structures cantilevered out from one, two or several load-supporting columns, to create an effect of airy solidity. Beyond rose a wooded upland: Llalarkno. To the north the land was planted to crops and orchards; to the south a parkland of meadows and enormous old trees heaved up to become a long range of ancient mountains.

A serene and pleasant prospect, thought Gersen. He crossed the field by a path of cemented sinter to the space terminal, a polygonal structure of black metal and glass with a central traffic and control tower. A sign directed him to a counter, where a uniformed clerk noted his personal particulars into an information bank, thus extinguishing a small yellow light on a display board: evidently the completion of a verification procedure initiated at the space fortress.

A public conveyance carried him into the center of town. At the Commercial Hotel he was offered room and bath adequate to his needs. His most immediate concern was money, of which he had none whatever. He placed a telephone call and discovered the local correspondent of Cooney's Bank, which Gersen immediately visited and was tendered a thousand svu on his letter of credit.

At a kiosk he bought a map of the city, then took a seat at a nearby sidewalk cafe.

A waitress came to take his order. Gersen pointed to a

table where a man sat with a frosty pale-green formulation. "What is that gentleman drinking?"

"That is our Cross-eye Punch, sir; it's fruit juice, sweet spirits of arrack and bangleberry rum, frozen and whipped."

"Bring me one of the same," said Gersen, and settled back to observe the inhabitants of Twanish. These were mostly Mongrels: folk of various types but all wearing similar garments: jackets striped vertically in dark or muted colors, with black trousers or skirts. The effect was one of formality and punctilio. There was a scattering of off-worlders: salesmen, agents and a few tourists. Gersen also saw Darsh, wearing clay-colored breeches and white blouses or white pajama-suits; and Methlen, set apart by their dark hair and olive complexions, their clothes and an indefinable ease of manner. An interesting mix of people, thought Gersen.

The waitress brought a chilled flask of Cross-eye Punch.

Gersen opened his map of the city, which he saw to be of no great extent. The streets and places of Twanish were carefully limned and labeled, but that area to the west designated as Llalarkno showed no detail whatever. The Methlen abodes and their avenues of ingress apparently were not to be exposed to the vulgar gaze. Gersen gave the faintest of shrugs. Methlen vanities were none of his concern.

The Cross-eye Punch was a success. At a signal the waitress brought a second goblet. "This should be ample to your needs, sir," she told him earnestly. "It is strong drink, and a stranger will not realize its authority until he attempts to stand erect. Sometimes these are known as 'Tickets to Redemption,' because when folk take more than is necessary they become obstreperous, and must be punished."

"I appreciate the warning," said Gersen. "How are these obstreperous ones punished?"

"That depends upon the offense, but often they are locked arm and leg into clouts, and children are allowed to pelt them with soft fruit, which often, so I fear, is spoiled and bad." The girl gave a shudder of distaste. "I for one never want to be made a public mock."

"Nor I," said Gersen. "Would you please bring me the telephone directory?"

"Certainly, sir."

Gersen turned the pages, and immediately found the entry

Kotzash Mutual, Skohune Tower, followed by the telephone code.

Gersen called the waitress and paid his score. "And where is Skohune Tower?"

"Look yonder, sir, across the park. Notice the building with the tall center portal? That is Skohune Tower."

Gersen sauntered across the park and approached Skohune Tower: a structure of eight levels, the floors of white concrete, the walls of glass, the load-bearing members four columns of black metal: a far cry from Dindar House at Serjeuz. For a bankrupt and debt-ridden concern such as Kotzash Mutual, Skohune Tower would seem a startlingly expensive address. From somewhere had come money: the *Ettilia Gargantyr's* insurance settlement? The sale of plundered Kotzash duodecimates?

Gersen crossed the avenue and entered the ground-level foyer: a glass enclosed area between the four columns. A directory instructed Gersen that Kotzash Mutual occupied Chamber 307 on the third level. Gersen considered the options open to him. He might walk into the Kotzash offices and assert control: a forthright act which certainly would arouse the notice of Lens Larque. There might or might not be a corresponding advantage for Gersen; certainly he wanted to act before Panshaw learned of Bel Ruk's death, which could only be a matter of hours.

Gersen crossed the foyer to the business office, where he discovered a whippet-thin Mongrel with keen features and alert black eyes, wearing the orthodox black trousers, a jacket striped in black, brown, dull mustard and maroon, and glossy black shoes. A brass counter plaque read: *Udolf Testel, Manager.*

Gersen identified himself as the field representative of Cooney's Bank. "We are seriously considering a branch here at Twanish," said Gersen in his most solemn voice. "I'll need a business address, and an office here might well serve my needs."

"I would be most happy to oblige you," said Testel, who seemed not only keen but also somewhat pompous and self-important. "Our occupancy is close to total; still I could offer you a suite on the second level, or a single room on the fifth." He produced charts and indicated the premises to which he referred. Gersen took the charts, studied them a moment, then examined the third-floor plan. Kotzash Mutual occupied a single room, 307, between a single room occupied by Irie Pharmaceutical Imports, 306, and the three-chamber offices of Jarkow Engineering: 308. "The third level would suit me best," said Gersen. "What is available here?"

"Nothing whatever."

"A pity. Either of these offices would exactly serve my needs." Gersen indicated "306" and "307." "Are the tenants permanently established? I wonder if they might be induced to move to the fifth floor?"

Testel bridled at this somewhat high-handed proposal. "I am certain that they would not," he said stiffly. "Mr. Coost of Irie is quite set in his ways. Mr. Panshaw in 307 works with Jarkow Engineering. Neither could consider moving: of this I am sure."

"In that case I'll look at the fifth level office," said Gersen. "If you'll give me the key, I'll make a quick inspection."

"Allow me to show the office," said Testal. "It is no trouble whatever."

"I prefer to look the place over alone," said Gersen. "Then I am not distracted in forming my opinions."

"Just as you like," said Testel in a nasal voice. He slid open a drawer, selected a key. "Number 510, to the right as you leave the lift."

Gersen rode the ascensor to the fifth level. The key, a strip of laminated metal, controlled the lock through varying permeabilities to magnetic fields. Such a key could not readily be duplicated, and would not facilitate entrance into 306, 307 or 308. Gersen, nevertheless, had noted the drawer in which the manager kept his spare keys.

Gersen made a quick inspection of 510, then returned to Testel's office on the ground floor and gave over the key. "I'll inform you of my decision presently."

"We shall be happy to serve you," said Testel.

In a back street Gersen located a locksmith's workshop, where he bought three blank keys similar to those used at Skohune Tower, and had them engraved respectively with the numbers 306, 307 and 308. He then returned to the spaceport and his ship, where he packed several types of eavesdrop equipment into a case. When he confronted Panshaw with the new circumstances, the ensuing conversations might well lead directly to Lens Larque, or at the very least provide some indication as to his whereabouts.

Back at the Commerical Hotel he dropped off his equipment. The time was now dusk and possibly too late to advance his program any further. Gersen, nevertheless, felt restless and on edge. Imminence was upon him; events were converging. He crossed the park to Skokune Tower, thinking, to make a reconnaissance. If Ottile Panshaw were on the premises, who knows where he might lead when he departed?

From the park Gersen counted windows. 306 still showed light. Mr. Coost of Irie Pharmaceuticals worked late. 307 was dark; Ottile Panshaw would be enjoying the evening elsewhere. 308, the offices of Jarkow Engineering, were also dark. Gersen crossed the street and looked into the foyer. The door into the business office stood ajar, and the diligent Udolf Testel still stood at the counter, frowning down at a ledger.

Gersen went to a telephone in the far corner of the foyer. He called Testel's office and heard the sharp declaration: "Skohune Tower; Manager's office."

Gersen pitched his voice at a quavering half-falsetto: "Mr. Testel, come at once to the roof garden! There's mischief going on; you must put an end to it! Come quickly!"

"Eh?" cried Testel. "What's all this? Who is calling, please?"

Gersen had broken the connection. He went to stand where he could watch across the foyer.

Testel came from his office on the run, his expression eloquent of concern and vexation. He jumped upon the ascensor and disappeared from view.

Gersen crossed to Testel's office, went behind the counter and slid open the key drawer. He removed keys from the slots labeled 306, 307, 308, and replaced them with the blank keys. He closed the drawer, left the office, crossed the lobby and departed Skohune Tower.

Pleased with his evening's work, Gersen dined at the Medallion Restaurant, which advertised *Classic Cuisine: Authentic Dishes in the Style of the Grand Masters*. Gersen, only mildly interested in abstruse gastronomy, put himself at the mercy of the waiter, who handed him a card edged in silver and black.

"This is our Grand Repast of today, sir, highly to be recommended!"

Gersen read:

Hors d'oeuvres of Ten Worlds
Broth with Aloe nuts and Water flowers,
in the style of Benitres, Capella VI.

Gratin of Pink Nard with Cress and Whitebait,
as served by Sigismond at the Grand Hotel,
Avente, Alphanor.

Prime Cutlets of the Five-Horned Darango,
imported from the Oxygen Marshes, Cuenos Notos.

Dumplings of Belsifer Root with Saffron,
in the
style of Farewell Station, Miriotes.

Relish of Mushroom Dry Saute,
Chilled Pineapple and Mango Chutney,
from the gardens of Old Earth.

Salad of Herbs and Greens,
dressed with oil of Mediterranean olives
and Alsatian vinegar.

Frivols, Flimsies, Flapdoodles,
as purveyed along the Esplanade at Avente.

Coffee from the Sunnyrain Highlands, Krokinole,
brewed to the instant in a porcelain pot and
served with a tot of Mascarene Rum,
in the style of Fat Hannah, at the Copus Spaceport.

The menu will be enhanced by five excellent wines,
appropriate to each service

The price of thirty svu placed this meal in the luxury category. Well, why not? Gersen asked himself, and instructed the waiter: "You may bring me this 'Grand Repast.'"

"At once, sir!"

The dishes were well-prepared, garnished expertly and served with a flourish. Perhaps they were indeed authentic, and so it seemed to Gersen, who had dined at many of the listed localities, and often had taken a tot of rum at Fat Hannah's on Copus. The clientele, so he noticed, was at least half Methlen. What if Jerdian Chanseth were to wander in? What would she think? What would she do? Gersen wondered what he himself might do. Nothing, probably.

He left the restaurant and strolled along the principal avenue of Twanish: a tree-lined boulevard known as The Mall, which, after a sweeping curve around Redemption Park, veered up into Llalarkno.

Few vehicles other than cabs moved along the streets. The Methlen system of control, so Gersen would learn, was simple:they imposed high licensing fees and built no roads except in the near vicinity of Twanish.

On impulse Gersen signaled down a cab: a small soft-wheeled vehicle with the passenger compartment to the front and the driver mounted behind.

"Where to, sir?"

"Llalarkno," said Gersen. "Just drive around a bit."

"You have no destination in mind, sir?"

"Quite right. Take me around Llalarkno and bring me back here."

"Well—I suppose it can be done, now that it's dark. The Methlen, and you wouldn't know being an outworlder, are jealous of their privacy. They don't like to see great charabancs loaded with tourists trundling about Llalarkno."

"So long as it's not illegal, I'll risk the trip."

"As you say, sir."

Gersen climbed into the passenger's compartment. The driver inquired: "Any particular place that you wish to see, sir?"

"Do you know the residence of Adario Chanseth?"

"Indeed, sir; the Chanseth house is named Oldenwood."

"When we pass Oldenwood, please point it out to me."

"Very well, sir."

The cab rolled off along The Mall, around Redemption Park, and up the incline toward Llalarkno. Weeping acacia trees obscured the lights of Twanish; almost at once Gersen felt himself in a new environment.

The road turned off across a wooded upland, winding among the Methlen homes. Gersen, perhaps prejudiced by his appraisal of Adario Chanseth, had expected splendor and display; somewhat to his surprise he found rambling old mansions built, so it was clear, for no purpose other than to please those who lived there. He glimpsed verandahs grown over with flowering vines, lawns and pools. Fairy lanterns floated through the gardens; tall windows of many panes glowed golden. The folk who lived in these homes, thought Gersen, would cherish them as if they were things alive. Children would never want to leave, but the eldest son must inherit and, heartsick or not, the others must leave. Gersen, who barely remembered his childhood home, grew melancholy. He could own such a home, if he so chose, as spacious and comfortable as any of these. The expense certainly was no obstacle, only the style of his life, which made such a notion no more than a far-fetched daydream. A pleasant daydream, nevertheless, upon which his mind lingered. Where would he choose to live, if circumstances so arranged themselves? Not on Alphanor certainly, nor anywhere along the Concourse, nor on any of the Vegan worlds, where such houses as these would not sit comfortably. Perhaps on Old Earth, or even here on Methel. With Jerdian Chanseth? The idea improved as Gersen considered it. Impossible, however.

Gersen called up to the driver. "Where is Oldenwood?"

"We are drawing near. There: Parnassio, the house of the Zames. There, Andelmore, of Floristys. And there is Oldenwood."

"Stop just a moment." Gersen stepped down from the cab and stood in the road. In a mood of even deeper melancholy he considered the house where Jerdian had lived her life. The windows were dark, except for a few watch-lamps; the Chanseths had not yet returned home.

The driver spoke. "Notice the house just yonder? That's Moss Alrune and a fine house indeed. It belongs to an old lady, the last of the Azels. She's priced the house at a million svu and won't take a dit less. Do you know of Lens Larque, the great corsair?"

"Naturally."

"One day he came wandering through Llalarkno, just as you now are doing and saw the house. He decided to buy; after all, what's a million svu to Lens Larque? He strolled through the garden, examining this and that, smelling the flowers, tasting the berries. Adario Chanseth happened to be abroad in his own garden, and spied the strange man. He called out, 'Hey there! What are you up to, in that garden?'

'I'm looking this property over, if it's any of your affair,' said Lens Larque. 'I've decided to buy.' Adario Chanseth roared out: 'Be damned to that! I'll never tolerate your big Darsh face hanging over my garden fence, not to mention your stinks and smells. Get out of Llalarkno and stay out!' Lens Larque roared back: 'Be damned to you! I'll buy where I like and put my face where I like.' Chanseth rushed into his house and called the security guards who of course hustled Lens Larque off the property; and there it still sits, vacant as ever, with no one willing to pay the million svu."

"And what ensued with Lens Larque?"

"Who knows? They say he went off in a rage, and whipped a dozen boys to soothe his feelings."

"And he's still on Methel?"

"Again, who knows? No one recognized him for Lens Larque while he dickered for Moss Alrune; his name was only mentioned later."

Through the trees Gersen could only glimpse Moss Alrune. On the lake beyond a glittering trail reflected from the moon Shanitra.*

Gersen climbed back into the cab, which proceeded around Llalarkno: through copses and dells, across moonlit glades, past the great old houses, to which Gersen paid no further heed. The cab returned down the incline and into The Mall. The driver's voice intruded upon Gersen's musings. "Where do you wish to go, sir?"

Gersen considered. Haste was of utmost importance, but he felt tired and out of sorts. Tomorrow morning would serve his purposes well enough. "Take me to the Commerical Hotel."

---

* The moon is named after a grotesque clown in the Methlen *opera bouffe*.

Chapter 13

From *People of the Coranne,* by Richard Pelto:

The Twanish Mongrels, reacting to the exclusivity of the Methlen aristocracy, have developed a counter-society, which is orderly, genteel and circumspect. Perhaps it should be noted here that "Mongrel" is not a Methlen term. The Methlen take note of only three sorts of people: Methlen, all other folk except the Darsh, and the Darsh. The term "Mongrel" was initiated by the *Twanish Scribe* facetiously to characterize the varied origins of the Twanish citizenry; the term came into vogue as an ironic reference to Methlen pretensions: a joke which of course passed the Methlen completely by.

Mongrels prefer to ignore their economic dependence on the Methlen. They like to think of themselves as energetic and hard-working entrepreneurs, with a general multi-racial clientele. Their society is essentially middle class and controlled by an exacting and fastidious etiquette.

Everything considered, Mongrel fantasies are no less flagrant than those of the Methlen, if of defensive origin. Mongrels like to think of the Methlen as frivolous, vain, self-indulgent and over-bred, in contrast to their own dignity, common sense and stability. The Methlen pageants are considered extravagant, ostentatious and faintly ridiculous as might be an array of strutting peacocks. Nevertheless, Methlen activities are the source of endless gossip among the Mongrels, and every Methlen of Llalarkno will be recognized by name when he or she comes down into Twanish.

The two peoples with their contrasting cultures live harmoniously. The Mongrels affect a contemptuous disdain for Methlen frailty; the Methlen pay the Mongrels no attention whatever.

Gersen arose early and took his kit to Skohune Tower. The foyer was empty and silent; the door into Udolf Testel's office was closed.

Gersen rode the ascensor to the third level. He passed 307 without so much as pausing; Ottile Panshaw's predilection for traps and alarms made his present errand impractical. At 308 he halted and, after a glance up and down the corridor, inserted his key. The door slid ajar. Gersen looked into the offices of Jarkow Engineering. He saw a large reception room, with a glass-walled secretary's office to the left and a hall to the right giving upon a glass-walled draughting room and a pair of private offices.

The chambers were empty. Gersen entered, closed the door behind him. The reception room contained a couch, two chairs, a table and shelves displaying models of space-mining equipment: carriers, diggers, grinders, centrifuges, hoppers, conveyer systems. The secretary's cubicle backed upon Ottile Panshaw's office. From his case Gersen brought a drive-needle and drilled a small hole deep into the wall. Into the hole he inserted a probe, so that the tip made contact with the outer skin of the wall in Ottile Panshaw's office. Under the secretary's desk he attached a recording machine inside a black box, which he connected to the probe with conducting films. He removed the back-plate from the secretary's telephone console, brought wires up from the black box and attached them to terminals inside the telephone.

He had worked quickly and efficiently; the time was still early. But as he replaced the back plate to the console, the door opened and into the reception room came a young woman in secretarial costume: a black skirt and a crisp prim blouse, candy-striped in purple, red and white. The secretary herself seemed not at all prim; in fact she was saucy, vivacious and pretty, with blonde curls fluffing out from under a white cap. At the sight of Gersen she stopped short. "And who might you be?"

"Communications technician, miss," said Gersen. "Your line has been showing irregular pulses; I've just set it right."

"Indeed." The girl crossed the reception room and tossed her handbag into a chair. "I've noticed something of the sort, especially on our calls out to Shanitra."

"Everything should proceed even and smooth now. There's one little part which often corrodes; we generally can fix it in five minutes and be gone before anyone arrives to work, but today I've been delayed."

"Fancy that. Well, I'm early this morning; I've got some letters of my own to write. Do you work all night?"

"Just when I'm on call. I only work part time; in fact I've been on Methel only a month."

"Oh? Where's your world?"

"I'm originally out of Alphanor, along the Concourse."

"I'd love to visit the Concourse! I'll be lucky if I get as far as Dar Sai, dog bite it!"

The girl was very composed, thought Gersen, and full of spirit, and also far from unattractive. "Working for a space mining firm as you do, I'd think you might be called on to travel everywhere."

The girl laughed. "I'm just a receptionist. Mr. Jarkow barely sends me to the store on errands. I suppose I could travel with him under special circumstances, if you know what I mean, but I'm not that sort."

Gersen picked up his case. "Well, I must be getting along." He hesitated. "As I say I'm a stranger in town and I know absolutely no one. Would you think me bold if I asked you to meet me this evening? Perhaps we could go somewhere pleasant for dinner."

The girl threw back her head and laughed, a trifle too loudly. "You are bold indeed. We Mongrels are a very proper folk, and I'm not so sure as to what you have in mind."

"Nothing more than what you can easily cope with," said Gersen, attempting an ingenuous grin, which had he known it, only twisted his dark face into a cunning leer.

The girl failed to notice. "Are you married?"

"No indeed."

"I really should say no and indignantly." She turned Gersen an arch side-glance. "But, well—why not?"

"Why not indeed? Where and when shall I meet you?"

"Oh—let's say the Black Barn, which is very gay, with dancing galore. Are you a nimble dancer?"

"Well—no. Not really."

"We'll repair that lack! At the tone of the evening hour. I'll wait just by the red door."

"Understood, except for how to find the Black Barn."

"My faith, you are a stranger indeed! Everyone knows the Black Barn."

"I'll find it without trouble. But let me ask your name."

"Lully Inkelstaff. Tell me yours."

"Kirth Gersen."

"What an odd name! It sounds quite medieval. Did you learn your trade on Alphanor?'"

"Partly, and partly here and there across space." Gersen took up his case. "I'd better go. We're not supposed to make calls during business hours. I wouldn't want to annoy Mr. Jarkow."

"You're too late," said Lully Inkelstaff. "I hear him in the corridor. Still, he's not one to worry overly much. He hardly notices anything—except me, I must say."

The outer door slid aside; into the office came two men: the first gaunt and gray, with narrow shoulders and a thin melancholy face; the second tall, ponderous and heavy-featured, with a pasty complexion and a profusion of unsuitable golden ringlets. He wore a loose and untidy Mongrel suit: black trousers, a jacket striped black, green and orange, which went ill with his complexion. The thin man went directly into the draughting office; Jarkow paused to rake Gersen up and down with a cold stare. He turned to Lully, who said in a cheerful voice, "Good morning, Mr. Jarkow. Allow me to introduce my fiancé Dorth Koosin."

Jarkow gave Gersen a nod lacking in amicability; Gersen bowed politely in return, after which Jarkow stalked off to his office. Lully put her hand to her mouth to stifle a titter. "The thought came to me on the instant. On occasion Mr. Jarkow attempts familiarities and I wanted to discourage him without a great drama. Sometimes he is really quite peremptory. I hope you don't mind."

"Not at all," said Gersen. "I am glad to be of service. But now I must go."

"I'll see you this evening."

Gersen left the office, and went directly to Chamber 307,

the headquarters of Kotzash Mutual. He tried the door and found it locked. Gersen rapped on the panel, but no one responded.

Gersen reflected a moment, then descended to the ground floor. Consulting the directory, he learned that Evrem Dai, Legal Consultant and Factuary-at-Law, occupied Suite 422.

Gersen rode the ascensor to the fourth floor and went to Suite 422. A clerk took him to an inner office, where Evrem Dai sat at a desk.

Gersen succinctly stated his business. Evrem Dai, as Gersen had expected, wanted several days in which to fulfill the requirements, but Gersen insisted not only upon haste but immediacy, and Evram Dai, after a moment's thought, prepared a document. He then used his communicator, spoke to several clerks and finally to a portly gentleman at an enormous desk fabricated from black jet and gold. Evram Dai displayed Gersen's Kotzash shares and the document he had prepared. The portly gentleman made an acquiescent motion; Evram Dai put the document into his communicator where it received a transmitted signature and seal.

Gersen paid a not inconsiderable fee and left Evram Dai's offices. He descended to the third level, arriving just in time to see Ottile Panshaw stepping into Room 307. Gersen ran forward and, catching the door before it slid shut, entered the office. Panshaw looked around with an expression of mild inquiry. "Sir?"

"You are Ottile Panshaw?"

Panshaw squinted at Gersen, head to the side. "Do I know you? I have the impression that somewhere we have met."

"Have you recently visited Dar Sai? Perhaps we met there."

"Perhaps. What is your name and what is your business?"

"I am a speculator. My name is Jard Glay, and I am the controlling stockholder of Kotzash Mutual."

"Indeed." Panshaw thoughtfully started for his desk. Gersen said: "A moment, Mr. Panshaw. I am now your employer. You are a paid employee of Kotzash Mutual?"

"Yes, that is so."

"Then I prefer that you use this chair while we talk."

Panshaw smiled wryly. "You still have not demonstrated that you are, in fact, the controlling stockholder."

Gersen produced the document prepared by Evram Dai. "I

have here an official attestation to this effect, together with a judicial order that you immediately relinquish into my custody all documents, records and correspondence pertaining to Kotzash business, together with all assets, including money, stocks, interests, contracts, real property, incidental property: in short, everything."

Panshaw's smile had become tremulous. "This is a most peculiar circumstance. Naturally, I am aware that you have been acquiring Kotzash stock. May I inquire as to your motives?"

"Why do you trouble to ask? You would believe nothing told you."

Panshaw shrugged. "I am not so skeptical as you appear to believe."

"No matter," said Gersen. "What is your nominal position here at Kotzash?"

"Managing Director."

"Who is the principal stockholder, after myself?"

Panshaw said guardedly: "I hold a rather large block of shares."

"And what is the principal business of Kotzash now?"

"Essentially, exploration for duodecimates."

"Be so good as to elaborate."

Panshaw made a delicate gesture. "There is nothing much to tell you. Kotzash controls various charters and exclusive rights, and we are trying to exploit them."

"Specifically, how and where?"

"At the moment we are concentrating upon Shanitra."

"Who has been making these decisions?"

"I, naturally. Who else?"

"Where is the money coming from?"

Again Panshaw's delicate gesture. "The subsidiaries have yielded good profits."

"Which you have not distributed among the shareholders."

"We desperately need working capital. The managing director must allocate funds to his best judgment."

"I intend to look carefully into every phase of Kotzash. As of now, I want all activities suspended."

"You seem to be in a position of authority," said Panshaw suavely. "You need only give the necessary orders."

"Exactly. Do you intend to continue in your present capacity?"

Panshaw's sensitive face became creased with perplexity. "You have surprised me; I need time to assess the situation."

"In short, you refuse to cooperate with me?"

"Please," murmured Panshaw. "Do not force unnatural meanings upon my remarks."

Gersen went to the desk. To one side rested the communicator screen and coding buttons. Behind stood a small filing case for current records. Much, if not most, of Kotzash's ramifications would be filed only behind the fragile forehead of Ottile Panshaw.

Panshaw sat in a melancholy reverie. Gersen watched him sidelong, now somewhat annoyed; in a sense he had outwitted himself. To give Panshaw scope to conduct a telephone conversation, presumably with Lens Larque, he must leave Panshaw alone in the office, thereby risking the destruction or alteration of Kotzash records.

An acceptable procedure suggested itself. He spoke in a reasonable tone of voice. "These changes must come to you as an unpleasant shock. Suppose I give you a few minutes to consider your position."

"That would be most gracious of you," said Panshaw, allowing no more than a trace of irony into his voice.

"I'll stroll up and down the corridor a time or two," said Gersen. "Sit at your desk, if you like, but please do not interfere with the records."

"Naturally not," said Panshaw indignantly. "Do you take me for a scoundrel?"

Gersen left the office, leaving the door pointedly open. He sauntered to the ascensor, then back, looking through the open door as he passed. As he had expected, Panshaw was talking earnestly into the communicator. Gersen could not see the screen which no doubt was blank in any case. Gersen walked on, to the end of the corridor and back, and Panshaw still occupied himself on the communicator, though now he frowned in nervous dissatisfaction.

Gersen made another tour of the passage, and when he passed the door again, Panshaw sat leaning back in his chair, placidly pensive.

Gersen stepped into the office. "Have you reached a decision?"

"Yes indeed," said Panshaw. "My legal adviser tells me that only two honorable courses of action are open. I can either depart the office on the instant, or I can hope to continue in a paid capacity with the company. I feel that I would only defeat my own purposes if now I withdraw in a fit of pique."

"Sensible, of course," said Gersen. "Am I to understand that you plan to cooperate with me?"

"That is correct, provided that we can come to financial terms."

"Before I can make an offer I must know more about the company; its resources, commitments and assets."

"Understandable," said Panshaw. "To start with, allow me to tell you this. Your instincts are superlatively keen. I blame myself for folly and vacillation; long ago I should have made sure of a controlling interest. I neglected to do so and now I must accept the penalty with as good grace as possible."

Gersen listened for that barely perceptible falsity which indicated a speaker's awareness of an eavesdropper. He heard nothing. "If circumstances warrant, I will retain your services at an appropriate salary. For the moment, please produce a comprehensive list of Kotzash assets."

Panshaw pursed his lips. "Such a list does not exist. We have a few thousand svu in the bank—"

"Which bank?"

"Sweecham's, just along the street."

"What of companies subsidiary to Kotzash?"

Panshaw hesitated. "We have working arrangements here and there—"

Gersen interrupted. "Let us put an end to this foolishness. You are congenitally unable to tell the truth, except, I suspect, under duress. I have done a certain amount of research. I know of Hector Transit, for instance, and I know of the settlement for the *Ettilia Gargantyr*. Where is this money?"

Panshaw showed neither discomfort nor embarrassment. "Most of it has gone to pay Jarkow."

"Pay him for what?"

"Explorations on Shanitra. We are making a massive effort."

"Why?"

"According to reports Shanitra carries somewhere a monster lode of duodecimates. We have been trying to locate it."

"Shanitra carries no duodecimates," said Gersen. "The Methlen would have won it long ago."

Panshaw gave an urbane shrug. "New lodes of duodeci-mates are constantly discovered."

"Not on Shanitra. Kotzash is now under my control, and I don't want Kotzash money wasted. Stop the explorations at once."

"Easier said than done. Certain phases have already been funded—"

"We'll get a rebate. Is there a contract?"

"No. I've worked on a basis of trust with Jarkow."

"Then perhaps he'll be reasonable now. Order an immediate halt."

Panshaw again gave his urbane shrug, then rose to his feet and left the office. Gersen immediately went to the communicator and made contact with Jarkow's office. The decorative image of Lully Inkelstaff appeared on the screen. Gersen had blinked off the communicator's eye and she looked in vain to see who was calling. She spoke: "Jarkow Mining. Who is calling please?"

Gersen kept silent. After a moment Lully flicked off her switch. Gersen however still controlled the line incoming to the Jarkow offices. He tapped a code against the microphone to activate his recorder playback.

First: a crackling sound, steps as Panshaw entered the office, and a moment later his own appearance and his initial conversation with Panshaw. Then the sounds of his departure from the office, and almost at once Panshaw's voice into the communicator. "News at this end. Bel Ruk failed. I've just had a visit from the new control. He's got a writ."

In response came a harsh voice which sent quivers along Gersen's nerves. "Who is he?"

"He calls himself Jard Glay. I've seen him on Dar Sai; I can't quite recall the circumstances. He's an odd fellow; I can't make him out."

A brief silence. Then again the ominous voice: "Play him easy. Watch him. In a day or two I'll have him taken up; then we'll learn who he is."

"It might be better to act at once," said Panshaw cautiously. "He could cause trouble. Suppose he knows of Didroxus Mining? Or the Hector Transit account? Or Theremus? He could block us out financially."

"How could he know?"

"Hector Transit is a matter of record on Aloysius. The accounts are all at Sweecham's."

"Work up a set of transfers dated yesterday. Kosema will handle the matter without difficulty."

"I can do that easily enough. Still something about this fellow alarms me. There he is now, watching me from the corridor."

"Let him watch. As soon as I show the face I'll deal with him. But first I must show the face."

"Very well." Panshaw's voice lacked conviction.

"In the meantime, cooperate with him—to a point. Discover what he's after; perhaps he'll teach us something to our profit. In four days, or perhaps five, we'll put an end to him."

"As you say."

Gersen tapped a code to his eavesdrop device, cut off the communication, then rose to his feet and went to the door. Panshaw should have returned from his visit to Room 308 by this time. Gersen went back to the communicator and once more called Jarkow's office. This time he allowed Lully to see his face. "It's I, your fiancé; remember me?"

"Oh yes. But—"

"Tell me, is Ottile Panshaw in your office?"

"He left just a moment ago."

"Thank you. Tonight at the Black Barn, don't forget!"

"I won't."

Gersen left the office, descended to the ground floor and went out to the street. A hundred feet north he saw a sign:

SWEETCHAMS BANK
Commercial Services . . . Interworld Transfers.

Gersen ran to the bank and entered through tall glass doors. An attendant approached. "Sir, how may I assist you?"

"Who is Mr. Kosema?"

"That is his office yonder. At the moment he is busy."

"The matter concerns me. I'll just step over."

Gerson crossed the lobby and entered Kosema's office. A pink pudgy man with a round face and a pouting pink mouth sat at a desk opposite Ottile Panshaw. He had been frowning down at a paper; he looked up with a nervous jerk. Ottile Panshaw smiled sadly.

Gersen took the paper from in front of Kosema. He saw it

to be an order transferring funds in the total of svu 4,501,
100 from accounts described as Kotzash 2: Theremus;
Kotzash 4: Hector Transit; Kotzash 5: Didroxus Mining; and
Kotzash 9: Wundergast Interests. The beneficiary of the order, dated yesterday, was the Basramp Investment Company.

Gersen stared at Kosema. "Are you participating with Ot-
tille Panshaw in felonious grand theft?"

"Of course not," spluttered Kosema. "I was about to inform Mr. Panshaw that I could not help him. How dare you
suggest such a thing!"

"I could suggest it to the authorities; I could show them
this order, which is on a Sweecham form."

"Absurd!" Kosema's voice cracked and quavered. "You
have no reason to suspect lack of fidelity."

Gersen gave a sardonic snort. "Look at these documents. I
am managing director of Kotzash."

"Yes, so it appears. Well, Mr. Panshaw has perhaps failed
to inform me—"

Panshaw rose to his feet. "I must be on my way."

"You will wait," said Gersen. "Sit down, if you please."

Panshaw hesitated, then resumed his seat.

"Mr. Kosema, I now notify you that Mr. Panshaw has no
further authority in regard to Kotzash moneys. I will challenge any drafts which you pay from this moment onward
unless they bear my signature."

Kosema gave a curt bow. "I understand perfectly. I assure
you—"

"Yes. Your unassailable fidelity. Come along, Panshaw."

Ottile Panshaw followed Gersen out to the street. "A moment," he said. "Let us go sit on that bench yonder."

The two crossed the Mall to the park and seated themselves upon a bench.

"You are an amazing man," said Panshaw. "I fear that
your acts will cost you dearly."

"How so?"

Panshaw shook his head. "I will name no names. But I will
tell you what I am now about to do. In two hours a Black
Arrow packet leaves Methel, bound for Saudal Suud. I plan
to be aboard. Take my advice and depart aboard the same
vessel. When a person whose name I cannot bring myself to
utter discovers that you have taken almost five million svu's

of money he regards as his own, he will treat you in a way I do not care to think about."

"I am surprised that you warn me."

Panshaw smiled. "I am a thief, a swindler, an extortionist. I am a thorough-going scoundrel. But when my self-interest is not involved I am apt to be decent, even generous. I am now taking flight, in a panic that this man will blame me for your deeds. You will never see me again, unless you join me aboard the *Anvana Syntro*. Otherwise you will be carried away to a secret place. There you will slowly and carefully be flayed."

"Tell me where to find this man. I will put an end to him."

Panshaw rose to his feet. "I don't dare so much. He never forgets a wrong, as you will learn. Do not ride in a cab; change your hotel every night. Don't go back to the Kotzash office; there's nothing there to interest you. He chose the office only because it was next to Jarkow."

"Did you order Jarkow to halt operations?"

"My word carries no weight with Jarkow. Tell me: where have we met before?"

"At Rath Eileann, in the Estremont, and at the Domus. Do you remember Benchmaster Dalt?"

Ottile Panshaw raised his eyes to the sky. "Good-bye." He walked rapidly away through the park.

Chapter 14

From *Life,* Volume III, by Unspiek, Baron Bodissey:

I am constantly startled and often amused by the diverse attitudes toward wealth to be found among the peoples of the Oikumene.

Some societies equate affluence with criminal skill; for others wealth represents the gratitude of society for the performance of valuable services.

My own concepts in this regard are easy and clear, and I am sure that the word "simplistic" will be used by my critics. These folk are callow and turgid of intellect; I am reassured by their howls and yelps.

For present purpose I exclude criminal wealth, the garnering of which needs no elaboration, and a gambler's wealth which is tinsel.

In regard, then, to wealth:

1. Luxury and privilege are the perquisites of wealth. This would appear a notably bland remark, but is much larger than it seems. If one listens closely, he hears deep and far below the mournful chime of inevitability.

2. To achieve wealth, one generally must thoroughly exploit at least three of the following five attributes:

a. Luck.

b. Toil, persistence, courage.

c. Self-denial.

d. Short range intelligence: cunning, improvisational ability.

e. Long-range intelligence: planning, the perception of trends.

These attributes are common; anyone desiring privilege and luxury can gain the precursory wealth by making proper use of his native competence.

In some societies poverty is considered a pathetic misfortune, or noble abnegation, hurriedly to be remedied by use of public funds. Other more stalwart societies think of poverty as a measure of the man himself.

The critics respond:

What an unutterable ass is this fellow Unspiek! I am reduced to making furious scratches and crotchets with my pen!
—Lionel Wistofer, in *The Monstrator*.

I am poor; I admit it! Am I then a churl or a noddy? I deny it with all the vehemence of my soul! I take my bite of seed-cake and my sip of tea with the same relish as any paunchy plutocrat with bulging eyes and grease running from his mouth as he engulfs ortolans in brandy, Krokinole oysters, filet of Darango Five-Horn! My wealth is my shelf of books! My privileges are my dreams!
—Sistie Fael, in *The Outlook*.

. . . He moves me to tooth-chattering wrath; he has inflicted upon me, personally, a barrage of sheer piffle, and maundering insult which cries out to the Heavens for atonement. I will thrust my fist down his loquacious maw; better, I will horsewhip him on the steps of his club. If he has no club, I hereby invite him to the broad and convenient steps of the Senior Quill-drivers, although I must say that the Inksters maintain a superior bar, and this shall be my choice since, after trouncing the old fool, I will undoubtedly ask him in for a drink.
—McFarquhar Kenshaw, in *The Gaean*.

The shrubbery behind Gersen rustled; he ducked, fell off the bench in a crouch. When he turned his small gun was in his palm, the nozzle protruding between first and second fingers.

A gardener in white coveralls looked at him in wonder. "Sorry I startled you, sir."

"Not at all," said Gersen. "I am a nervous man."

"So I noticed."

Gersen moved to another bench and sat where he could see in all directions. He long had felt himself a man apart from all others, with a certain destiny; often he had known horror and rage and pity, but fear, when it entered his mind, came strangely.

Gersen examined himself with detachment. Fear had affected Tintle, Daswell Tippin, Ottile Panshaw, and now himself. Well, why not fear? The thought of a flaying, with Lens Larque wielding Panak, was horrid enough to frighten a corpse.

Gersen sat motionless, discouraged and despondent. The sources of his mood were clear enough. He had become enamoured of Jerdian Chanseth; he envied the Methlen their beautiful homes. Both emotions had broken against his harsh and obsessive purposes like waves breaking against a rock. And now with Panshaw gone, his single link to Lens Larque had frayed to a broken strand or two. One of these strands was Jarkow. Or he could allow himself to be captured and taken to visit Lens Larque, at which thought his skin crawled.

Gersen reviewed the events which had brought him to Twanish. They led from Rath Eileann and Tintle's Shade to Serjeuz, Dinkelstown and finally to Methel. He had expended vast exertion, but what had he achieved? Nothing of consequence. What had he learned? Only that Lens Larque, for reasons unknown, had engaged Jarkow Engineers to an unreasonably thorough investigation of the moon Shanitra.

So then, he asked himself gloomily, what next? He had not yet inspected Panshaw's office, which in any event was probably a waste of time; indeed Panshaw had specifically told him so. With no great enthusiasm Gersen returned to Skohune Tower and Room 307. Sliding back the door, he scrutinized the room, which already felt disused and dead. To capture a man, the easiest method was narcotic gas. Gersen sniffed the air, which smelled fresh enough. He checked the door casing for sensors, looked along the rug for a hump which might indicate a mine. The rug itself might be woven of explosive fibers, which would upon contact break him into fragments.

Carefully he entered the room, and avoiding the rug, sidled to the desk. Using elaborate precautions, he explored Panshaw's files, where he found the various leases, enabling certificates, licenses and grants which originally had been declared Kotzash Mutual's only assets. Most carried a terse notation written in red ink: "worthless." The Shanitra lease awarded Kotzash Mutual sole and exclusive rights to "explore, test, develop and exploit all valuable substances present upon the surface or within the interior," and prohibited "all other persons, agencies and entities, including manned or unmanned mechanical devices" from trespass upon Shanitra for the term of the lease, which ran for the term of twenty-six years.

Interesting, thought Gersen, if not particularly illuminating. The key question remained unanswered: why would Lens Larque invest so much time and money on Shanitra?

Gersen found nothing more to interest him. The details of payments made to Jarkow, or other engineering firms, were nowhere in evidence; presumably they resided in a bank computer.

Gersen called Sweecham's Bank, and after a series of formalities with which he patiently complied, he was rendered the code which controlled Kotzash financial records.

For half an hour Gersen studied the information presented to him and in the end knew little more than before, although the magnitude of payments made to Jarkow came as something of a surprise. For over a year Kotzash had honored monthly invoices from Jarkow in sums ranging from svu 80,-500 to svu 145,720. The payments then dropped off to svu 42,000. Whatever the search, it seemed to be dwindling and phasing out.

On sudden thought, Gersen looked into the city directory. Jarkow Engineering must necessarily maintain an equipment yard, employment and bookkeeping facilities, transport docks, even a warehouse.

In the directory under "Jarkow" Gersen discovered four entries: a residential address for "Lemuel Jarkow," another for "Swiat Jarkow," "Jarkow Engineering" in Skohune Tower, and "Jarkow Corporation Yard," on Gladhorn Road.

Gersen put away the directory, leaned back on the chair and tried to formulate a plan of action. Ottile Panshaw had served as a kind of indicator, registering the presence of Lens

Larque as a buoy marks the location of a reef. With Panshaw gone, Gersen himself became the key to Lens Larque's whereabouts, in the same sense that a staked-out lamb is the key to the presence of a tiger. Gersen winced. Far better that he seek out Lens Larque than that Lens Larque seek him out.

The only investigation which seemed even remotely propitious was contained in the question: why did Lens Larque invest so much effort on Shanitra?

Jarkow might know, but Jarkow would certainly tell Gersen nothing. The melancholy draughtsman might also know. Jarkow's employees—those who had worked on Shanitra—might know.

Gersen, prickling with the need for action, jumped to his feet. He crossed the room, slid the door open a trifle, looked up and down the corridor, which was empty. He descended to the street. Gladhorn Road, according to his map, angled away from the Mall and curved to the northeast.

A cab swung to the curb and halted, as if soliciting his custom. Gersen continued along The Mall, and presently glanced over his shoulder. The cab, old and quite ordinary, distinguished only by a faded white stripe around the skirt, moved out into the traffic and was gone. The driver had been a bulky flat-faced man of uncertain age and unknowable racial background.

Gersen performed a set of procedures designed to frustrate any tracer mechanism which might have been put upon him. On Gladhorn Road he stepped into a clothing store, where he bought gray twill trousers, a pale blue shirt, a belted brown jacket, and a black cloth cap, which he donned on the spot. Leaving his former garments on the premises, he went out on the street, now in the guise of an artisan.

Gladhorn Road curved to the east, past small shops and miscellaneous enterprises: rooming houses, taverns, restaurants, dim stores dealing in curios, apothecaries, barbers, public clerks. At the outskirts of town Gersen came upon the Jarkow corporation yard, where Jarkow maintained his equipment: conveyors, rotary torches, gantrys, vertical stabbers, thrusts, loading pods, a pair of mobile cranes. To one side stood a row of small buildings. The first showed a sign EMPLOYMENT OFFICE. Across the doorway hung a second sign: NO HIRING TODAY. Beyond were a payroll office and tool warehouses then a small landing field, on which rested a pair of weatherbeaten personnel carriers and a heavy cargo lift.

For want of a better occupation, Gersen entered the employment office. Behind a counter sat an old man with a scarred brown face. "Sir?"

"I saw the sign," said Gersen. "Does that mean there'll be no hiring tomorrow?"

"That's my guess," said the clerk. "We're just closing down a big job and there's nothing else on the boards. In fact we've laid off most of our crew."

"What's the job you just finished?"

"Big exploration job, up on Shanitra."

"Did they find anything?"

"Friend, whatever they found I'm the last man they'd tell."

Gersen turned away and sauntered back out to the street. Opposite he noticed a ramshackle building decorated with extraordinary lightning bolts of black and white on a background of brick red. The roof supported a large sign as garish as the building itself: a crescent moon with a naked girl reclining in the concavity; she held aloft a goblet of pale liquid from which floated electric sparks. The sign displayed a legend: STAR-WANDERER'S INN.

Gersen crossed the street. The music of a euphonium, played with gusto and decision, waxed louder as he approached. In his farings across the Oikumene Gersen had known many such taverns, where he had witnessed many strange events and heard many odd tales, not a few of them true.

He entered a long low-ceilinged room, heavy with beer fumes. In the far corner a hatchet-faced old woman in a gown of black tinsel, her skin toned white, her hair dyed blue, played the euphonium; at the other end was the bar: a single slab of petrified wood. In between groups of men and a few women sat at wooden tables. Alone at a table to the back sat a large Darsh, brooding into a huge tankard of ale.

Gersen went to the bar. A shelf to the rear displayed a multitude of beer mugs, imprinted with as many emblems. Gersen saw a number of familiar labels: *Vergence* and *True Companion* from Alphanor; *Obladense* and *Old Subterranean* from Copus, *Smade's Own* from Smade's Planet; *Bass Ale, Hinano, Tusker, Anchor Steam* from Earth; *Mahogany Select* from Derdyra, *Edelfrimpschen* from Bogardus: Gersen felt

himself in the presence of old friends. In the spirit of the
time and place he requested a flask of the local brew, *Hangry's White Ale,* which he found eminently palatable.

Turning, he looked around the room. At a large trestle
table sat a group of men whose conversation identified them
as employees of Jarkow Engineering. They had consumed
considerable beer and spoke in loud positive voices, making
no effort to dissemble their opinions.

"—told Motry that if he wanted me on that man-killer
he'd have to give me back my swamper and also some kind
of shroud to bar the dust. He promised, and I ran the dingus
for a month and got scabs and red-nose and all else, and then
I find that Motry gave my swamper to old Twaidlander, who
runs that little tri-nozzle about two hours a day, and never
dirties a finger."

"Motry's a strange one. You got to handle him right."

"Well, I don't work for Jarkow any more and I might just
explain things to Motry."

"He's still up on the job, with the technician."

"The two of them can blow each other up, for all of me."

Gersen took a seat at the table. "You gentlemen all work
for Jarkow?"

An instant silence while he was appraised by six pairs of
eyes. One said curtly, "Not now. The job's washed out."

"So I was told at the hiring office."

One man said, "You arrived on the scene about a year
late."

Another grumbled: "You didn't miss much. Bad food, low
pay and Claude Motry for superintendent."

"And no bonus!"

Gersen said thoughtfully. "Not much chance of a bonus
unless they found a lode of black sand."

"They couldn't find black sand because there's none out
there. Everybody knows that, except the rich lunatics who
paid the bills."

Gersen suggested: "Maybe they weren't looking for black
sand."

"Maybe not, but what else is there to look for?"

Another argued: "Even so and irregardless they never did
a proper exploration. All shallow tunnels, no deep probes.
Where they'd hope to find sand is deep, and nowhere did we

tunnel deep. More of a mesh or a network, as if they were looking for something shallow."

"Out in Section D we went down a good half-mile, before we made our horizontals."

Gersen spoke for a round of drinks and the workers gave him their cordial best wishes.

Somewhat to the side sat a young man wearing workman's breeches with a fine green jacket and yellow shoes. In a quiet voice, to no one in particular, he spoke a single word: "Twittle."

One of the workmen nudged Gersen. "Watch this now. Watch the Darsh."

Gersen looked at the Darsh who as before sat staring into his beer.

"Pfit," said the young man in yellow shoes.

The Darsh brought his hand to the tankard and began to flex heavy red fingers.

"Pfat," said the young man.

The Darsh lowered his head between his shoulders, but still did not raise his eyes. The young man jumped to his feet and went to the door. Along the street came a stout gentleman with a moony face, a pair of glossy mustaches, wearing a fine Mongrel suit.

"Phut," said the young man, and quickly ran off down the street. The Darsh jerked to his feet and lumbered out the door. The stout gentleman attempted to move aside but the Darsh seized him, threw him to the ground, kicked his round rump, poured a mug of beer over his head, then slouched off down the street.

The gentleman in the black suit sat up, to stare in perplexity this way and that. Slowly he rose to his feet, shook his head in wonder and continued on his way.

The workers returned to their conversation. "The strangest job I ever worked," said one. "I've mined twenty-six asteroids, and never wasted ten minutes on such a block of pumice. All surface scum, so I told Motry. He wouldn't listen."

"He never cared one way or another, so long as Jarkow paid his wage."

"Not Jarkow; somebody by the name of Kotzash."

"Whatever, they had us boring like weevils through cheese, and now they're satisfied at last!"

A newcomer had come to stand by the table. "Don't be too sure! We just got finished today laying out ropes of dexax— Motry and the technician are arranging the wires. Once they blast, Motry says we'll go back and tunnel some more. I asked him: 'Motry, what in the name of Delilah's hind leg are we looking for? Then I could keep my eyes peeled.' He just give me his sarcastic grunt and says: 'When I need your advice I'll ask for it.' 'Take it anyway, Mr. Motry,' I say. 'It's free!' And he says, 'Free advice is worth what it costs, and how come you're standing here advising instead of working?' 'Because, Mr. Motry, I've finished my job.' 'Then punch out your ticket and take the carrier down to land. The job is done for now!' So I come on down, and just now got my pay. There's nobody left up there but Motry and Jarkow and a couple of technicians rigging some kind of radio contact."

Gersen sat a few minutes longer and presently decided that the workmen knew no more about the Shanitra project than he did himself. He took his leave, and returned up Gladhorn Road the way he had come. At the clothing shop he resumed his usual garments and walked along the Mall to the Commercial Hotel. Before entering his room he took careful precautions for fear that someone might have visited him, leaving an unpleasant surprise. He found nothing out of the ordinary.

He took his lunch in the hotel restaurant, hardly noticing what he ate. During the last few hours much had occurred, but nothing from which he could derive meaningful information.

He left the restaurant and went out on the Mall, watching to right and left. He saw nothing to threaten him, unless— was that cab with the white stripe around the skirt the same cab which had accosted him earlier? He could not be sure. He crossed the Mall and went into the park. For ten minutes he walked the gravel paths, wondering what to do next. Lens Larque was somewhere near at hand: perhaps in a space vessel, perhaps on Methel itself.

Gersen's mind had become tired; he was bored with his problems and saw no way to escape them. On impulse he went out to a side street, where he signaled down a passing cab: one which displayed no faded white stripe around the skirt. He told the driver; "Take me out to Llalarkno."

As before the driver made difficulties. "That's like a big

private park. The Methlen don't like visitors; in fact they put probation points against any cab they catch with tourists."

"I'm not a tourist," said Gersen. "I am an interworld banker and a man of great importance."

"All very well, sir, but the Methlen draw no such distinction."

Gersen produced a five-svu certificate. "I am also able to pay the fare."

"As you say, sir. But if I am approached and notified, then you must pay the impositions."

"Agreed," said Gersen. "Take me to Oldenwood, the Chanseth house."

The glades and dells of Llalarkno worked magic upon Gersen's nerves. As he looked off at the half-hidden houses, his fears and compulsions began to seem unreal.

At Oldenwood the driver slowed the cab. "The Chanseth residence, sir."

"Stop just a moment," said Gersen. The driver reluctantly obeyed. Gersen threw open the door and stood up on the boarding flange. Past a bank of flowering shrubs and a sprawling candle-nut tree a lawn sloped down to Oldenwood. Somewhat beyond the house Gersen glimpsed a group of young people dressed in white, yellow and pale blue. They seemed to be watching a game, perhaps tennis or badminton, played beyond Gersen's range of vision.

"Come, sir," said the driver in a voice of urgency. "Banker or even interworld financier, they won't like you peering and staring. They have a mania for privacy, these Methlen."

Gersen returned into the cab. "Drive over to Moss Alrune."

"As you wish, sir."

At Moss Alrune Gersen descended from the cab and despite the driver's anxious protests, walked around the grounds, appraising the house, the meadow which sloped down to the lake, the surrounding trees. He heard no sound but a faint trilling of insects.

Gersen returned to the cab. "Take me back into Twanish."

"Thank you, sir."

Gersen alighted at the Carina-Crux Bank where he arranged for the purchase by Cooney's Bank, through its affiliate, the Carina-Crux Bank, of that property known as Moss Alrune, from the estate agent representing Cytherea Azel.

Chapter 15

From The Avatar's Apprentice, in *Scroll from the Ninth Dimension*.

On that fateful afternoon the very skies showed portents: a lurid gloom in the east, a cloud of meaningful shape over Ymmyr Marsh in the west.

Since dawn's first flush Marmaduke had paced the parapets, overlooking the horde which cloaked Maninguez Plain. Everywhere showed the flux of sinister purpose. Along Shadim Road manciples drove their war-wagons: Cham River could not be seen for barges loaded with engines, tormentors and gibbets. Halfway up the Yar swarmed the multitudes; from north to south their beacons flashed.

At last Holy Bernissus, in stately robes, stepped out upon the parapets. He raised high his arms in benign salute, but the hordes expressed a hateful sound which, mingling from all quarters, produced the dull wavering roar of stormy surf.

Bernissus shook his head in sorrow and drew somewhat back. For moments he gazed across the plain, stroking his beard.

Marmaduke reverently came forward. "Holy Sir, it seems that we two stand alone against this vindictive multitude."

Bernissus uttered Words: "It is well."

Marmaduke stood back in perplexity. "Most Excellent! Illuminate my ignorance, if you will! How may we find satisfaction in these lonely conditions?"

Bernissus spoke Words: "In good time all will be made known."

"I am grateful for the assurance," said Marmaduke. "In sheer truth this odious horde has unnerved me."

"Felfaw cannot prevail," were the Words, "even though he has wrought a great and busy mischief."

"Holy Appodex: allow me to enumerate the victims of his cruel hoax. Of the horde now pullulating across the plain, all are either Devariants or Oblatics, with the exception of ten thousand Cathars. Many know syllables of the Unspeakable name. Yonder stand the Purple Myrmidons, yonder the Hypogrotes of Lissam, yonder the Glames, who at least show us the etiquette of facing forward inasmuch as they go into battle with naked backsides. The Swans of Porving cluster around their Magnates; they menace us with standards on high! I recognize Obus of Thraw, Vilnisser, the Red Cockatrice, Pleighborn, Flynch and Sandsifer of Hutt. Not ten days ago they burned blue incense at fanes along the Wayvode!"

Once more Bernissus moved forward to stand in majesty, the wind blowing back his robes and white beard. Raising arms on high he issued a slogan, which whirled down Maninguez Plain and broke against the Yar in flashes of lightning. The enemy quailed but presently took courage and thrust high their standards. They shouted: "The Decretals must be altered! We nominate Felfaw for the Column! Bernissus, falsest of the false, must be cast down!"

Bernissus spoke gentle Words: "Not all are malign. In this case, bad leads good."

"The swords of both sorts are long and sharp," declared Marmaduke. "I fear that these noble parapets must burst asunder with only the two of us on defense. Where are the faithful? Where Helgebort and the Indefatigables? Where Nish and Nesso, and Little Mouse? Where the Verv-ils?"

"Their destinies lie elsewhere," were the Words. "They are the cadres; they will teach and counsel; they will declaim the Panticles, and prepare the onset of the Second Realm. So let it be!"

"Blessed Bernissus! What must be my role in the days to come?"

"Each plays his part. I go now to the Oratory to devise an irresistible Slogan, to send these poor jackals reeling. For the nonce you must patrol the parapets. Post high the standards, dislodge ladders, defy the foe."

"I will do all needful," declared Marmaduke staunchly. "But, Beneficence, make haste! The enemy awaits only the sign."

"All will be well." With deliberate tread Bern-issus descended to the Sacred Chamber.

The sign came down; the legions gave a tremendous yell and advanced upon the parapets.

Marmaduke called into the passage: "Beloved Bernissus! The sign has come down from Acher-nar; the legions are upon us! Their swords are thrice-honed steel; they carry lances, catapults and war-hooks; they raise ladders to scale the parapets! I have posted the standards; my slogans have created havoc, but I am one against eight hundred thousand. I will necessarily be cut into minute pieces, as each warrior vents his zeal upon my single corpse! Ineffable, the time is at hand!"

Marmaduke listened but heard no response. Anxiously he descended the passage and called the holy Name, but his voice rang hollow through empty chambers. Down to the uttermost foundations he went, and through a seep-hole crawled out upon the marsh. He fled to the north and presently overtook Bernissus, who, with robes gathered high and with thewed legs thrust-ing back the mire, made ponderous but steady progress north toward Warram Forest.

Gersen descended from his room to the lobby of the hotel and looked out the front windows into the street. Three cabs stood at the curb, apparently waiting for custom. The first, which showed a weathered white stripe around the skirt was driven by a swarthy flat-faced man with black curls and ears clipped to points. Gersen seated himself where he could watch the street.

A man and a woman left the hotel. They approached the first cab, but were refused service. They tried the second and then the third with similar results, and finally hailed a cab cruising along the street.

Three cabs in a row, each equipped with a tank of narcogen? Possible, thought Gersen: quite possible indeed.

He stepped from the front door and stood a moment before the hotel as if in cogitation. From the corner of his eye he noticed that all three drivers had become alert. Gersen paid them no heed. He crossed the Mall and walked into the park. From behind a copse of snuff-brush he watched the cabs. The first remained in place; the second and third slid hurriedly away around the Mall.

Gersen returned to the Mall a hundred yards west of the hotel where he flagged down a passing cab, definitely not one of those which had been waiting in front of the hotel.

"Take me to the Black Barn," said Gersen.

The cab swung about and instead of climbing the incline toward Llalarkno, turned south and out into the country.

The Black Barn stood in the middle of a field a half-mile from town: a circular building with low plank walls and a vast conical roof surrounded by a black iron weathervane in the shape of a crowing rooster. Lully Inklstaff had not yet arrived.

The sun sank behind the far hills, leaving a sky of tangerine and gold; and now Lully Inkelstaff appeared, wearing a black and white gown, with a great puff of red gauze pinning the blonde curls at the back of her head. She greeted Gersen with a cheerful wave of the hand. "I don't think I'm too late—just a few minutes perhaps, which is quite good for me. Have you been inside?"

"Not yet. I thought I'd better wait here for you."

"Just as well. It's so easy to miss connections; it happens shamefully often. And—must I admit it?—I'm usually to blame. Shall we go in? I think you'll be amused. Everyone likes the Black Barn, even the Methlen. They're always here in force. Wait till you see their strange dancing! But come!" Lully took Gersen's arm with an almost affectionate cordiality, as if they had been friends for years. "If we're in luck my favorite table will be waiting for us."

They passed through a pair of iron-bound plank doors and into a foyer furnished with dilapidated old farm implements. To right and left were stalls, from which protruded the heads of simulated farm animals.

A ramp led down into the main chamber past a pair of rickety old wains. Hundreds of tables encircled the dance floor, with a bandstand to the back now occupied by a pair of musicians in animal costumes, playing tamboura and oboe.

Lully led the way to a table which Gersen found no different from any other, but at which Lully settled herself with an exclamation of happy satisfaction.

"You'll think me silly, but this is my good luck table. I've had such merry times here! We're sure to have a wonderful evening!"

"You make me nervous," said Gersen. "Perhaps I won't match up to the occasion. Then you'll be annoyed with both me and the table."

"I'm sure not," said Lully. "I've decided that we shall enjoy ourselves and the table had best mind its manners."

Definitely a brisk and determined young woman, thought Gersen; best that he also mind his manners.

Lully, cocking her head to one side, seemed to divine something of Gersen's misgivings. She said breezily: "On the other hand, tragedy might stalk us; anything is possible. We might fall down while we're dancing—"

"Dancing?" inquired Gersen in alarm. Lully seemed not to hear.

"—and then I'd simply have to try another table until this one decided that the old ways were best. Are you hungry?"

"Yes indeed."

"So am I. Let me order, because I know exactly what's good."

"By all means," said Gersen. "Whatever you wish."

"First we'll have a dish of relishes and some pickled smelt, then chipes with black sauce, with a double dish of ramp savouries, and cottrell cutlets. Does that suit you?"

"Perfectly."

"The chirret is very good here, but perhaps you prefer beer?"

"What is chirret?"

"It's a very nice damson cider and not at all strong. Sometimes folk make such fools of themselves trying to dance after drinking Black Barn beer."

"Chirret, then, by all means, although as to the dancing—"

Lully already was signaling a waitress. Like all the other waiters and waitresses she wore festival peasant costume: a voluminous black and green blouse over a blue skirt with red stockings and black gaiters. Lully ordered decisively, specifying exactly how the dishes should be prepared and served. Almost immediately the waitress brought a jug of chirret, and next dishes of nuts, salted sea-flakes and pickled smelt.

"We're early," said Lully. "The crowd hasn't really arrived. In an hour there'll be almost too much activity and we'll hardly find room to dance. First we'll eat and talk. Tell me all about yourself and the places you've been."

Gersen laughed uneasily. "I hardly know where to start."

"Anywhere will do. I've become interested in eidolology and I can't at all understand your skarmatics. They're contradictory; you would seem an unusual man!"

"To the contrary, I'm very ordinary: clumsy and awkward as well."

"I don't believe a word of it. Incidentally, have you decided to settle here at Twanish? I do hope so!"

Gersen smiled thoughtfully, reflecting upon Moss Alrune. "Sometimes I'm tempted to do so."

Lully sighed. "It must be wonderful to travel the stars! I've never been anywhere. How many worlds have you visited?"

"I don't know exactly; I've never counted. Dozens and dozens, at least."

"I'm told that every world is different, that spacemen, even if they don't know where they are, can look at the sky, smell the air and instantly pronounce the name of the planet. Can you do that?"

"Sometimes. But I'd be fooled as often as not. Tell me about yourself. Do you have brothers and sisters?"

"Three of each. I'm the oldest and the first to take a job. I've never before considered marriage; I've always had such jolly times, it seemed a shame to change."

Gersen's sensitive antennae quivered and jerked; he became more uneasy than ever. "I also intend to avoid marriage for the forseeable future. Tell me about your job."

Lully wrinkled her nose. "It was nicer before the Kotzash job. I liked old Mr. Lemuel Jarkow very well indeed. Mr. Swiat Jarkow is not above making himself familiar."

"Do many Darsh come in to see Mr. Jarkow?"

"Not many; very few in fact."

"Perhaps a large Darsh came in with Mr. Ottile Panshaw."

Lully pursed her lips, shrugged. "I don't remember. Is it important?"

"I've seen Mr. Panshaw somewhere before. I think on Dar Sai."

"Very likely. Kotzash was originally a Darsh company. These are such mysterious questions. In fact you're a mysterious man. I wouldn't be surprised if you were with IPCC. Are you?"

"Of course not. If I were, I'd hardly be allowed to advertise it to the first pretty girl who asked."

"That's true. Still, you certainly don't seem an ordinary technician."

"When I'm off-duty, my personality changes," said Gersen, in a strained attempt at facetiousness.

Lully examined him with great intentness. "Why have you never married? Has no one ever selected you?"

Gersen shook his head. "I wouldn't dare ask anyone to the kind of life I lead."

After a thoughtful moment Lully said: "At Twanish it's customary for the woman to suggest marriage to the man, which is only proper etiquette. It's different elsewhere; so I'm told."

"Yes, that's quite true." Gersen sought for some way to change the subject. "I see some Darsh over by the entrance. Do they come to the Black Barn?"

"Of course! They're asked to sit over yonder, under the ventilator where their odor won't offend anyone." Lully watched the two Darsh sidling across the room. "They're almost barbarians. They never dance but just hunch over their tables gulping food."

"Where do the Methlen sit?"

"Over beside the bandstand. They usually come in carnival costumes; it's a rather foolish fashion with them. . . . Such a strange folk, always playing games, acting out parts, pretending and skylarking. No doubt it's great fun if you're wealthy and live in Llalarkno."

"I should think so. Would you like to marry a Methlen?"

"Small chance! In fact, I'd never dare to ask one; they're ever so persnickety, don't you agree?"

"Yes indeed."

"They have their own customs of course, but no real etiquette. Would you marry a Methlen girl if she asked you?"

"It depends on the girl," said Gersen, his mind elsewhere. He hurriedly amplified his remarks. "Naturally I don't expect to marry anyone."

Lully gave his arm a little pat of admonishment. "You've got a good job now; it's time that you settled yourself."

Gersen smilingly shook his head. "I'm definitely of the wrong temperament. . . . Look: there comes the orchestra."

Lully glanced at the musicians. "It's Denzel and his Seven Barnswallows. A most peculiar name, since they are only five. I don't like it when things are misrepresented. Still they are quite proficient, especially at step-toes and prances. . . . What are your favorite dances?"

"I don't know any dances whatever."

"How odd! No patterns, no jigs, no gallops?"

"Not even a slow march."

"We certainly must remedy that! It's simply shameful! I could never ask you for marriage!" Lully broke into laughter. "On the other hand, I might go lame, then where would I be with a jigging husband? . . . Here comes our food, and we don't want to think of marriage on empty stomachs."

The orchestra, consisting of flatsoon, bass-pipe, guitar, dimple-horn and tympanillo struck up a tune and folk went forth to dance. The multiplicity of their techniques amazed Gersen. To the first tune they performed an intricate whirling reel punctuated by kicks and leaps. To the next tune they coursed back and forth in a hopping loose-kneed glide; to the third tune they practiced a series of evolutions ending with four dancers, backs pressed together and arms thrown back, performing a high-kneed running-in-place exercise.

Gersen commented upon the versatility of the dancers. Lully looked at him with wide-eyed wonder. "I forgot that you're not a dancer! We do dozens of steps; its considered hacky to dance the same step twice. Wouldn't you like to learn a simple little polka?"

"Well, no. Not really."

"Kirth Gersen, you're really a shy man! It's time someone took you in hand. I think that we'll just prescribe dancing lessons for you, starting tomorrow."

Gersen sought for an adequate reply, but was distracted by the arrival of a group of Methlen. As Lully had remarked, most of them wore pierrot costume, with pompons on their white hats and long slippers with turned-up toes. They trooped gaily to that area reserved for their patronage.

Presently some came out to dance, keeping well apart from the Mongrels. They used a variety of steps, dancing in pairs in a fashion far less energetic than the mode of the Mongrels.

Gersen scanned the group but saw no one he recognized. Meanwhile Lully talked of this and that, pointing out acquaintances, explaining dance techniques, commenting upon the delicacy of the chipes and the excellence of the smelt. Gersen tried to divert the conversation to Jarkow's office, with little success.

At the conclusion of the meal, with the orchestra playing a merry tune and the dancers performing an intricate interweaving at a fast skipping pace, Lully became restless. She turned shining eyes upon Gersen. "Tomorrow evening I'll teach you this step!"

Gersen shook his head. "I can't possibly be on hand."

Lully spoke in a reproachful voice: "You are seeing another girl?"

"Of course not," scoffed Gersen. "I have a business appointment."

"Then the next night! I'll prepare a little supper and we can make a good start."

"I'd make a poor student," said Gersen. "In fact, I suffer from dizzy fits; dancing would certainly bring them on."

"You are joking with me," said Lully sadly. "You are seeing another woman; there can be no reasonable doubt."

Gersen searched for new excuses, but was interrupted by the arrival of one of Lully's friends, a young man wearing a stylish suit of tan and black.

"Why aren't you dancing?" he asked Lully. "The orchestra is at its best."

"My friend doesn't dance," said Lully.

"What? Surely he wouldn't want you to waste your evening! Come, they're starting *Stampede of the Golliwogs.*"

"Do you mind?" Lully asked Gersen.

"Not at all!"

Lully and her friend went briskly out upon the floor and soon were partipating earnestly in the dance. Gersen watched a moment without great interest. His mind wandered; he leaned back in his chair contemplating the stagnant state of his affairs. Doubts, indecisions, reverses hindered him everywhere. He had lost the initiative against Lens Larque, who indeed was now moving against Gersen himself. The danger had become imminent. So far he had evaded the rather casual attempts to capture him; no doubt they would become more direct. If Lens Larque grew impatient, a sliver of glass projected from across the street would instantly abate the nuisance created by Gersen's activities. As of now, Lens Larque would seem only irked and resentful; Gersen might expect possibly another day before Lens Larque set to work in earnest. . . .

Gersen's reverie was interrupted by the arrival of a second group of Methlen. He wondered if Jerdian had returned to Llalarkno, and he wondered if he would see her. . . . Almost as he thought her name she turned and he saw her face. Like her friends she wore carnival costume: a snug white garment covering her from neck to feet, with blue pompons down the front, eccentric slippers and a conical white hat topped by a pale blue pompon, pulled at a tilt halfway down across her dark curls. She looked so fresh and appealing and innocently gay that Gersen's heart rose up in his throat.

Without troubling to think he rose to his feet and crossed the room. She turned her head and saw him; for a moment they looked eye to eye. Her party had now started off across the room; Jeridan hesitated, darted a quick glance after her friends, then came to where Gersen stood in the shadows. She spoke in a husky whisper. "What are you doing here?"

"For one thing I've been hoping to see you." Gersen put his hands under her arms, drew her close and kissed her. After a moment she disengaged herself and drew back. "I thought I'd never see you again!"

Gersen laughed. "And I knew that you would. Do you love me still?"

"Yes, of course. . . . I don't know what to tell you."

"Can you leave your group and go off with me?"

"Now? It wouldn't be possible. I'd cause a scandal." She

looked across the room. "In a moment my escort will come to find me."

"He'll think you've gone to the restroom."

"Perhaps so. What an undignified pretext for meeting a secret lover!"

"Can I meet you later tonight, when you've left here?"

Jerdian shook her head. "We're planning a midnight supper for guests, I couldn't possibly escape."

"Then tomorrow, at noon."

"Very well, but where? You can't come to Oldenwood; my father would be ungracious."

"In front of Moss Alrune, on the side facing the lake."

She looked at him in surprise. "We can't meet there; it's a private property!"

"Nevertheless it's vacant and no one will molest us."

"Very well then. I'll be there." She looked over her shoulder. "Now I must go." Again she looked over her shoulder. "Quick." She stepped close to him and raised her face; they embraced. Gersen kissed her once, twice; then, breathless and half-laughing, she pulled away. "Until tomorrow noon!" She went quickly off after her party.

Gersen, turning, met the shocked and unfriendly gaze of Lully Inkelstaff, just emerging from the passage leading to the lady's restroom. Wordlessly she swept off to the table she had shared with Gersen, snatched up handbag and cloak and marched away to join her friends.

Gersen gave a rueful shrug. "At the very least, I've avoided tomorrow's dancing lesson."

Chapter 16

Gersen paid off the score and departed the Black Barn. To one side a half-dozen cabs awaited passengers. The cab first in line carried a faded white stripe along the skirt. Gersen casually turned away, and stood as if awaiting someone from within. How had he been tracked to the Black Barn? Had he been tagged with a tracer? Perhaps a daub of stuff which, in response to a search ray, returned a signal? . . . Tonight he would scrupulously bathe and change all his clothes.

Tonight—if he arrived at his hotel alive. Most definitely he would use none of the cabs along the rank. Gersen sauntered slowly back and forth with an air of a man preoccupied; arriving at an area where he could no longer see the cabs, he ran off down the road to Twanish.

The night was clear and dark. Constellations strange to Gersen hung in the sky and showed the road as a pale ribbon with dark fields to either side. As Gersen ran his body seemed to come alive; his whole soul expanded. This was the existence he was meant for and where he felt easy: running through the night across a strange world, with danger behind and himself the very embodiment of retaliatory danger. His vapors and dreary misgivings were gone; he felt the Gersen of old . . . Against the sky loomed a tall copse of trees. Gersen stopped short to listen. From the Black Barn, now almost a quarter-mile distant, he heard the whisper of music, and saw the lights of a cab. Gersen looked to the side of the road opposite the trees. He saw a shallow ditch and, beyond, a clump of weeds. He jumped the ditch and flung himself flat behind the weeds.

The cab came at speed, lights blazing along the road. Coming abreast of the trees, the cab stopped abruptly, almost beside Gersen. But the attention of the driver and occupants was fixed upon the trees, not the clump of weeds which barely concealed Gersen.

The driver spoke in a soft voice: "He's not down the road. He couldn't have come much farther."

From the compartment stepped three men; Gersen could see only their silhouettes in the glow reflected back from the headlights.

The driver spoke again: "He's hiding in the trees, unless he took to the fields."

One of the passengers, a short squat man, spoke in a plangent bass: "Turn so the lights shine into the trees."

The driver did so, backing the cab almost into the ditch.

The short squat man said, "Ang, around to the right. Dofty, around to the left. Keep out of the light, get him alive. That's important. Bird wants him alive."

Gersen rose up from behind the weeds. Soundlessly he jumped the ditch. Climbing the two steps to the control booth, he thrust his adder-tongue stiletto into the nape of the driver's neck. Pincers cut the vertebral nerve, inducing instant death. Gersen lowered the corpse into the foot-space, and seated himself at the controls. The short man stood in the road to the left of the cab: a man with whom Gersen wanted earnest and candid conversation.

Three minutes passed. Gersen sat with his sliver pistol in hand, waiting. Ang and Dofty emerged from the trees. They walked forward into light from the cab: Ang, a crooked angular young man with a long high-bridged nose and a short black beard; Dofty, burly and baby-faced with eyes peering through slits. Gersen had often met their like Beyond, in disreputable back-street taverns or working at their trade, as now.

The short squat man took an impatient step forward. "Nothing?"

"He's not there," said Ang.

Gersen waited until the two were close in front of the cab, then, with neither qualm nor compunction, he discharged his weapon once, twice, driving splinters of explosive glass through the foreheads of Ang and Dofty, and once again at the short man's elbow as he spun around. The short man's gun dropped upon the road.

Gersen jumped down from the driver's seat. "I'm the man you're looking for."

The short man said nothing, but stared at Gersen, his face contorted in pain.

Gersen spoke in the most casual of voices: "Have you ever

seen a man die by cluthe? No? Yes? You can choose cluthe, or I'll shoot you in the head. Which?"

"Shoot," whispered the short man.

"Then answer my questions. If you had caught me, what were you to do with me?"

"Bind you with tape and take you to a shed."

"Then what?"

"I would call for instructions."

"Who gives you instructions?"

The short man merely stared. Gersen stepped forward, his hand in a glove. He raised his hand, extended his arm. "Quick!"

"The Bird."

"Lens Larque?"

"You said the name."

"Where is he now?"

"I don't know. I take my orders by radio."

From the direction of the Black Barn came new lights. The short man lunged toward Gersen, who shot him accurately in the forehead. Gersen carefully replaced the fearful glove in its socket, then turning away, saw in the reflected light a weathered white stripe around the base of the cab. He ran off down the road toward Twanish.

The cab from the Black Barn, finding its way obstructed, halted. Gersen, pausing to look back over his shoulder, saw the driver and occupants alight, to stare in horror at the corpses.

At the Capricorn Cafe, overlooking Redemption Park, halfway between the Commercial Hotel and Skohune Tower, Gersen sat with a pot of tea assessing the events of the evening. His mood, he was pleased to note, had become less troubled. Activity had flushed the stagnant channels of his mind. The four killings? He regretted only that he had teased so little information from the short man. He thought of Jerdian and felt a warm excitement; he thought of Lully and laughed aloud. . . . Under Lully's desk at Jarkow Engineering reposed the recording apparatus he had installed so short a time before. Directed into the Kotzash office it now served no purpose. Much more advantageous if it could record conversations at Jarkow's office.

Gersen looked toward Skohune Tower, which at this hour showed only the dim illumination of night bulbs.

Gersen finished his tea. He went to the hotel, picked up his bag of equipment, returned to the street and sauntered across the park to Skohune Tower. The lobby was empty. He rode the ascensor to the third floor and using his key to Room 308, entered the offices of Jarkow Engineering.

Just inside the door he halted to listen. No sound, no indication of human presence. He stepped into Lully's cubicle, where he found and detached the recorder unit. Optimally, so he decided, the sound probe should be located in Jarkow's office.

Gersen installed the microphone under Jarkow's desk, where he discovered a set of implements which startled him. Gersen recalled an old aphorism: "He who sups with the devil should use a long spoon." Jarkow, working as he did with Lens Larque, had installed several versions of the "long spoon" where it could help him most.

Gersen worked quickly and efficiently, and in half an hour arranged the system to his satisfaction, with the recorder attached to the Kotzash telephone and microphones at vantage places around the room. He packed his tools, and started to leave, but at the draughtman's office stopped short. He opened the door and looked in, to find the usual paraphernalia: plotting machines, superficial integrators, automatic scribers, a pattern library. Work in process lay spread out on a table: page after page of charts, columns and rows of figures. Each page carried a notation: Section 1A, Section 1B, with the last page labeled Section 20F. Under the table Gersen saw a pair of peculiar objects: the first an irregular mass of chalky substance about a foot in diameter. The surface had been marked off into approximately one hundred areas, each labeled in blank ink, after the same scheme as the pages had been labeled. The second object was an expanded replica of the first, made of a light transparent substance, and similarly limned into small areas. Under the surface ran a myriad scarlet threads, curving, bending, twisting, humping, in no obvious order or pattern.

Most odd, thought Gersen. He picked up the object, looked at it this way and that. Most odd. Most curious. . . . Gersen gave a sudden cry of uncontrollable laughter.

Was such remarkable and magnificent foolishness possible? He thought back across the months, and a hundred items of information suddenly ranged themselves into coherent order.

Gersen replaced the transparent object. He took his case

and left the offices of Jarkow Engineering. He had achieved
his purpose. Conversations to be recorded in Jarkow's office
could not fail but be interesting.

Without incident Gersen returned to the hotel. The tattletale he had arranged on the door to his room was in place
and undisturbed. Gersen entered, closed and locked the door,
bathed and went to bed.

Gersen spent a restless night. Faces floated through his
mind: Lens Larque: the caricatures, drawings and blurred
photograph. Poor broken Tintle and his spouse, Daswell Tippin, Ottile Panshaw, Bel Ruk, Lully Inkelstaff, Jerdian Chanseth. . . .

In the morning Gersen ordered breakfast up to his room,
then, assailed by doubts, ate none of it. Dressing with care,
he descended to the ground floor, slipped out upon the Mall,
went to the Capricorn Cafe and there took his breakfast. Today was to be an important day. At noon: to Moss Alrune
and Jerdian. Later—who knows? Possibly a meeting with
Lens Larque. He returned to the hotel and went up to his
room. The tattletale had been disturbed. Putting his ear to the
door Gersen heard a set of odd sounds. With the most exaggerated delicacy he slid the door ajar, to find a chambermaid
setting his room to rights.

He entered, bade her good morning; a few minutes later
she withdrew. Gersen immediately went to the telephone. He
called the Kotzash office and activated the recording device.
To his ear came those four conversations which had been
recorded that morning. First, a call from Zerus Belsaint of
Stellar Fortress Security Association, requesting conversation
with Mr. Jarkow.

"Sorry," said Lully in a pert voice. "Mr. Jarkow is not
present."

"When do you expect him?"

"I don't know, sir. Perhaps tomorrow."

"Please mention that I called, and I'll try again tomorrow."

"Very well, sir."

Next to be heard was a call from Jarkow inquiring for Ottile Panshaw.

"He hasn't been in, sir."

"What?" Jarkow's tone was sharp. "Has he left a
message?"

"Not a word! No one's called but a Mr. Zerus Belsaint who wants to consult you."

"A Mr. Zerus who?"

"Mr. Zerus Belsaint of the Stellar Fortress Security Associates. May I tell him when you'll be able to see him?"

"I'll be in this afternoon late, but I won't talk with Belsaint. He'll have to wait. If Panshaw calls, have him come to the office and don't let him leave."

"Yes, sir."

Gersen next listened to Lully's private conversation with a friend where he learned more than he cared to know. Lully described her previous evening's adventures, using images and metaphors which Gersen found unflattering. "And with a Methlen girl, would you believe it?" Lully's voice was pitched in tones of outrage. "I can't imagine what sort of a man he is! I gave him a most awful look, simply withered him! Then I went off with Nary. We danced three suites and a great gallop. And that's not all! On the way home, we came upon a frightful murder—in fact, four murders, of a cab driver and three passengers. They lay around the road like so many dog carcasses. I've had a night I won't forget!"

"Who was the Methlen girl?"

"That giddy Chanseth bit. You see her everywhere."

"Yes, I know of her."

The conversation ended, and the final call came through: from Motry, Jarkow's works superintendent. "Mr. Jarkow, please."

"He's not here yet. He'll be in later today."

"I'm just down from Shanitra. I called in to report final checkout. He can pass the word on to his principals. Will you give him the message?"

"Certainly, Mr. Motry."

"Don't forget now!"

"Naturally I won't forget! In fact, I'll put a note on his desk this minute."

"That's the system! Quite proper, my girl! I'll look into the office tomorrow morning."

"Very good, Mr. Motry. I'll tell Mr. Jarkow."

Thereafter the line was dead. Gersen sat back in the chair and reflected. Today must be the day. He looked out the window. The weather was cool, with Cora-light slanting down from an autumnal sky. The uplands of Llalarkno showed indistinct through haze; the town, the park, the entire landscape seemed suffused with a melancholy serenity, which Gersen found consonant with his own mood. Problems had been solved; mysteries had revealed themselves to an effect so ludicrous, cruel and wild that Gersen's mind veered away.

Gersen considered the conversations he had overheard. Jarkow expected important visitors during the afternoon: who could they be? . . . His thoughts shifted to Jerdian Chanseth, and brought him a twinge of hollow uncertainty. What would she be thinking? Now, this very instant? Gersen, so astute, crafty and resourceful, found himself besieged by doubts and anxieties. He saw her as he had seen her first, in her dark green frock and dark green stockings, the dark hair curling over her ears and across her forehead. Her only notice of him had been a haughty glance; how different now their relationship! Gersen's heart melted within him . . . He checked the time: less than an hour to noon, not to early to set out for Moss Alrune.

Gersen considered the cabs waiting near the hotel. Unlikely that any of these could be considered threats; nevertheless he crossed the park and flagged down a cab cruising the street. As always, he discovered resistance, and the driver consented to the journey only when Gersen agreed to sit far back in the shadow of the interior where he could not be seen.

In the road by Moss Alrune Gersen alighted and paid the fare; the driver wasted no time in departing.

Gersen walked back along the road to the entrance arch. Great trees of a type unknown to him overhung the stone wall and cast a dapple shade; the air was still and silent. To right and left of the arch, stone pillars supported the busts of nymphs cast in bronze; their eyes looked unseeingly down at him.

He passed under the arch and into the grounds. The driveway curved up to a broad portico; beyond, a path led off around the house into the gardens, where Gersen so far had not explored. He walked among confections of flowering shrubs and carefully groomed trees, and presently came to a low stone wall. On the other side spread the grounds of Oldenwood. Gerson looked out across the lawn, now occupied by a pair of small dark-haired girls, naked except for white skimmer hats decorated with flowers. They saw Gersen and paused to stare. Their frolicking became more sedate. Presently they ran off to a more secluded area.

Gersen turned back the way he had come, wondering if ever his own children would run so blissfully across the lawns of Moss Alrune. . . . He went around to the front of the house. On the steps sat Jerdian, looking pensively across the water. She rose to her feet; he put his arms gently around her and kissed her; she acquiesced, without fervor.

For a few minutes they stood, then Gersen said: "Have you spoken of me to your family?"

Jerdian laughed sadly. "My father does not think well of you."

"He hardly knows me. Shall I go talk to him?"

"Oh no! He'd be frigid . . . I really don't know what to say. All last night I thought about you and myself, and all this morning. . . . I'm still confused."

"I've been thinking too. I see three possible courses. We can take leave of each other, finally and forever. Or you can come away with me—now, if you like. Tomorrow we'll leave Methel and go off across space."

Jerdian sighed and gave her head a slow dismal shake. "You don't know what it is to be Methlen. I'm a part of Llalarkno, just as if I had grown here, like a tree. I'd be forever lonely away from my home, no matter how much I loved you."

"Or I could stay here on Methel and make my home here, with you."

Jerdian looked at him dubiously. "Would you really do that for me?"

"I have no other home. Llalarkno appeals to me; why shouldn't I live here?"

Jerdian smiled ruefully. "It's not all that simple. Outworlders aren't often made welcome, if ever. We're very exclusive, as I'm sure you know."

"I've already arranged that part of it. We already own a home."

"Here? On Methel?"

Gersen nodded. "Moss Alrune. I bought it yesterday."

Jeridan looked at him in amazement. "The price was a million svu! I thought you, well, a poor adventurer—a spaceman!"

"So I am, after a fashion. But hardly poor. I could buy a dozen Moss Alrunes and not even notice it."

"I'm bewildered."

"I hope you don't think the worse of me for not being poor."

"No. Not really. You're more of a mystery than ever. Why did you risk your life fighting that great Darsh at hadaul?"

"Because it had to be done."

"But why?"

"Tomorrow I'll tell you everything. Today—the time isn't quite right."

She looked at him searchingly. "You're not a criminal? Or a pirate?"

"I'm not even a banker."

Jerdian, looking past Gersen, became rigid. A furious voice called out: "Hoy there, fellow! What are you doing here? Jerdian! Whatever is this?" Without waiting for an answer Adario Chanseth signaled to a pair of burly footmen. "Take this fellow and pitch him into the street."

The footmen advanced confidently. A moment later one lay face down in a flower bed, the other sat nearby numbly holding his bleeding face. Gersen said: "You threw me out of your bank, Mr. Chanseth, but this is my property and I don't care to be molested."

"What do you mean, your property?"

"I bought Moss Alrune yesterday."

Chanseth uttered a harsh laugh. "You bought nothing very much. Have you read the Llalarkno charter? No? Then you are in for a surprise. Llalarkno is a private domain, and retains basic ownership in perpetuity. You bought no title; you bought what is in effect a lease, which must be validated by the Llalarkno Trustees. I am one of these. I don't want your outlander face hanging over my garden wall, staring at my children, no more than I'd tolerate that Darsh blackguard."

Gersen looked at Jerdian, who stood with her hands twisting and tears running down her cheeks. Chanseth glanced at her. "So that's the way of it, eh? A romantic drama. Well, put the role away and out of your head. You're a wayward little creature; your imagination leads you into situations which you can't control. The drama is over; here you must stop. It is time you were learning propriety. Go home at once."

"Just a moment," said Gersen. He went to Jerdian and stood looking down into her tear-stained face. "You don't need to obey him. You can come with me—if you choose to do so."

Jerdian said in a low voice, "He's probably right. I'm a Methlen and I'll never be anything else. I suppose I might as well face up to it. Good-bye, Kirth Gersen."

Gersen bowed stiffly. "Good-bye." He turned to Adario Chanseth, who stood stonily nearby, but could find no words to express his feelings. He turned on his heel, strode down the drive, passed under the arch, and the bronze nymphs gazed down with blind eyes.

The road was empty. Gersen walked southward toward Twanish, with the grounds of Oldenwood to his right. He turned a single glance across the sloping lawn. The two little girls, now wearing frocks, noticed his passage and paused in their play to watch. Gersen continued, through the quiet woods, at last down the slope to the Mall, and around to the Capricorn Café. He felt hungry, thirsty, tired and depressed; he threw himself down at a table and made a meal of bread and meat, then sat with a pot of tea, staring across the park.

The episode had run its course. Emotions, hopes, gallant resolves: all past and gone like sparks on the wind.

The pattern, Gersen reflected, was that of a simple tragicomedy in two acts: tensions, conflicts, confrontations on Dar Sai, a brief interlude while the settings were shifted, a surge to the climax at Moss Alrune. The dynamic thrust to the production had been provided by Gersen's folly. How absurd to think of himself against the bucolic background of Moss Alrune, participating in the Methlen frivolities, no matter what his wistful yearnings! He was Kirth Gersen, obsessed by inner imperatives which might never be satisfied.

The drama was ended. The tensions had resolved; the matters at conflict had settled into equilibrium with a ponderous lurching finality. Gersen managed a bitter smile as he sipped his tea. Jerdian would not suffer very long, or very painfully.

Gersen rose to his feet and went to the hotel. He bathed, changed into spaceman's gear. He called his recording device, and heard another of Lully's personal calls, to a Nary Balbroke, and another call from Jarkow, again inquiring after Ottile Panshaw, in a sharper voice than before.

"He's not called, Mr. Jarkow."

"Very strange. He's not in the office next door?"

"The office has been empty all day, sir."

"Very well, I won't be in until late afternoon; I've got

some important business. You go home at your usual time. If Panshaw calls, leave me a note."

"Yes, Mr. Jarkow."

Gersen switched off the communicator. He looked at his chronometer: Lully would presently be leaving the office.

Gersen made his preparations, checking and rechecking with meticulous patience. Satisfied at last he departed the hotel and walked across the park, arriving at Skohune Tower just in time to see Lully trot briskly out upon the street and march off up the Mall. Gersen went into the building, rode the ascensor to the third floor, and went directly to Room 308.

He put his ear to the door. No sound. Inserting his key he slid the door open and surveyed the interior. The rooms were empty. He stepped into the reception room and closed the door.

He went to Jarkow's office and looked inside. Empty, as before. Gersen crossed the hall to the draughting room, and seated himself to the side.

He waited. Half an hour passed. The shafts of Cora-light entering by the west windows began to approach the horizontal.

Gersen grew tense. The seconds went past with an almost audible thudding.

He became tired of sitting. He went to stand where he could look through the glass partition, both toward the outer door and, by turning his head, into Jarkow's office. The situation was not to his satisfaction; he felt overly conspicuous. Closing the door, he dropped to his knee and with his knife cut a small slit in the lower panel, allowing him a slantwise view into Jarkow's office.

Steps in the hall. Gersen listened: a single man. Whoever might be Jarkow's "important visitor" he had not yet arrived.

The door slid back; into the outer office stepped Jarkow. Gersen, standing behind a cabinet, watched through a niche in a stack of books.

Jarkow came into the office carrying a small case. He stopped, looked into Lully's cubicle, scowled. An ugly harsh-looking man, thought Gersen, rendered even more so by his elaborate blond hairpiece. But by no means a man to be taken lightly. Muttering under his breath, Jarkow went heavy-footed to his office. Gersen dropped to his knees and out of sight.

Looking through a slit, Gersen saw Jarkow go to his desk where he opened the case and brought out a black box surmounted by an amber button. Jarkow placed the box in the precise center of his desk, then went to sit in his chair. He leaned back, turned to look moodily out of the window across the park toward Llalarkno.

Gersen stepped out of his hiding place and into the hall. Jarkow heard a sound; he jerked about to see Gersen entering his office. His heavy eyebrows lowered, his yellow-gray eyes became narrow. For a moment he and Gersen stared at each other. Gersen took three slow steps forward, so that he stood almost in front of the desk.

Finally Jarkow spoke: "Well, who are you?"

"My name is Kirth Gersen. Have you ever heard of me?"

Jarkow gave his head a jerk. "I know something of you."

"I took Kotzash away from Panshaw. I instructed him to halt all proceedings on Shanitra. Presumably he notified you."

Jarkow nodded slowly. "He did so indeed. Why have you gone to such effort?"

"To begin with, I wanted the Kotzash money. Yesterday I transferred almost five million svu to my own account."

Jarkow's eyes narrowed even further. "In that case, I will render my bill to you."

"Don't trouble yourself."

Jarkow seemed not to hear the remark. He took the black box from the center of his desk and moved it to the window ledge beside his chair. "So: what do you want with me?"

"A few moment's conversation. Are you expecting company?"

"Perhaps."

"We'll have time for a chat. Let me tell you something about myself. I was born at a place called Mount Pleasant, which was subsequently destroyed by a syndicate of slavers. One of the group was a certain Lens Larque: a murderer, thief and general blackguard. This Lens Larque is Darsh, and originally bore the name Husse Bugold. He became an outcast, a 'rachepol' and lost an ear. His other ear he lost only recently, at Tintle's Shade in Rath Eileann. How do I know? I cut it off myself. Madame Tintle probably cooked it into next day's ahagaree."

In Jarkow's eyes yellow lights were flickering. He rose suddenly to his feet. In a well-modulated voice he said: "Your language offends me, inasmuch as I myself am Lens Larque."

"I am aware of this," said Gersen. "I have come to kill you."

Lens Larque reached under the lip of his desk. "We shall see who kills whom. First I will break your legs." He squeezed, but no answering fan of power spurted forth; Gersen had disconnected the circuitry during his visit.

Lens Larque muttered a guttural curse and from his pocket drew a weapon. Gersen fired his own pistol, exploded the weapon out of Lens Larque's hand. Lens Larque roared in pain. Lurching around the desk he threw himself forward. Gersen swept up a chair, thrust it into Lens Larque's face. Lens Larque thrust it aside with a sweep of bull-strong arms. Gersen stepped close, kneed Lens Larque's abdomen, slapped the back of Lens Larque's neck with his right hand. He stepped back, ducked a massive blow, then kicked Lens Larque's knee, pulled him off balance and sent him sprawling to the floor, where the blond hairpiece fell away to reveal a ridged skin-bald scalp and vacant ear-holes.

Gersen leaned on the edge of the desk and pointed his pistol at Lens Larque's midriff. "You are about to die. I wish I could kill you a dozen times."

"Panshaw betrayed me."

"Panshaw is gone," said Gersen. "He betrayed no one."

"Then how did you know me?"

"I saw your face in the other room. I know your plan, and why you used Kotzash. All to no avail."

Lens Larque clenched his muscles and tried to seize Gersen's feet, but performed only a feeble cramped movement. He stared up at Gersen. "What have you done to me?"

"I have poisoned you with *cluthe*. The back of your neck is now burning. Your arms and legs are already paralyzed. In ten minutes you will be dead. As you die, think of the harm you have inflicted upon innocent people."

Lens Larque gasped. "The box yonder—give it to me."

"No. I take pleasure in thwarting your plans. Remember Mount Pleasant? There you killed my father and my mother."

"Take the box," whispered Lens Larque. "Pull the guard back; press the button."

"No," said Gersen. "Never."

Lens Larque began to thrash across the floor as his viscera

knotted and cramped. Gersen went to the reception room and waited. The minutes passed. The sounds continued as Lens Larque's muscles coiled, knotted and pulled in different directions. His breath came in stertorous gasps. After nine minutes he lay twisted in a grotesque contortion. At ten minutes he ceased to breathe, and a minute later he was dead.

Gersen, sitting on the reception chair, drew a deep breath, and released it. He felt old, sad and tired.

Time passed. Gersen rose to his feet, went back into that room he had known as Jarkow's office. Twilight was deepening to night. Over Llalarkno rose the moon Shanitra, in its full phase.

Gersen picked up the black box. He held it a moment, weighing it, feeling its power. Contrary impulses thrust at him. He remembered Adario Chanseth's austere face. Gersen laughed mirthlessly. Lens Larque had labored long to achieve his most sardonic trick. Should such toil and expense be wasted, especially since Gersen shared all of Lens Larque's motivations?"

"No," said Gersen. "Of course not."

He slid back the guard sleeve and put his finger on the amber button.

He pushed.

The surface of Shanitra erupted: chunks fell away with majestic deliberation; fragments sprayed in different directions; a cloud of dust created a nimbus glowing in the Coralight.

The dust dissipated. The disrupted material settled into new configurations. The irregular surface of Shanitra had now taken on the similitude of Lens Larque's face: the ear lobes long, the scalp bald, the mouth twisted into a leer of idiotic mirth.

Gersen went to the communicator. He called Oldenwood and was put into contact with Adario Chanseth.

Chanseth peered at the screen. "Who is calling?"

"Go out into your back garden," said Gersen. "There's a great Darsh face hanging over the garden wall."

Gersen broke the connection. He left Skohune Tower and went to the hotel, where he paid his bill and departed.

A cab took him to the spaceport. He went out to his Fantamic Flitterwing, climbed aboard, and departed the planet Methel.